A Christmas Star

The Cape Light Titles

CAPE LIGHT

HOME SONG

A GATHERING PLACE

A NEW LEAF

A CHRISTMAS PROMISE

THE CHRISTMAS ANGEL

A CHRISTMAS TO REMEMBER

A CHRISTMAS VISITOR

THE CHRISTMAS COTTAGE

A CHRISTMAS STAR

A WISH FOR CHRISTMAS

A Christmas Star

A Cape Light Novel

Thomas Kinkade

& Katherine Spencer

BERKLEY BOOKS, NEW YORK
A Parachute Press Book

F
KIN

THE BERKLEY PUBLISHING GROUP
Published by the Penguin Group
Penguin Group (USA) Inc.
375 Hudson Street, New York, New York 10014, USA
Penguin Group (Canada), 90 Eglinton Avenue East, Suite 700, Toronto, Ontario M4P 2Y3, Canada
(a division of Pearson Penguin Canada Inc.)
Penguin Books Ltd., 80 Strand, London WC2R 0RL, England
Penguin Group Ireland, 25 St. Stephen's Green, Dublin 2, Ireland (a division of Penguin Books Ltd.)
Penguin Group (Australia), 250 Camberwell Road, Camberwell, Victoria 3124, Australia
(a division of Pearson Australia Group Pty. Ltd.)
Penguin Books India Pvt. Ltd., 11 Community Centre, Panchsheel Park, New Delhi—110 017, India
Penguin Group (NZ), 67 Apollo Drive, Rosedale, North Shore, 0632, New Zealand
(a division of Pearson New Zealand Ltd.)
Penguin Books (South Africa) (Pty.) Ltd., 24 Sturdee Avenue, Rosebank, Johannesburg 2196, South Africa

Penguin Books Ltd., Registered Offices: 80 Strand, London WC2R 0RL, England

This is a work of fiction. Names, characters, places, and incidents either are the product of the author's imagination or are used fictitiously, and any resemblance to actual persons, living or dead, business establishments, events, or locales is entirely coincidental. The publisher does not have any control over and does not assume any responsibility for author or third-party websites or their content.

PRINTING HISTORY
Berkley hardcover edition / October 2008
Berkley trade paperback edition / November 2009

ISBN: 978-0-425-22993-4

The Library of Congress has catalogued the Berkley hardcover edition as follows:

Kinkade, Thomas, 1958–
A Christmas star: a Cape Light novel / Thomas Kinkade & Katherine Spencer.
p. cm.
ISBN 978-0-425-22358-1
1. Cape Light (Imaginary place)—Fiction. 2. New England—Fiction. 3. Dwellings—Fires and fire prevention—Fiction. 4. Christmas stories. 5. Domestic fiction. I. Spencer, Katherine. II. Title.
PS3561.I534C475 2008
813'.54—dc22

2008019834

PRINTED IN THE UNITED STATES OF AMERICA

10 9 8 7 6 5 4 3 2 1

To Ellen Steiber
With endless thanks for your magical, editorial touch and for your
cherished friendship.
—A.C.

DEAR FRIENDS

⌒✦⌒

$\mathcal{T}$HIS CHRISTMAS AS WE GATHER AROUND THE HOLIDAY dinner table, I gaze at my loved ones, their faces aglow in the golden light of the candles, and feel truly blessed for my family and my faith.

Faith unites families, and families inspire faith. It's difficult to imagine one without the other. How marvelous Christmas is then—a time that we honor both as we come together and celebrate so joyously!

This year our friends in Cape Light will also come to realize how great a role faith plays in one's family, though the lessons for them won't be easy. Our old friends Sam and Jessica Morgan will face a heartbreaking loss when their beloved house goes up in flames. Their trust in each other—and in God—will be tested.

We will also meet some new friends like Jack Sawyer and Julie Newton, who are not looking forward to the holidays. But perhaps a simple wish on a Christmas star can bring them together. Perhaps love can heal battered hearts and lift up weary spirits.

So follow me to the village of Cape Light, where the townspeople invite us into their homes year after year to enjoy the comfort and warmth of their friendship, their families, and their faith.

Merry Christmas!

Thomas Kinkade

Chapter One

~⌒~

EVERY YEAR JESSICA AND SAM MORGAN HAD THE SAME
debate. Jessica liked to put up their Christmas tree the weekend after Thanksgiving. Sam liked to wait.

Some years, when she had been busy with her job at the bank
and taking care of their two boys, or if they'd had their family over
on Thanksgiving Day, Jessica was content to put the task off. At
least for a week or two. But this year Sam's sister Molly and her
husband, Matt, had hosted Thanksgiving, and Jessica wasn't working at the bank in town anymore. When the weekend arrived, she
had nothing to think about but getting a jump start on the holidays.
Starting with the tree.

This year, Jessica had a plan.

On Sunday afternoon, while Sam predictably sat in front of
the TV, mesmerized by a football game, Jessica bustled around
the kitchen and quickly put on a pot roast—one of her husband's

favorite dinners. She set it simmering on a low flame, then headed for the attic to begin the slow but steady process of moving the many boxes of decorations down to the living room.

She felt like an ant, focused and persistent, slowly and quietly transporting her treasures, one by one.

Her older boy, Darrell, now fourteen, sat by his dad's side, cheering and yelling at the TV as their favorite team, the Patriots, battled an arch rival. Tyler, who was four, played with trucks in his bedroom. He was still interested in his mother's activities and was intrigued by the attic. He seized any excuse to get a peek at the mysterious, shadowy space, and without Jessica knowing, he followed her up the attic stairway.

"What are you doing?" he asked, poking his head up from the opening in the floor.

"Taking down the Christmas decorations. Want to help me?"

"Okay." He climbed to the top of the steps and took a small box from her hands.

"Take this down, carefully. I'll get some more."

Jessica was glad to have a helper. Tyler wasn't able to carry much, but his company and questions made the task go faster. By the time the home team declared victory and the pot roast was ready, all the cartons had been brought down and opened up.

"I love opening the boxes. It's like seeing everything for the first time. Isn't it?" Jessica smiled at her son as she peered in a particularly mysterious carton. She always meant to label everything when she put the boxes away but somehow never got around to it.

"Like a toy that got stuck under the bed," Tyler observed.

"Yes, that's what's it like," Jessica agreed. "Exactly."

Jessica and Tyler had started unwrapping music boxes, papier-mâché angels, and Jessica's prized collection of snow globes.

A *Christmas Star*

The big cushioned rocking chair was pushed aside, and the colorful satin tree skirt spread out on the floor where the tree would preside. Tyler played with the tree stand, trying to fit the pieces together. He almost had it, too, Jessica noticed. He was mechanically inclined, just like his father.

Sam walked in and found them busy at work. "What's all this? Is it Christmas around here already?"

Jessica glanced at him over her shoulder then turned back to the box of hand-carved wooden angels she had just discovered. Sam had made the angels for her the first year they were married, the first year they had a Christmas party in their house. She loved the handcrafted figures, each one unique and full of expression. They meant so much to her. She always put them on the fireplace mantel surrounded by fresh greens and small white candles.

She removed one angel and set it on the lamp table. "If we waited until you were ready, we'd be putting up our tree on Christmas Eve."

"Like one of those smart families, you mean?" He picked up a snow globe, shook it, and watched the flakes swirl. "I hear you get a great bargain on a tree that way."

"Looks like we have to wait until next year for a discount. Everything is set."

"I thought we were going to get a fake tree. One with the lights and ornaments already attached. You just pop it open like an umbrella—"

Sam gestured, demonstrating. Jessica knew he was only teasing her. He knew she would rather have no tree at all if she couldn't have a real one.

"I thought we could go to the tree farm tonight." She closed the box and glanced at him.

"So soon?"

She had a feeling he would say that. Even the expression on his handsome face was no surprise. They had been married more than five years now. "We can take a ride after dinner. To Sawyer's."

"It might snow. I just saw the weather report."

"I heard it, too. Just a few flurries. The boys want to get the tree tonight, don't you, guys?" She turned, appealing to her sons who had both flopped on the couch and were batting at each other with Christmas pillows.

Sam gave her a look. *I know it's not the boys, Jess. It's you,* he was saying. She smiled and pretended not to notice.

Tyler turned to his father. "Can we, Dad? Look, I fixed the tree stand. Almost."

"Good job. How about you, Darrell? Don't you have homework or something?" A logical question. Though Jessica detected a hopeful note.

Darrell, in his first year of high school, had a more reserved reaction than his little brother. But Jessica guessed he would vote for her side. In a cool way, of course.

"I finished most of it. I can go." He shrugged, not looking at either of his parents.

Sam glanced over at her. "Nice work, Mrs. Claus."

"Oh, don't look that way. It will be fun. Dinner's ready. Can someone set the table?"

She left the living room, smiling. Sam and the boys followed her into the kitchen.

I should have tried that tactic before, Jessica thought. *That was even easier than I'd thought.*

With the tree search in mind, the family ate dinner quickly. They each carried their dishes to the sink and helped clean up. Sort of, Jessica conceded, as she left the pots to soak in the sink.

Wearing down jackets, scarves, and gloves, they piled into Sam's big SUV and headed out to Sawyer's Tree Farm, about ten miles away on the other side of Cape Light.

It was a frosty night, with patches of midnight blue sky and bright stars showing through tattered clouds. Jessica could smell snow in the air. But they would be back home by the time it started, drinking hot cocoa and hanging the ornaments. Jessica felt a familiar sense of happy anticipation. She couldn't help it; she always got excited when they set off to find the tree.

Sam glanced at her. "I wonder if Sawyer is even open this year. We might have to try a new place."

"Oh, I hope not." Jessica tugged off a glove. "But you might be right. Jack hasn't been the same since his wife died. Last year he just had the trees. No Christmas shop, or the extras for the kids. I guess Claire was the one who did all that."

Darrell was too big for those amusements, but Tyler would miss it, Jessica thought.

Sam glanced at the back seat, where Darrell was in his own zone, hooked up to his iPod, and Tyler played with an action figure. Reilly, a yellow Lab mix, sat between the boys, panting as he always did on car rides. Darrell's arm was protectively slung around the dog's shoulder. He had asked Jessica to get Reilly a doggy seatbelt, but she hadn't quite gotten around to it.

Jessica didn't know why they had to bring the dog every year, but Darrell—who had fixed upon Reilly in the animal shelter, even though the hound was getting on in years and not at all what they'd had in mind—insisted that Reilly be included in family events. Every year Darrell would take Reilly out on his lead at the Christmas tree farm and let him sniff the possible trees for approval.

Jessica guessed that she and Sam were having the same thought at that moment. How quickly the boys were growing up. Growing away from them. It had been difficult for her to have a baby. They had just about given up when Darrell came into their lives, a nine-year-old more or less abandoned by his family. They had decided to adopt him just as she became pregnant with Tyler.

Lately, she and Sam had been talking about having another child. After Sam's sister Molly had a baby about six months ago, they had both realized that they, too, really wanted more children. That was the real reason she quit working at the bank. That and a wish to spend more time with the boys before the years slipped past. They had so many after-school activities now, it was a full-time job just chauffeuring them around.

She was thirty-eight. Some women were just starting at her age, she kept reminding herself. But considering her history, she wondered if it would happen. She and Sam had decided they wouldn't go to any extremes. Just let nature—and God's plan for their lives—take their course. Jessica really hoped she would get pregnant soon. She kept picturing a little baby girl in her arms by the Christmas tree next year, though she tried not to get her hopes up too much.

"Is this it?" Tyler's excited voice drew Jessica out of her thoughts.

"It certainly is," Sam said, turning up the long, wooded drive that led from the main road to the farm property. At the top of a hill, the drive forked in two directions, one side leading to an old white farmhouse and the other toward acres of cultivated land, where trees and shrubs had been planted in long rows.

In front of the fields, about a quarter acre was surrounded by a frontier fence. Row upon row of Christmas trees of all kinds, shapes, and sizes stood waiting to be taken home and decorated. There was a small wooden shed to one side, large enough to hold just one or two people, a stool, and a cash box. Jessica noticed a sign on a chalkboard, listing the types of trees and prices. Balsam, spruce, Scotch pine, Douglas fir. Next to that was a brass bell with a rope pull that would call Jack if he was up at his house. If you really wanted him. If not, some customers just chose their trees and left the money. Things were done casually out here in the country.

Some distance behind the Christmas tree area, Jessica saw the small red barn. A faded sign that read NORTH POLE WORKSHOP hung over the white double doors at a crooked angle. She could remember the barn once filled with decorated wreaths, handmade ornaments and stockings, and baskets full of home-baked cakes and chocolates shaped like stars or reindeer.

Outside the barn, a large white horse with furry hooves would stomp around his yard, tossing his mane and tail, impatient to pull a cartload of children through the woods. If there was enough snow on the ground, Jack would hitch up a long wooden sleigh, covered with lap robes and jingling bells, and the children would get the ride of a lifetime.

Jessica remembered taking both her sons on those sleigh rides through the woods at night. The moon had been full and the snow-covered trees had looked edged with pure silver. It made her sad to see the place looking so bleak now. The shop was closed and the area with the Christmas trees had no decorations, not even a wreath or a bow. Just a few spotlights shining down so customers could shop at night.

"Looks like we're the only ones here tonight," Sam noticed as they climbed out of the SUV and headed for the trees. His words made white puffs in the frosty air. "How do you want to do this? Every man for himself, or do we walk around together?"

"It's too confusing if we run off in different directions," Jessica said. "I think we should look at the Douglas firs first. They don't dry out as quickly as the other kinds."

"Good point. Our tree has to hold on to its needles a *long* time." Sam looked at her, his brown eyes sparkling under dark brows.

Jessica smiled but didn't answer. She followed as Sam led the way to the maze of trees.

They had been browsing for a while when Jessica looked up to find Jack Sawyer walking toward them. At least she thought it was Jack. She hardly recognized him. His head was bowed under a knit cap pulled down low over his forehead. He looked like an old man, though she knew he was only a few years older than she was, in his early forties. His bearded face and mismatched, worn clothes made him look tired and defeated. So did the expression in his dark brown eyes. He stared at her, unsmiling.

"Hello, Jack. We're just looking for a tree." Jessica felt silly saying something so obvious. But the way he stared at her, and his blank expression, made her nervous.

"Sure. Take your time." He glanced over at Sam, who was conferring with the boys and Reilly. They seemed to have narrowed the search down to two or three choices. "Your older boy shot up, didn't he? He's getting big."

Jessica nodded. It had been a struggle the past two years to keep Darrell in blue jeans that didn't start riding up his shins like clam diggers. "He's fourteen. He grew about four inches this year."

"That's the age. He'll be even taller before you're through."

Jack sighed and rubbed his bearded chin. She wondered if he was thinking about his own son, David. David had left town, she heard, shortly after his mother died. Jessica wasn't sure what the young man was doing now, whether he was away at school or working somewhere. Something in Jack's demeanor made it hard to ask him any personal questions. He and his wife were members of the same church she and Sam attended, but she never saw Jack there anymore. She didn't really know him that well. She suspected his life was not easy, out here all alone now. He seemed unhappy and she suddenly felt sorry for him.

"Jess . . . can you come over here? I think we have a winner," Sam announced.

Jessica turned to join her family, relieved to end the awkward conversation.

A short time later, Jack lifted the large Christmas tree the Morgans had chosen onto a makeshift table near his work shed. It was just a sheet of plywood over two sawhorses. The first snowflakes had begun to fall, large, fat white feathers. They clung to the tree branches and to the top of Jack's hat and beard. He didn't seem to notice.

"You picked a tall one," he noted as he wrapped the tree in nylon webbing.

"My wife likes a tall tree." Sam glanced over and grinned at her. "We always have to saw off a few feet to get it to fit inside the house."

"Oh, Sam." Jessica shook her head. That wasn't true. Well . . . an exaggeration, for sure. Her husband loved to tease her. She was used to it by now.

With Sam's help, Jack tied the tree to the roof of the SUV and they were all set. Jessica had also found an untrimmed wreath for the front door and some pine roping, which Sam tossed inside. The boys and dog climbed in the back, and they were soon headed home as the snow began to fall steadily.

They were all talking and laughing together on the way home, the boys anticipating a snow day off from school tomorrow. The ride back went by quickly, and Sam soon turned down their own drive, nearly hidden on the wooded road.

Jessica loved the way the old house looked in the winter, coming into view from behind the trees. Especially tonight, with its peaked roof, porch pillars, and gingerbread molding edged with a fresh snowfall, its lines were graceful and welcoming. She loved the way it would soon look decorated for Christmas, like an illustration in a picture book.

It was beautiful now, a Victorian jewel, but the house had been deserted and just about falling down when Sam bought it at an auction two years before he and Jessica started dating. A carpenter and woodworker, Sam had a real vision for it and had done most of the restoration with his own skillful hands and heart.

Jessica had concentrated on the interior. Together they had created a masterpiece. It was a lot to keep up, that was true. But Jessica wouldn't have traded their antique treasure for the largest, most lavish mini-mansion to be found.

When they pulled up to the back door, Sam shut off the car and hopped out. "Darrell, help me get this tree down, will you?"

Jessica ran ahead to open the side door. "It's still early. We can put it up and decorate tonight. All the boxes are out." When Sam didn't answer, she added, "It's a big job. It's good to get it done early."

Carrying the tree toward the house with Darrell on the far end, Sam shook his head. "Don't give me that, Jess. Don't even try to tell me you're just being efficient or that the *boys* want to do it. I know you love to trim the tree. I know it's all you."

Jessica was grateful for the darkness that hid her smile. "I guess you got me," she admitted.

Sam laughed, a deep, warm sound that had done so much to make her fall in love with him.

"Yeah, I know. Lucky me." He quickly leaned over and kissed her cheek.

* * *

NOT LONG AFTER THE MORGANS DROVE OFF, JACK HAD SHUT OFF the spotlights and carried the metal cash box back up to his house. He pulled off his jacket, gloves, and hat, and tossed them in a heap in the mudroom. Then he walked into the kitchen and put the kettle on to boil.

The kitchen was an unholy mess. Pots and dishes were piled high in the sink, with more scattered across the counter and table. He looked in the cupboard for a clean mug, then ended up rinsing out one he found on the windowsill. There was more clutter on the table, boxes of cereal and crackers, a jar of jam and one of peanut butter, along with some more dirty dishes, piles of unopened mail, and old newspapers.

He had never been much of a housekeeper and lately had even less interest in keeping up. It just didn't seem worth the bother, living here alone.

It had been a busy weekend. Lots of families shopping for trees. The early birds, his wife, Claire, used to call them. "More early birds," she would say, peering out the window. "We'd better get out there, Jack."

But the sight would make her happy. She loved to sell the wreaths and decorations that she made. She loved to help each family select just the right tree for their holiday. She loved to talk to the children about Santa Claus and what presents they were hoping for.

Sometimes Jack missed her so badly it hurt, an aching feeling, deep in his bones. During the days after Claire had passed away, he wondered when the pain of missing her would fade. Now he knew. Never.

Having poured his water for the tea, he wrapped his big chapped hands around the warm mug and sat perfectly still in the silent house. He saw the snow falling past the window, a white veil fluttering in the darkness. *Flurries, my foot.* He knew what a heavy snow looked like coming down. He would be stuck in here by the morning. The weather forecasters, with all their satellites and radar and colored maps, still couldn't get it right.

He sighed and closed his eyes. As if that made a difference. He could die in his bed tonight. Nobody would find him for days. No one would know. Or care. No one in the entire world would miss him. David, *maybe.* If he ever found out. If he was even still alive. The only reason Jack stayed here at all was in the hope that David would get in touch. A hope that grew slimmer with each passing day.

If I left, Jack thought, *what would I do? Where would I go?*

Anywhere people don't celebrate Christmas. That was at the top of the list.

He hated Christmas now. He didn't know how he had survived it, two years in a row without Claire. He hated selling the trees to all these happy families. Like those Morgans, without a care in the world. They didn't know how good they had it. He had been like that once. A smiling idiot. So naive and trusting—of people, of life. He'd had no idea how quickly things could change. How his happiness could vanish in the blink of an eye, like snowflakes melting on your hand.

Each day that brought him closer to Christmas felt like salt rubbed in his wounds. He had been part of a happy family once, his wife and their boy. They had been his entire world, though perhaps he hadn't fully understood how important and how fragile that world was. He had wasted so much time fretting about his landscaping business and the nursery.

Then they were taken from him. Just like that. First Claire. Then David. He hadn't appreciated his blessings at all, not really.

He remembered those days now in this house, as if it had all happened in a dream.

He pushed the memories away and took a sip of his tea, gone cold in the cup. Living alone here, not talking to anyone sometimes for days, he lost track of time. Not just a few minutes here and there, but large swaths of a day would pass him by. He would look up and realize he had been in a daze, drifting in his thoughts for hours. He knew that wasn't good. And the way he had let things go around here—not good at all. He had to pull himself together before he crossed a line. Before it was too late. If only he knew how. He tried sometimes, he really did. But he didn't seem to have the energy and focus anymore. He didn't seem to have the heart.

He flipped open the metal cash box and slowly counted out the take for the day, more to have a constructive task to focus on than any real interest in his profits. He piled the bills in neat stacks on the table—ones, fives, tens and twenties. He didn't bother counting the coins, just scooped them up and tossed them in a shoe box he kept on a nearby shelf. He had a few of those boxes around the house, and he intended to take them to the bank someday. He felt sure the bank teller would laugh at him, would wonder if he kept all his money stashed in a mattress. Maybe that's why he never did it. He wrote a small note, recording the total, then put a rubber band around the bills and stuck the stack in a drawer in his desk.

It wasn't very late, but he didn't feel like watching TV. Thanksgiving was barely over, and already the Christmas shows and holiday commercials had taken over the airwaves. A tsunami of false, forced warmth and cheer. The TV screen just might remain blank and silent until the New Year, Jack reflected.

He strolled around the house and shut off the few remaining lights. He would be pushing the snowblower tomorrow, that was for sure. A few extra hours of sleep wouldn't hurt. He loved to sleep. It was the only time he didn't have to face his solitary existence. Sleep was oblivion, a blessing.

He stood in the parlor and stared out at the night and the falling snow. He wondered if his wife was in heaven, watching him. He wasn't sure if he believed in heaven anymore but if anyone deserved to be there, it was Claire. She had a truly beautiful soul, kind and good hearted. She saw the best in everyone. She went to church and even prayed at night, before she fell asleep. From time to time, he had gone to church, too. Just to please her. But after she died he didn't keep that connection. The pastor there, Reverend Something-or-other, tried a few times to reach out to him, but Jack wasn't interested in hearing any of those comforting clichés. Someone telling him his wife was in a better place, or that it had been her time. How was that supposed to make him feel better?

Maybe there is no heaven, he thought, turning away from the window. *Maybe there's just nothing more than this here and now. A harsh conclusion on a cold night, my friend,* he told himself. *I think it's time you went to bed.*

He was about to turn off the porch light and head back to his room near the kitchen when he heard a sharp knock on the door. He felt his temper rising. There were some crazy people—young couples mostly—who came shopping for Christmas trees at all hours of the night. As if they expected him to be a twenty-four-hour convenience store. He had a good mind not to answer, but he knew that type never took the hint. They would only knock louder.

And so they did in the time it took for him to reach the door and turn the handle.

He yanked open the door, about to tell whomever he found on his doorstep where to get off.

A wide-eyed woman stood staring back at him. She wore a blue down jacket, the hood pulled over her head, soft brown curls slipping out from the edges and framing her face. One hand was stuck deep in a pocket. The other circled a small child who clung to her leg.

The sight threw him off. It was not at all what he expected to see. He realized he was staring and cleared his throat. "Are you here for a tree? I'm closed."

The woman shook her head. "I realized that. I'm sorry to bother you, sir, honestly." The way she'd called him "sir" made Jack flinch. Made him feel old and grouchy. Which he was, he realized. Older than her, anyway.

"I had some car trouble on the road, right in front of your house. I managed to get it partway up the drive before it just went dead. My cell-phone battery is gone. We saw your light on and walked up. Could I trouble you to use the phone?"

He nodded quickly. "Sure. Come on in." He stepped aside to let them in. The child, a little girl, clung so fiercely to the woman's leg that the mother walked with a stilted gait.

She smiled at him then looked down at the little girl. "My daughter, Kate. She's very tired."

He stared at the child a moment, fascinated by her puffy pink jacket, trimmed in white fur with prancing unicorns embroidered on the front. He suddenly looked back up at the woman.

"My name is Jack. Jack Sawyer." He stretched out his hand, remembering his manners. Then he shuddered at the sight of his chafed skin and broken nails, stained black from the tree sap.

She didn't appear to notice. She seemed relieved by the gesture and shook his hand firmly. "Julie Newton. Nice to meet you."

She pushed her hood back and her hair sprang free. Jack could see it had been gathered in back with some sort of clip, but most of it had come loose. She brushed it back nervously with her fingers. Then she looked back at him. She had beautiful eyes, large brown ones that seemed to telegraph her every thought. He could see she felt wary of him. Or nervous. Or both.

He stepped back quickly and cleared his throat. "The phone is in the kitchen," he said, leading the way to the back of the house. They stood at the kitchen doorway and he flicked on the light.

The disaster scene he had so easily ignored earlier stretched out before them. He could have sworn he heard the woman muffle a gasp.

"Sorry for the mess. It's been a hectic weekend. I've been outside working a lot. . . ." He stepped over to the table and scooped up as many dirty dishes and cups as he could handle.

"Don't worry. Please. Don't fuss." She stood stiffly in the doorway, not daring to venture in.

Of course, she knew this level of mess had not happened over the weekend. It couldn't even happen over an entire week. A mess like this was like a Category 4 hurricane, Jack thought. It took time and the right conditions to amass.

He swept a pile of newspapers and magazines off a stool by the phone, then wiped the seat with a dish towel for good measure. "Have a seat. Here's the phone," he said, handing her the receiver.

She forced a smile and stepped forward, her little girl stuck to her side as if by Velcro. She eyed the chair for a moment, sat, and then hoisted the child into her lap, though the girl seemed a bit big for such treatment.

"I'm not sure who to call. Is there a tow service you know of? Or a taxi?"

Jack was surprised by her question. Of course, she needed to have her car towed. But when she had said she wanted to make a call, he thought she meant to call her husband, or someone equally significant in her life, to come get her.

Jack ran a hand through his hair. "The service station in town will send out a truck. But not at this hour. We don't have much of a taxi service around here either. A few cabs by the train station, but I doubt they're running now. Where do you need to go? I can give you a lift."

"Oh, no. I couldn't ask you to do that." Julie Newton shook her head. She looked down to find her daughter touching something sticky on the table and quickly pulled the little hand away.

Jack rubbed his cheek then smoothed down his scraggly beard with his hand. He looked worse than the kitchen. No wonder this woman was afraid of him. "Where were you headed when the car broke down? Is anyone expecting you?"

"We're on our way to Long Island from Maine," she explained. "My brother lives there with his family." She took a breath. Jack wondered if she would say more, or if that was all the explanation he would get.

"Long Island is a long way from here. Were you planning on driving through the night?" An ambitious schedule, he thought. The town of Cape Light was north of Boston and about five hours from Long Island. The drive was even longer in bad weather.

Julie shrugged. "I was going to stop somewhere. I don't really like driving in the snow," she confessed.

"Looks like you've stopped here." He glanced at her then back at the cluttered counter. He picked up a cereal box and stashed it in the cabinet. As if that would help; he almost laughed at himself out loud.

"Maybe you can give us a ride to town? To a motel or something?"

"There's a motel on the highway. But it's a long way, especially in the snow. And that place has been looking pretty run-down lately. I wouldn't recommend it," he added.

The little girl was dozing now, her head resting on her mother's chest. The woman stroked her daughter's hair. The soft curls matched the mother's, in miniature, he noticed. He studied Julie's profile, her high cheekbones and wide mouth. She looked tired, too, he thought, but it only seemed to add to her loveliness.

Jack crossed his arms over his chest. "You can stay here. I guess." His tone was gruff, offhand. "There's a guest room upstairs, two twin beds."

She looked shocked by the offer and he instantly regretted it.

"We couldn't do that. . . . It's too much trouble for you."

"No trouble. It's the cleanest part of the house," he added, with a wry smile. "I never go up there anymore." He paused and met her glance. "I realize I'm a complete stranger and you're thinking, *What if he's a nutcase or something?* There's a solid lock on the door and I sleep down here." He pointed to his room, a short distance down the hallway.

She hesitated. "I'd hate to bother you like that, Mr. Sawyer."

Again he silently winced at her polite title; it seemed to age him.

"Call me Jack. And it's no bother. Honest." He glanced at her, feeling self-conscious and annoyed. He suddenly saw himself through her eyes, what he was—what he'd turned into living alone here these last two years.

A messy, half-crazed, eccentric old man. Though he knew now, in the bright kitchen light, he wasn't all that much older than she was. Though unquestionably attractive, he guessed her age to be in the mid-thirties. He was only forty-two, for goodness sake. But

the way she looked at him, he felt sixty-two. He turned to the cluttered counter again and matched the coffee can with its plastic lid,
clumsily pushing it on until it fit.

"Okay . . . I mean, thanks. I'm grateful for your help. Really,"
she said.

She rose from her chair, cradling her little girl against her body.
The child looked too heavy for her to carry easily, and Jack thought
he should offer to take her. Then he stopped himself. The little
girl probably wouldn't like it, and her mother probably wouldn't let
him anyway.

"Okay, follow me. I'll get you some sheets and blankets. It
might be a little cold up there," he warned as they headed back
toward the staircase.

"No colder than sleeping in my car. Which is where we would
have ended up if you weren't here."

I'm not really here, lady, he wanted to say. *This is just an illusion.
A really good impression of a person I used to know.*

Just as he had promised, the guest room was clean and neat,
with twin beds separated by a night table and an oval rug in
between. The walls were pale blue and the curtains were off-white
linen with blue ticking stripes. Painting the room had been one
of the last projects his wife had taken on, just before she got sick.
Claire, who had been full of energy up until then, loved to do work
around the house, even painting and refinishing furniture.

The bedroom was a far cry from the mess downstairs, and Jack
could tell Julie was relieved.

He quickly retrieved some linens and blankets from the hall
closet and began to make up the beds. Julie gently laid her daughter down on one bed and helped him with the other. When the first
was done, she moved her daughter over and they set to work again.

Their shoulders brushed for a moment as they both tugged cases over pillows. Jack forced himself not to look at her.

She quickly stepped back. "That's fine. I can finish up. You've done enough. Really."

He nodded and stepped back toward the door. "Can I get you anything from your car? I have to go out again anyway . . . to check the trash. Animals."

His explanation wasn't entirely true. Weeks had gone by without him worrying about raccoons. Lately, he would hear the sound of them raiding his garbage in the middle of the night, and all he felt was weary resignation. *Fine, let them have their raccoon smorgasbord.* But he suspected Julie did need some items from her luggage. All women did. And it was still snowing out there.

Julie stood up from where she had been working on the bed and brushed a strand of hair off her cheek. "If you're going out anyway, I could use the blue duffel bag in the backseat. My car is about halfway down the drive. It's unlocked."

"Okay, I'll get it for you."

She nodded. "Thank you, Jack. You've been very kind."

He shook off her thanks. At least she hadn't called him sir or Mr. Sawyer again.

"I'll leave the bag at the top of the stairs. If there's anything else, let me know."

He felt her watching him. He walked out of the room and down the stairs, then headed outside. He stood on the porch a moment and took a long, deep breath. The air was frigid. He felt the sharp cold travel deep in his lungs. Then felt his head slowly clear.

The snow was falling heavily now. It was definitely not just the flurry the weather report predicted. There would be a few inches on the ground by the morning. Jack strode down the drive that led to the road and looked for Julie's car. He wore only a flannel shirt and a down vest, but felt oblivious to the cold and snow. He hardly noticed it, his thoughts still spinning.

He wasn't used to being around a woman. That's all it was.

She and the girl would be gone in the morning, as soon as the tow trucks were running. *So no reason to go off the deep end, pal,* he coached himself.

But the woman and her child sure put a surprise twist in his evening. He had to admit that much.

"SO HOW DO YOU LIKE OUR TREE THIS YEAR, MRS. CLAUS? DOES it meet with your approval?"

Sam and Jessica sat close together on the couch in the living room, their arms around each other. The tree was trimmed, the hot cocoa and cookies gobbled up completely. The boys had long gone to bed, and now the only lights left on in the entire house were the banked embers in the fireplace and the tiny bulbs hidden in the branches of pine.

"I think it's the prettiest we've ever had."

He laughed quietly. "You always say that, Jess."

She laughed, too, and settled her cheek against his chest again. "Well, why even ask me then if you know what I'm going to say?"

He kissed the top of her head. "Because I love to tease you."

"I know that," she murmured. She sighed and was silent a moment, content just to sit quietly, sharing this special time with her husband. "Jack Sawyer still sells the best trees. But I felt sorry for him. He seemed so sad and lonely out there. . . . He looked awful," she added. "I hardly recognized him."

"I know what you mean. Losing his wife has been hard on him."

"Where's his son? I didn't want to ask. It seemed too personal."

"I'm not sure. I think David left town a few months after Claire died. That must have been hard on Jack, too."

Jessica sighed. "I hope our boys don't move far away from us when they grow up. I know they each have to go out on their own, but I don't want them too far away. Especially at the holidays."

Sam squeezed her closer. "We have years to worry about that yet, Jess. Darrell just started high school."

"I know, but time goes by so quickly. Even faster as you get older. Don't you get that feeling sometimes? I feel as if we just got married and moved into this house. It's all gone by in the blink of an eye."

"I know what you mean. Maybe that's because we're happy. We have to count our blessings. Let's try to relax and make the most of the holidays this year. And the time we have left with the kids still growing up. Maybe, if we're lucky, we'll have another baby soon."

He peered down at her. Jessica avoided his glance. She was hoping she would get pregnant this year. She knew Sam was, too, but she didn't like to talk too much about it.

"We are very blessed," she said carefully. "It seems wrong to ask for more. There are so many people facing the holidays who hardly have anything to feel happy or grateful about."

Sam nodded, not saying anything. Then he pulled her closer and they kissed. Her marriage and loving Sam were at the top of her list of blessings. It didn't seem so long ago that she had met Sam and fallen head over heels for him, though at the time she was sure their romance would never work out. They were opposites in so many ways. At least, on the surface. But defying probability—and her mother's disapproval—they were married. Sam had changed her life and all her plans. Their life together had turned out to be much more wonderful and fulfilling than anything she had ever imagined.

They were so lucky, Jessica thought as she held her husband close. It was times like this when she had to remind herself that her worries were so trivial. Sam was better at that. He helped her keep life in perspective, to focus on the good and cultivate a thankful heart. She had to remember that. Especially at the holidays.

CHAPTER TWO

ᴊessica woke slowly, feeling confused. She stared
into the darkness. She heard Sam breathing deeply beside
her, then some other sound.

The smoke alarm. Shrieking over and over.

Could it possibly be?

She sniffed the air. She smelled a faint whiff of smoke. They'd
had a fire in the fireplace tonight. Would that set it off?

She shook Sam's shoulder. "Sam, wake up. The smoke alarm."

Sam rolled on to his back and stared at her. Even in the darkness she could see his expression change swiftly.

He bolted upright then practically leaped out of bed, his eyes
wide. "Quick, grab some shoes. I'll get Darrell, you get Tyler. Meet
me at the head of the stairs."

Sam was up and out of bed. She saw him fumbling on the

nightstand, grabbing his cell phone, then he scooped up a pair of sneakers as he dashed down the hall.

Jessica grabbed her robe and slippers but didn't stop to put them on. She ran into Tyler's room and flipped on the lights, then ran to his bed. He squinted at her, one arm raised against the sudden burst of light.

"What'd you do that for?" he mumbled sleepily.

"Get up, honey. Get up now." She tried her best not to scare him but couldn't keep the urgent note from her voice.

On the floor by his bedside, she found a pair of sneakers and a sweatshirt. She tugged him up, nearly pulling him out of the bed by his arm.

"You have to get up, Tyler. We have to go. Right now!" She tried not to shout or sound hysterical. But it was impossible. She could smell the smoke clearly now. It was no fluke from the fireplace ashes.

"Mommy, what's the matter?" Tyler stared at her, his voice shaky and confused as he stumbled out of the room.

"We have to get out of the house. Just stay with me. Don't let go of my hand." She put him in front of her, pushing him down the hallway toward the stairs.

"Come on! Come on, you two!" Sam shouted. He stood at the top of the staircase with Darrell. "I think we can still get out the front door. Let's go!"

They descended the stairway in single file, walking as quickly as they could without bumping into one another. She heard Sam on his cell phone. He had called 911 and was talking to the operator. Tyler was scared. He cried softly, but thankfully kept moving.

"—Yes, on Beach Road. Number six-oh-nine. You can't see the

house from the road," Sam said. "There's a mailbox at the bottom of the drive. It says Morgan. . . ."

The smoke grew thicker, absorbing the light. The smell was nearly overpowering. Jessica heard Darrell coughing and then Tyler. Tyler paused on the stairs and she pushed him forward.

"Don't stop. Just keep going."

She heard Sam cough but could hardly see the outline of his body now. "Quick, everyone. To the front door then run down to the end of the drive and wait for me. Try to cover your mouth with something—your bathrobe or pajamas."

Sam ran ahead and opened the door. Jessica saw Darrell fly through the smoke, then Tyler followed. She rushed past Sam, using the edge of her robe to cover her mouth. Her eyes stung and she could hardly breathe as she pushed out of the house into the cold air.

She heard the door slam then felt Sam grab her arm. Together, they ran across the snowy lawn. Her bare feet froze instantly. But she hardly felt it. She saw the boys and felt a great relief in her heart. They had all made it out. Thank God.

Tyler was shivering and crying. Darrell had his arm around his little brother's shoulder. Jessica ran to them. Tyler pointed to the house, unable to speak.

Jessica turned. The house was glowing, the windows on the first floor lit by an eerie yellow light. Smoke poured out of the back windows and chimney. A window at the back of the house burst. The sound of splintering glass and crackling flames shooting out made Jessica jump back and reach for her children.

"Oh, dear Lord . . ."

"Daddy, did you let Reilly out? He was right behind me," Darrell said. A note of alarm peaked in his voice. "I don't see him. . . ."

Sam closed his eyes slowly, and Jessica knew that in the urgency of saving his sons, he had forgotten the dog.

Darrell stared at Sam for a long moment. Then he turned and raced toward the house, kicking up snow with every flying step.

Jessica screamed, "Darrell, no! Sam! Get him! He's going back inside!"

Darrell dashed toward the house at full speed. Sam chased after him. Jessica saw his feet slip in the snow and knew that Darrell would make it to the porch before his father could catch up.

"Darrell, stop!" Sam's voice was hoarse, anguished. "You stop right now! Don't you dare go in there. . . ."

Jessica watched Darrell pull the front door open. A cloud of black smoke poured out as he rushed inside and disappeared instantly.

Sam took the porch steps two at a time and ran into the burning house right behind him.

"No! Stop!" Jessica covered her mouth with her hand. Beside her, Tyler sobbed. Jessica knelt down and put her arms around him. She buried her face in his shoulder for a moment, not daring to see if Sam and Darrell had come out.

"Dear God . . . please. Please let them come out of that house right now. Please God. . . . I'll never ask for another thing in my life. I promise."

Jessica stared at the house, blinking back tears, the simple, heartfelt prayer running in a silent loop through her mind.

"Mommy?"

"Shhh . . . just a minute, Ty. Just a minute . . ."

She patted her little boy's shoulder and bit down on her lip, her gaze fixed on the burning house. She could hear sirens in the distance, coming closer. But the fire was growing even faster, the smoke dense and black. More windows had burst on the first floor, and flames seemed to leap out from all sides.

"Darrell! Sam!" She cupped her hands around her mouth and screamed at the top of her lungs. "Come out! Please! Come out now!" she shouted.

Tyler turned and buried his face against her leg.

Finally, she saw them. Not at the front door where her gaze had been fixed, but coming around the side of the house.

She nearly collapsed with relief at the sight. "Look Tyler, they're okay . . . and they have Reilly."

Sam walked with his arm around Darrell's shoulder. Darrell carried the dog in his arms. Reilly looked limp. Jessica wondered if the poor dog had made it after all.

Sam and Darrell's faces and pajamas were covered with black soot. Darrell was coughing loudly but wouldn't give Sam the dog.

"Thank God!" Jessica ran to them, her bare feet slipping in the snow. She put her hands on Darrell's shoulders and stared at him, suddenly conscious that he was now almost as tall as she was. She wanted to give him the scolding of a lifetime for disobeying her. All she could do was cry.

Darrell stood with his head hanging down, staring at Reilly. "He can't breathe, Mom. He needs oxygen."

Sam put his hand on Darrell's shoulder. "The fire department is here. Don't worry. They'll take care of him."

The fire trucks had arrived. Jessica turned to see two large red trucks pull up and roll right past them. They parked close to the house, and firefighters in long black coats, hats, and boots, jumped out from all sides.

They began unfastening the ladders and pulling out hoses. Jessica recognized Fire Chief Rhinehardt.

"Everyone out of the house?" he asked, hurrying toward them.

Sam nodded. "Yes, we're all here. I think my son inhaled too much smoke." He glanced back at Darrell, who sat in the snow, cradling Reilly in his lap and coughing harshly. "And the dog, too. He can't breathe."

"We'll get them some oxygen right away." Rhinehardt turned to the house. "Looks like the fire started around back. We'll pull the pumper over and start there," he said, starting back to his crew. "It's moving fast. I can see it's already reached the second floor. You folks were lucky."

Sam sighed. He looked over at Jessica, who stood a little distance away with the boys. "Yes . . . we were. Very lucky."

An ambulance pulled up and parked behind the fire trucks. Two EMTs climbed out and rushed over to them. "How are you doing? Anyone injured?" one of the workers asked.

Jessica shook her head. "My son's having trouble breathing. He inhaled a lot of smoke."

The EMT walked over to Darrell and crouched down beside him. "How are you doing, son?"

Darrell tried to speak but could only cough in answer.

"Let's get you in the ambulance and take a look at you."

"My dog needs help, too," Darrell managed.

"I can give some oxygen to your dog. Sure thing." He gently stroked the dog's head. "What's his name?"

"Reilly." Darrell rubbed his hand over his eyes. Jessica rested her hand on his shoulder. She could see he had been crying.

"Don't worry. We'll help Reilly. Just come with me."

The other EMT had handed Jessica blankets, and she wrapped them around herself and Tyler then followed Darrell to the ambulance. She sat inside the ambulance with her younger son while

Darrell was given oxygen. The med tech fixed a small mask over Reilly's muzzle and carefully administered some to him, too.

Darrell let the dog lie on the stretcher while he sat on a narrow bench on the side of the vehicle and stroked the dog's head. The sight made Jessica start crying all over again.

She turned her head and saw Sam standing by one of the trucks, talking to a firefighter. The fire now completely consumed the house, top and bottom. A light wind blew most of the smoke away from the front of the house where they stood. But the black clouds still hung in the air, the soot raining down from the sky, coating the newly fallen snow. The snow in the front yard had been trod to mud by all the firefighters rushing about.

Jessica could hardly stand to look at their house burning, but she couldn't take her gaze away from it. The crackling sound as the fire consumed the wooden structure, the firefighters shouting as they battled the blaze. From time to time, she heard more windows explode or something crash inside the building. Perhaps it was the floor caving in, she thought, or walls falling down.

It was a nightmare. One she couldn't wake up from. Everything she owned, everything she needed. Heirlooms from her family and Sam's, all their records and photos and books. All her jewelry. All the boys' clothes and toys and silly little things she had saved since they were small—their school art projects, Tyler's teething ring, and Darrell's Little League awards. Everything that was of any value to her or her family was in that house. Burning before her very eyes. Going up in smoke.

How could this be happening?

It seemed impossible.

She watched a fireman standing at the top of a ladder swing

a long ax and hack a hole in the roof. Then others on the ground directed the spray of water from the hose into the attic.

Even though the house was already filled with flames and smoke, purposely breaking through the roof somehow seemed such a violation. It made the entire effort to stop the fire seem so . . . hopeless.

Sam walked back to the ambulance and looked up at her. "How are you doing, Jess?"

"We're doing okay," she replied, though she hardly felt that way.

He jumped up and sat next to her then put his arm around her shoulder. "They've called Essex for backup. Another pumper and crew should be here soon."

Soon would be too late, Jessica thought. It was already too late.

"How's Darrell?" he asked.

Jessica glanced back at the boys. "Better. He's stopped coughing. I'm not so sure about Reilly. Thank God, you two came out alive. I lost years off my life waiting for you."

"It was a miracle to get out the first time. I guess we have a lot to be grateful for."

Jessica looked up at him and saw the shadows from the fire flickering on his face. She nodded but didn't answer. She didn't feel very grateful right now. Not with their entire house burning down in front of them.

But how would she be feeling if Sam and Darrell had not come out of the house together? Or if one or both of them had perished inside? She looked down and sighed. Hadn't she been begging God just moments ago to save her husband and son? It was horribly ungrateful to add footnotes now.

A police cruiser came up the drive, followed by a dark blue Jeep

Cherokee, her sister Emily's vehicle. Emily was the town mayor; Jessica realized someone must have called her.

"We'll be right back," Jessica told the boys as she and Sam started over to where Officer Tucker Tulley was getting out of his car.

"I heard the call on the radio," Tucker explained, his face grim. "For a minute, I didn't realize it was your place. Then I called your sister and headed straight over."

Emily, wearing snow boots and a long down coat that was buttoned over her pajamas, ran toward them. "Oh, Jess, Sam . . ." She glanced at the house then hugged Jessica, squeezing her tight. Emily was always so controlled and coolheaded, even in a crisis. The sight of the burning house had really shaken her, Jessica realized. "Everyone okay?"

Sam nodded. "We all got out fine, thank God."

"Then Darrell ran back inside for the dog," Jessica added, "and Sam ran in after him. But . . . here we are."

Tucker peered into the ambulance. "Kids. They don't realize the danger."

"Jessica, you must have nearly died waiting for them to come out."

"I nearly did," Jessica admitted. Emily hugged her again. "He loves that dog so much," Jessica said quietly. "I hope Reilly makes it. He's not breathing very well, even with the oxygen."

"How is the crew doing? Is it under control?" Emily asked.

"They're doing their best," Sam said quietly. "A truck from Essex should be here any moment."

Emily stared at the house, transfixed by the sight of the leaping flames and smoke. Jessica noticed the expression on Emily's face; it wasn't a good sign. Jessica knew her sister had seen many fires, large and small. She could probably tell if anything would be left of their house or if the firemen had gotten there too late.

Emily suddenly turned away from the fire and looked back at Jessica. "You must be freezing. Come home with me. No sense standing out here all night. There's nothing more you can do."

Jessica didn't answer. She didn't know what she wanted to do—or what she should do. What was the proper way to behave when your house was on fire?

"Emily's right," Sam said. "Why don't you and the boys go back to her house? I'll stay here with the firemen."

Jessica didn't like the idea of being separated from Sam right now. After he ran into the house following Darrell, she didn't want to let him out of her sight. But she knew it made sense to get the boys inside somewhere. It wasn't right to have them watch their house burn to the ground.

Maybe she didn't have to see that either, she decided.

"Yes, you're right. I'll take the boys to Emily's. Let me get them. . . ." She walked back to the ambulance. Sam and Emily followed. Tucker Tulley was already there, talking to the EMTs.

Tyler sat wrapped in a blanket, his head leaning back against the wall, his eyes closed. Sam climbed inside and picked him up, then carried him toward Emily's car.

Darrell looked up at his mother and aunt. "Darrell, Aunt Emily's here," Jessica said. "We're going back to her house."

Darrell's hand stroked the dog's silky flank. "What about Reilly? He's still not breathing so well. I think he needs a vet, Mom."

Jessica felt overwhelmed. She didn't know what to do about poor Reilly. How could they possibly find a vet at this hour?

"There's a twenty-four-hour veterinary clinic on the highway," Emily said. "I'll ask Tucker to take Reilly there. Would that be okay?"

Darrell nodded. "I guess."

He gently lifted the dog. Reilly moved his head with effort and licked Darrell's hand.

Sam came back to the ambulance and helped Darrell carry Reilly down. Jessica saw Emily talking to Tucker, and then the two of them returned together.

"Put Reilly in my car," Tucker said to Sam. "I'll bring him right to the clinic," he promised.

"Thank you, Tucker." Sam had the dog now and carried him toward the cruiser.

Tucker followed them. "No trouble. It's the least I can do."

Jessica watched as the dog was carefully set in the backseat of the police car. Sam put his arm around Darrell as Tucker drove away, his emergency light flashing.

Darrell pressed his head to his father's shoulder, then after a moment, stood up straight again. He was trying to be a man, but it was hard, Jessica realized. He was really just a boy. She felt tears in her eyes and blinked them away. She felt bad about Reilly, too. But she loved Darrell so much. She thanked God again that he wasn't hurt.

"Come on, Jess." Emily came up behind her and coaxed her toward the car. "Tyler woke up, he wants you. Sam will take care of Darrell."

Jessica nodded and followed her sister. She wanted to look at the house but forced herself not to turn her head.

She knew what it looked like.

She would never forget the sight.

JACK WOKE TO THE SMELL OF COFFEE. HE DIDN'T IMMEDIATELY remember that he had guests. He rolled on his side, listening to the sounds coming from the kitchen. He heard Julie's voice almost whispering, then Kate's, higher pitched and louder. He climbed out of bed and headed for the bathroom that was adjoined to his bedroom.

He had not always slept in the downstairs room. It had been David's bedroom when he was a teenager. But after Claire died, Jack didn't feel right going back to the room they had shared. Once David was gone, Jack had ended up in here. He hadn't changed a thing. His son's sports posters and high school souvenirs still hung on the walls. The clothes he had left behind were pushed to the back of the closet.

Jack sometimes wondered if camping out here was just a way to feel close to David. To keep his hope alive.

He emerged from the shower and ran his hand over his bearded cheeks. He hadn't trimmed his beard in a long time. There hadn't been any reason to bother. But today he found a small scissors in the medicine cabinet and made a few snips. He gave up almost at once. There was a lot of gray mixed in his beard now. He had hardly noticed that before. Then again, he had never worn a beard while Claire was alive. She hated that look on men. But now it seemed more convenient.

He combed back his wet hair, noticing the length. He ought to get a haircut. One of these days.

Back in the bedroom, he found a clean pair of jeans and a waffle-knit Henley shirt in a laundry basket. He pulled on a clean denim shirt over that. He didn't bother to check his appearance in the mirror as he pulled on socks and work boots. He wasn't any fashion model from a mail-order catalogue, but at least he looked cleaned up. Cleaner than last night, anyway.

When he walked into the kitchen, Julie looked up and her

eyebrows rose in surprise. Embarrassed by her reaction, he quickly turned to pull a mug from the cabinet.

"Coffee smells good," he said. "Did you sleep okay?"

"Very well, thank you. Looks like a few inches of snow fell last night."

"Yes, it did pile up." He peered out the kitchen window then turned back to the table. Kate, who was eating a bowl of Cheerios, shyly glanced up at him.

"I gave Katie some cereal. I hope you don't mind."

"Of course not." He shook his head and sipped the coffee. It was strong, the way he liked it.

He stood watching Katie gobble up her cereal and remembered that he had heard them late at night, down in the kitchen. Julie was quietly feeding the little girl a snack. He realized then that they must have been hungry and he should have offered them something before they went up to bed. His manners were rusty, that was for sure.

"I'm just going to fix myself some eggs and bacon . . . and toast and stuff." He pulled open the refrigerator, scanned its meager contents, and began pulling out the breakfast ingredients. "Would you like some?" he asked Julie.

She shook her head, but Katie was staring at him, her spoon dangling in the air. She sure looked interested in the menu.

"How about Katie? She'd like some bacon, I bet."

Julie glanced at her daughter. "She's fine."

Katie's expression fell. Jack turned back to the stove and turned on the gas burner. He didn't want to overrule her mother, but he could practically see the child's mouth watering.

"Well, I have to finish this up. It's not worth keeping a few pieces in the fridge. I'll cook it all and if she doesn't want it, I'll save it for a sandwich or something."

Julie sat back in her chair but didn't say anything. Jack glanced at Kate. Her face looked relieved and then he actually saw a flicker of a smile.

"Finish your cereal. Then you can have something else," her mother said quietly.

Kate got back to work on her Cheerios while Jack whisked up a pan of scrambled eggs and cooked the bacon in a skillet. A few minutes later, he set two platters on the table, one filled with eggs and bacon, the other with a pile of toast.

Julie took out plates and silverware. "We're usually in too much of a rush in the morning to eat a real breakfast."

"No rush today," he pointed out. "Help yourself."

He caught Kate's eye and winked at her. She stared at him then slipped a strip of bacon onto her plate.

Julie gave up arguing. She dished some eggs and bacon onto Kate's plate and slid the rest on to her own.

"You need a good breakfast. We'll need to do some digging to get your car out," Jack predicted.

"Oh, you don't have to bother. Just give me a shovel. I can do it."

Jack tried not to laugh. Her car was on the part of the hill where the snow drifted the highest. From what he could see last night, the tires were bald and wouldn't get traction if it had snowed saltwater taffy. *If* he could even get the old thing started.

"What exactly was wrong with the car? You didn't say."

Julie shrugged and sipped her coffee. "It was making this funny sound. Then a light started flashing on the dashboard."

Could be anything, he thought. "It would cost a lot to have it towed from here. Let's try to start it up and get it into town. I'll follow you to the service station."

"I guess it would be best to drive it if I can." He could tell from her expression that money was an issue.

Julie finished her breakfast and started clearing the plates and loading the dishwasher.

"Don't bother with that. I'll do it later," Jack said.

"It's okay. You made breakfast. I don't want to leave you with a big mess," she insisted.

He watched her a moment then turned to look at Kate, who was remarkably quiet for a little girl. He guessed her age to be about five. Maybe a bit younger. She was still eating her bacon, holding a strip between her fingers and working down the slice in small mechanical bites. It reminded him of David when he was little. He had done the same thing.

Jack sighed and sipped his coffee. "I bet you have a lot of snow in Maine by now," he said to Julie.

She was scrubbing the frying pans and turned from the sink to glance at him. "We sure do. We were living in Carlisle. It's a very pretty town just south of Bar Harbor. They made a movie there a few years ago."

"Sounds nice. So you don't live there anymore?" he asked, trying to get her story straight in his mind. "Are you moving to Long Island permanently?"

She nodded. "I don't really want to. But I lost my job and I was divorced two years ago."

"What kind of work do you do?"

"I'm an art teacher. The school district had budget cutbacks and I was the last one hired, so . . ."

"That's too bad." He could see her as a teacher. She had a certain way about her. Quiet and able. He could see her managing a roomful of noisy kids without getting flustered. It was a tough break to lose a good job like that, especially this time of year.

"I don't really want to go down to New York. My brother's house is not that big, and it's going to be difficult. But we had to move out of our apartment, and he offered to help. I need a few months to get back on my feet," she added. Jack could tell from her voice that this was hard for her to admit. "It will just be temporary. I'll take any kind of job. It doesn't have to be teaching."

"Oh, sure. That shouldn't take long." He meant it, too. She was so bright and well-spoken. Anyone would hire her.

He got to his feet, grabbed a broom, and began sweeping up. He wondered about Katie's father. Julie hadn't mentioned a husband, only an ex-husband. Didn't divorced fathers need to send some support money for their kids? Of course he knew a lot of men didn't live up to their responsibilities. Perhaps that was the case here. But he had asked enough questions for now.

A few minutes later, they were all warmly dressed and headed down the hill to Julie's car. Jack carried the snowblower, and Julie carried a shovel. Kate wore her pink unicorn jacket, Jack noticed, this time with matching waterproof pants and rubber snow boots. Her hood was pulled up, tied tight, and a scarf was tied around her neck. She also wore thick waterproof mittens, clipped onto her coat sleeves.

Thrilled with the snow, she awkwardly ran ahead in her snow gear. Then she slipped and began sliding down the hill on her bottom. Her mitten-covered hands waved in the air like pink flippers.

Julie ran after her and helped her up. Kate seemed surprised but didn't cry. Julie got her back on her feet and they started down the hill once more.

Kate quickly broke away from the grown-ups and repeated the

performance, falling on her bottom and sliding down the hill, this time on purpose.

Julie called after her, and Jack touched her arm.

"She's okay. Just having a little fun. I should have looked for a sled or something. I'm sure I have one somewhere."

Julie glanced at him, a warm look in her soft brown eyes. "That's okay. You've done enough."

He hadn't done much, he thought. Just given them a place to sleep and some scrambled eggs. But it was nice of her to say.

When they reached her car, it was as bad as he expected. Maybe worse. He got to work with the snowblower and then they used the shovel. Julie got Kate working on a snowman, so she was well occupied and out of the way.

Finally, the door on the driver's side was clear and he was able to climb inside. He turned the key in the ignition and at first heard just a click. Then the engine revved up and finally turned over.

"Good job!" Julie jumped up and clapped her hands.

Jack felt like a hero, though he knew it was silly to even smile back at her. Big deal. He started the car.

Now to get it out of here. That would really be a feat worthy of applause. He left the engine running and climbed out. With all the heavy clothing on, he'd started to sweat. He wiped his hand over his brow and took a look at the car.

"Let's just let the engine run a minute and warm up. Then you get in and I'll push."

She glanced at him. "Are you sure?"

"It will be okay. It's going to need a push to get back on the road. There's no way those tires are going to grip the snow."

It was surprising the car had even passed inspection, Jack thought.

Julie nodded. "All right. If you think that will work."

"It's worth a try."

Julie slipped behind the wheel and shut the door. "Just tell me what to do."

"When I say, 'Go,' hit the gas. Just give me a second to get back there."

"Okay." He saw Julie ready herself. She gripped the wheel and stared straight ahead, as if she were behind the starting gate at the Indy 500.

Jack shook his head. She was so . . . sweet. It got to him; he couldn't help it. He got behind the car, gripped the bumper on one side, and leaned his weight into it. "Okay, go!"

Julie hit the gas and he pushed with all his might.

The car lurched forward. He was gratified for a moment . . . then fell forward, scrambling to keep his balance. He felt his ankle turn painfully inside his boot as he came down hard on the icy snow.

He bit his lip, stifling a shout, then rolled to his side and quietly groaned. The pain was intense.

Julie shut the engine and jumped out of the car. He tried to get up but could barely come to a sitting position.

She knelt down next to him. "What happened? Are you all right?"

"My ankle. I twisted it."

"Oh, dear." She sat back on her heels, her brow wrinkled in concern.

"I don't think it's too bad," he said. "Sometimes these things just pass if you work them out."

When it came to physical injuries, Jack was king of the "work out the pain" school. He took a breath, stretched out his leg, and forced himself to flex his foot. Another searing bolt shot through his leg. He tried not to grimace but couldn't help it.

Julie looked alarmed. "I hope you didn't break it."

"That makes two of us." He winced, knowing he had sounded

sharp. "It's not broken, just a sprain." *I hope,* he added silently. "I'll be okay after I get up and walk around a little."

Julie's mouth twisted. He could tell she didn't think that was a very good idea, but she didn't say anything.

Jack swung himself around so he was facing uphill, then tried to lever himself up with his arms and his good leg. One hand slipped out from under him and he suddenly felt Julie slip her arm around his back and pull him up.

She was stronger than she looked, a lot stronger. He turned his head slightly and glanced down at her. She was suddenly so close. He felt very awkward.

Finally, he was upright, balanced on one leg. "I'm okay now. Thanks."

She didn't let go. "You can't get up the hill on one leg. Even if you do think you're Superman."

He almost smiled, except the pain made that impossible. She was right. He needed her help. "Okay, let's try it. But you need to tell me if I'm too heavy."

"You'll know, don't worry."

Kate had been working on a snowman and now ran over to see what was going on. Jack could tell from her expression that she was confused.

"Jack fell in the snow and hurt his ankle," Julie explained between their hip-hop steps up the hill. "I have to help him."

"Oh." Kate stared up at Jack. He tried to force a smile, but it was hard. Every time he touched his injured leg to the ground, it throbbed with pain.

"You run up ahead and open the door for us, okay?" Julie told her.

Kate's expression brightened. She was excited to have such an important job. "Okay. I can do that."

She dashed off, quick as a bunny hopping through the drifts. Jack paused and watched her. He glanced down at Julie. "How are you doing? Need a rest?"

"I'm fine. I think it would go faster if you just relaxed and leaned on me. I'm pretty tough, Jack. I won't break."

He nodded. He had been forcing himself not to lean on her completely. He was worried about hurting her. And it had been a long time since he had been this close to a woman. She probably didn't realize that, he thought.

Her shoulder felt fragile and feminine under his arm. Her hood had fallen off and wispy curls framed her rosy cheeks. The flowery scent of her hair was another distraction.

"Okay, let's get going again." He stared straight ahead and shifted more weight her way. Step by step, they finally made it to the house, where Kate waited by the open door.

"Oh my. She's letting all the heat out of the house. I'm sorry," Julie said.

"No big deal. She's just trying to help."

They had reached the porch and Jack grabbed for the railing. With Julie on the other side, he hopped up the few steps and finally staggered inside. He spotted the nearest chair and quickly landed with a loud grunt.

Julie followed, her cheeks red and her eyes bright. She shrugged off her jacket and quickly smoothed her hair back.

"I'll get you some ice. You need to elevate your foot." She headed for the kitchen with a purposeful stride.

Jack bent to remove his boot. His clothes were soaking wet with melted snow, and he felt chilled to the bone. He even felt chunks of snow stuck in his beard and quickly swatted them away.

That was the least of his problems right now. His ankle was so tender, it hurt just to remove his shoe and sock. When he looked up, he saw Kate nearby, staring at him.

"Once I fell down the stairs," she told him. "My arm hurt so much. The doctor took a picture of it. Then he put a cast on me."

"Really?"

Kate nodded. "It was pink. I drew pictures on it."

Jack stared back at her. "I don't have to go to the hospital. I don't need a pink cast. It's not that bad."

He hadn't meant to sound sharp, but Kate shrank back, then ran to Julie as she returned to the room.

"Put your leg up on the table." Julie took a cushion from the couch, set it on the coffee table, and Jack lifted his leg up. She settled the ice pack on his ankle. Her touch felt soft and gentle on his bare skin. "I can see where you twisted it. It's already turning blue."

"Great." Jack glanced down at his foot. What a morning. He wished he was alone. Completely alone again. He hated the feeling of her standing there, staring at him.

A glass of water suddenly appeared in Julie's outstretched palm, with some aspirin. "I found these in the medicine cabinet."

"Thanks." He took the pills and water without looking at her. "I'm not so sure about that car making it to town. I can't follow you now, either. I think you need to call a tow truck."

"Okay. How about calling a doctor? I think someone should take a look at your leg."

"I'll keep the ice on awhile. I'll be fine." He stared straight ahead.

Julie walked around him and sat on the couch. She leaned forward, facing him. She waited. He didn't say anything more. Or even look at her. "I can't leave you here like this," she said finally. "What if your ankle is broken?"

"It's not broken, I'm telling you. I'm fine." He didn't mean to argue with her, but he could hear the sound of his temper rising.

She blinked, her mouth a tight line. If she'd had any friendly feelings for him at all, he could see he was now making a very bad impression. His true colors showing, he thought glumly.

"I feel responsible for your fall, Jack. I'm not going until I know you're taken care of. Do you want to tell me where to find your doctor's phone number? Or should I just look in a phone book and pick one out?"

Man, she was one stubborn woman. You'd never guess it to look at her. He glared at her, his jaw set. But she didn't back down.

Of course he didn't blame her for his fall. He should have been ready for the car to pull away. He hadn't been paying attention. No use in arguing about that now, though. Maybe if he called the doctor, she would leave.

"There's a list of numbers on the wall, near the key rack. It's Dr. Harding. I can speak to him," he added.

"Fine." She marched past him, Kate following like a little puppy.

He had agreed to the call just to get her moving. He knew what Harding would say. Ice on and off for a few hours. Keep it elevated. Wear an Ace bandage. He'd had enough of doctors when Claire was sick. He avoided them now as much as possible.

Julie came back with the phone and the number written on a small scrap of paper. He dialed and the receptionist connected him to Dr. Harding.

He looked over at Julie while he waited for the doctor to come on the line. She stood with her arms crossed over her chest, listening to every word. She wore jeans and a dark blue green sweater today that zipped up the front and had a hood. He tried not to notice how the color complemented her fair complexion and reddish-brown hair.

"Hello, Jack. What can I do for you?" Matt Harding asked.

Jack described his accident. "I'd rather not come in. No need. Just wanted a few pointers on home care," he said casually.

"I don't think that's a good idea, Jack. If you have a fracture or a bad sprain, you'll need a cast so the ankle will heal correctly. From what you've told me, sounds like it could be a real injury."

For goodness sake! Just what he didn't want to happen. He glared at Julie then back at the receiver. "It doesn't hurt that bad, honest."

Dr. Harding ignored his reply. "I can see you this morning. Come in any time before noon. I have an X-ray machine right in the office. You won't have to drive around unless you need a cast, then I'll have to send you to a specialist. There's a good one in Essex."

Jack let out a long, exasperated breath. "I guess I'll come in then. If you think it's necessary."

"I do. Do you need help getting here?"

Jack hesitated a moment then said, "That's okay. I think I can get someone to drive me." He glanced at Julie and she nodded, finally looking satisfied.

He looked away quickly. Just what he didn't want to happen. Again he wished he had been alone. He would have managed fine without all this . . . fuss. Over nothing.

He ended the call and put the phone on the table. "He can see me this morning. I guess we'd better get it over with."

"Yes, let's." Julie rose from the couch. She picked up his boot and sock. "This sock is soaking wet. I'll get you a dry pair. Where do you keep them?"

"That's all right." He snatched the wet sock from her hand, tired of being fussed over. "Let's just get going."

Julie didn't say anything. She took the phone and went back into the kitchen. He tried to pull the sock on, but it was too wet and it hurt his ankle to struggle with it. He stuck his bare foot into his boot, trying hard not to groan aloud again. He hadn't taken off his coat, so putting it back on was not an issue. He put his right foot on the floor and tested his ankle.

It hurt something fierce. He would need Julie's help to get outside and into his truck. He turned as she walked into the room with Kate at her side, both bundled for the outdoors again.

He pulled himself up, balanced on the chair, then reached into his pocket for his keys and handed them to her. "Ever drive a truck?"

She shook her head, a small smile tilting up the corners of her mouth. "Don't worry. I'm sure I can manage. They say trucks these days drive just like cars."

"This one is ancient. It drives like a tank."

He had reached the door, stumbling along, supporting himself on the furniture.

"It will be an adventure, I guess." She pulled open the door and offered him her shoulder for support.

He paused and peered sideways at her. He had no choice and she knew it. He put his arm around her shoulders and they hobbled out of the house, side by side, Kate following close by.

Jack grabbed the railing while Julie locked the door. He squinted at the brilliant sun and clear blue sky.

It had been a long time since he'd had an adventure. He wasn't sure he was ready for one.

CHAPTER THREE

*W*HEN JESSICA WOKE UP SHE THOUGHT SHE WAS IN HER bedroom. Why did the bed feel so lumpy? she wondered. Her eyes felt dry and irritated, as if she had been out on the beach on a windy day. Then she smelled smoke, in her hair. On her skin. She sat up quickly and nearly cried out loud.

It all came back to her in a horrifying rush. The sight of their house burning. The billows of black smoke rising into the night sky. The sounds of the firefighters, their hoses and axes, as they fought the fire. Unable to control it.

She was lying on the foldout bed in her sister Emily's house. The mattress was thin and uncomfortable.

Sam lay next to her, deep in sleep. His face was scrubbed clean but his fingernails were black, she noticed. He was fully dressed and she didn't recognize the clothes—baggy jeans and a hooded sweatshirt with the name and insignia of some boat club across the front. Her brother-in-law Dan's clothes. Jessica was wearing Emily's blue terry cloth bathrobe and a borrowed nightgown underneath.

She glanced at the clock. Eleven in the morning. She couldn't remember the last time she had slept this late, but she still felt exhausted and foggy-headed. They had stayed up for hours last night. No one could sleep. The boys had been terrified and Tyler had finally dropped off in her arms. Sam had sat up with Darrell, who waited to hear progress reports on Reilly from the clinic.

Emily and Dan had stayed up with them, keeping them company. Though there wasn't too much to talk about. They had been lucky to get out of there alive. So lucky, they kept telling each other.

Now Jessica sat on the edge of the bed and felt the cold floor under her bare feet. *I could have been dead this morning*, she thought. *We all could have been*. A headline for the Cape Light *Messenger*: "Local Family Perishes in House Fire." The realization was chilling.

She squeezed her eyes shut and clasped her hands together, saying a quick, silent prayer. *Thank you, God, for saving my family. I thank you from the bottom of my heart and soul for keeping all of us safe from the fire. Especially my children.*

"Jess . . . what are you doing?" Sam stroked her back, mumbling his words.

"I'm thanking God we're alive this morning. And our children are safe and no one was hurt last night."

"Yes, thank God." Sam sighed. "Come here a second. Don't rush off."

She turned to him and he gently pulled her down. She rested next to him, her head on his chest, and he stroked her hair. "I still can't believe it," she whispered.

"I know. Neither can I."

"I keep thinking we're going to get the boys up, go home, and it will still be there. As if nothing happened."

"Yeah, me too. It's hard to get your mind around it. Even though we saw it happen. We watched the whole thing."

Jessica didn't answer for a long time, her mind filled with the image of the house, the yellow and orange flames flaring up against the dark sky. The charred and blackened wood.

"Do you think there's anything left?" she asked.

"Sure there is. People rebuild after fires all the time. I practically built that house from the ground up when I bought it. I can do it again, don't worry."

His words reassured her a bit. "What about our things? All of our . . . everything. We ought to be able to find some of it that isn't ruined, don't you think?"

"I don't know, Jess. It's not just the fire. It's the water. And the smoke."

"But I'm sure there are a few good things that didn't get ruined completely. I mean, there has to be. A few things we could clean off? Dry out?" The thin, desperate edge in her voice surprised her.

Sam patted her shoulder. "Sure, honey. We'll find things. I'm not sure when we can go back though. I'll ask the fire department. I have to call this morning, first thing."

Jessica closed her eyes. "Sam . . . this is such a nightmare. I can't believe it."

"I can't believe it either. We just have to be thankful that no one was hurt. Or worse. What if we woke up this morning and—" He turned and looked at her. "I don't even want to say it."

She knew what he meant. He didn't have to say it. What if something had happened to one of their children? Or Sam, himself?

Their belongings, even their beautiful old house, it was all just stuff. She had to keep some perspective, Jessica reminded herself. Things could have been so much worse.

She nodded quickly and sat up. She wiped her eyes with a tissue. "I'm going to see how the boys are doing. They must be up by now."

"Okay." Sam nodded and sat up.

When she reached the door, she glanced back at him. He sat on the side of the bed, rubbing his hand over his messy hair. He was so precious to her. He was part of her heart and soul. What if he and Darrell had never come back out of the house last night? She couldn't imagine what she would feel right now. Jessica thought she wouldn't be able to go on living.

As she had guessed, the boys had both gotten up before her. She saw Darrell in the family room, staring blankly at the TV, and found Tyler in the kitchen with Emily and Dan. Tyler ran to her. He hugged her around the waist, squeezing tight and burying his face in her side. She'd managed to put a clean T-shirt on him last night but he was still wearing his dirty pajama bottoms. There had been no way to get him into a bathtub last night. Jessica had barely been able to wash his face and hands.

"It's all right, honey," she soothed him. "Everything's going to be okay." She crouched down next to him. "Did you have any breakfast?"

He shook his head. "Aunt Emily is making pancakes."

"Uncle Dan is making them," Emily corrected. The large wooden table was set with six places, and Emily added a big jug of pure maple syrup and a butter dish. "Aunt Emily is just supervising."

"Your aunt has a talent for that." Dan turned and smiled at

Jessica. She tried to smile back but it was difficult. She blinked and looked away.

"Mom." Tyler tugged on her sleeve. "Jane went to preschool," he reported, talking about his younger cousin. "Do we have to go to school today, too?"

School? Jessica had forgotten all about that. She shook her head. "No, honey. You aren't going to school today."

For one thing, the boys had no clothes to wear. And any school books that had been in the house . . . She tried not to think about the house. She poured herself a mug of coffee and left the room to look in on Darrell.

He sat in a rigid position, his arms crossed over his chest, staring at the TV. He had been too upset to sleep last night. He camped out by the kitchen phone and called the emergency vet clinic every hour. Jessica had coaxed him into the shower at one point and, finally, wearing some more of Dan's borrowed clothes, which floated on him ten sizes too big, he had fallen asleep in the living room.

Jessica moved aside a pillow and blanket and sat down next to him. "Darrell? Want some breakfast?"

He shook his head. "I'm not hungry."

When was the last time she had heard him say that? Since Darrell had hit adolescence, she couldn't keep enough food in the house. "Have you heard anything more about Reilly, honey?" she asked quietly.

He shook his head. "The doctor said he's still the same. He's not doing too good, Mom."

Darrell didn't look at her when he spoke, his eyes glassy and bright. She put her arm around his shoulders and hugged him. He was getting so big. Where had the time gone?

She remembered when he had first arrived in their life. Sam had been volunteering at the New Horizons Center and Darrell had come for a stay there. He had latched on to Sam, following him around like a puppy. Sam had loved him from the start and seen only good in the boy. Only the beautiful potential.

But Darrell had been in lots of trouble back in Boston, which was how kids ended up at New Horizons. He had been truant from school and picked up for shoplifting. His mother had a drug problem and had left him in the care of his grandmother while she went into a rehab program. But Darrell's grandmother was up in years and had a heart condition. She was in no shape to watch over a nine-year-old boy who was hurting so badly from his mother's abandonment.

Jessica had been hurting back then, too. She and Sam were trying to start a family and she had experienced a miscarriage.

She could hardly believe it now, but at first, she hadn't wanted to adopt Darrell. She didn't want a half-grown, troubled, mischievous boy. She had wanted a tiny baby. Of her own. Sam had tried to understand, but the conflict had been a great stress on their marriage. She had actually thought it was best to send Darrell back to his mother.

At one point, it seemed as if Darrell was gone from their lives forever. Jessica found out she was pregnant but still felt a horrible ache inside. She quickly realized what had happened. She missed Darrell. She loved him, as much as if not more than Sam did, and wanted to raise him as their own. His natural mother did not give him up for adoption that easily. But finally it had all worked out and Darrell came to live with them forever, on a beautiful Christmas morning five years ago.

That had been her special, most spectacular gift to Sam.

Except, of course, when she had given birth to Tyler, just about nine months later.

Now she rubbed Darrell's back, not knowing what to say. He was too old now for her to soothe him with gentle lies about the dog. "I'm sorry about Reilly. I know how much you love him. We all do. He's getting good care. Maybe he'll improve today."

Darrell nodded. Then he turned to her. "Can I go see him, Mom? I bet he's afraid, all alone with a lot of strangers."

"Sure. Someone will take you over. I'm sure he'll feel better when he sees you," she said honestly.

What about the cars? she wondered. Were their cars ruined by the fire, too? They had been parked so close to the house. It was possible. She rubbed the back of her neck. This was all too much to think about. She couldn't handle it.

Emily called, announcing the pancakes were ready. Jessica patted Darrell's leg. "Come on into the kitchen. Try to eat something. I don't want you to be by yourself in here."

Darrell nodded, shut off the TV, and followed her. Sam was already at the table, helping Tyler fix his pancakes. Tyler kneeled on his seat and carefully poured the syrup from the large bottle, making a smiley face on the top of his pancakes. Jessica suddenly realized Tyler had no idea what had really happened. He had seen the house burning but didn't quite get it. A blessing, in a way, she thought.

"That's the way, buddy. Easy does it," Sam coached his younger son.

"Tyler, I didn't realize we had an artist in the family," Dan said. "A young Jackson Pollack."

"He's a wonderful artist," Jessica bragged as she took a seat. "Didn't you ever see our art gallery on the refrigerator?"

"Yes, I have." Dan nodded. "Very impressive."

Jessica glanced at Tyler and the smile froze on her face.

Lost.

All those beautiful pictures Tyler drew, all the colors and strange, fantastic creatures and flowers and rainbows.

She swallowed hard, trying to keep a normal expression. She had been so careful to save their artwork and special projects. The stories and poems they brought home. Cards they made for her and Sam for Mother's and Father's Day. She had a special box, filled to the brim with their creations.

Just a pile of ashes now, she was sure. She took a bite of a pancake, but that tasted like ash in her mouth now too.

Emily came in and took the seat next to Jessica. "Did you call Rhinehardt yet?" she asked Sam.

"I did. He has to call me back," Sam answered.

"I don't think they'll let you back in the house today," Emily said. "They're probably still investigating the cause. And the insurance investigators have to come, too."

"You called the insurance company last night, right, Sam?" Jessica turned to him. They had both been in shock. Still were. It was hard to remember if they had taken care of any of these important details.

"I did. But I need to call our agent this morning. He might have been trying my cell and the power ran out."

And he didn't have the cord anymore to charge it, Jessica realized. Not until he could find a replacement. She had left her cell phone in the house, in her purse, which had been on her dresser. She wished now she had thought to grab her handbag. It held so many important pieces of identification and all her credit cards. But last night, focused only on getting her children out of the burning house, such things hadn't seemed important.

As if reading her mind, Emily said, "When you're feeling up to it, we can go over to the mall, Jess, and get some clothes for the kids. And for you and Sam."

"Oh . . . okay. That's a good idea." She glanced at Sam. "Do you think we can get into our bank account without official ID?"

Sam laughed at her. "You're the banker. You tell me, hon."

She sighed. She mostly enjoyed her husband's sense of humor, but sometimes it rubbed her the wrong way. Like right now.

"Don't worry, Jessica. I'll take care of everything. You can pay us back anytime," Emily said softly.

Jessica met her sister's gaze and telegraphed a silent thank-you. Emily was nearly ten years older. They hadn't been close growing up, partly due to their age difference and different temperaments. But in the years since Jessica had returned to Cape Light, she and Emily had grown very close. Now she cherished her sister's friendship and support. Their own mother had never been very warm or nurturing, and Jessica knew that Emily tried to make up for that.

"I called Mother while you were still sleeping," Emily said, as if reading her mind. "I hope you don't mind. I thought she should hear it from us, before the neighbors told her. You know how fast news like this gets around. She's going to call back later, to speak to you."

"What did Lillian say?" Sam asked. "Probably something like, 'I always told them that rickety old house would either fall down or blow away in a tornado.'" Sam made his voice thin and high, imitating his mother-in-law perfectly.

"Not quite that bad," Emily replied, hiding a smile. "But you're close."

Jessica glanced at her husband, who sat drinking his coffee. She hoped that he wasn't blaming himself now for choosing an old house for their family. She could never blame Sam for this, no matter what absurd ideas her mother came up with.

"Don't pay any attention to her, Sam. Please. Not now, of all times."

Sam nodded. "Guess I'd better start making some calls. I have a long list to work through." He rose from his seat, coffee mug in hand.

Jessica tilted her head back and looked at him. "Can I help you? I can call some places."

"That's okay. You ought to get the boys cleaned up and go out with Emily. You do need to go shopping for us. They have to go to school tomorrow."

Tyler made a face and poked his pancakes with his fork.

"Sorry, pal. But this isn't an ordinary day," Sam tried to explain. "Tomorrow, we all get back on track."

How easy he made that sound, Jessica thought. As if they had just hit a small bump in the road. A slight detour.

She doubted they would get on track tomorrow. Or any day soon. She had no idea how they would even find the track at this point, they had been blown so very far off course.

IT WAS PAST NOON BY THE TIME THEY FINISHED THE PANCAKES. Jessica went upstairs and took another shower, this time giving her hair a double lather of shampoo to get out the smoky smell. She didn't linger in the bathroom. Others were waiting their turn for the shower. Emily and Dan's house was small and already felt crowded.

She slipped into the guest room and quickly dressed in some of Emily's clothes. She felt awkward and even a little embarrassed in the blue pants and maroon sweater top. But what could she do?

Not only was her sister taller and larger, but their taste in clothes was so different.

Jessica sat on the edge of the foldout bed and roughly combed her hair, trying not to think about all her favorite clothes and shoes—everything in her closet and dressers—lost in the fire. The firefighters had come quickly. Maybe she could find some salvageable things in the rubble.

As she came down the stairs, she realized visitors had arrived. She heard Molly, Sam's younger sister, talking to Emily in the kitchen. When she walked in, they both stopped talking and stared at her. Jessica felt self-conscious but tried to smile at her sister-in-law.

"Jess! You poor thing . . ." Molly ran over and threw her arms around Jessica. Jessica stood there stiffly, then patted Molly's shoulder. "Thank God you're all okay!" Molly said, stepping back. "What a tragedy. What a nightmare for you. . . ."

Jessica started to speak, but Molly was all worked up now. There was no stopping her, Jessica knew.

"How are the boys? They must be terrified. They—"

"The boys are doing okay," Jessica cut in. "I don't think Tyler understands yet what really happened," she added quietly. "He just asked me when we were going to go home. He wants to play with his video games."

Molly nodded and sighed. "Kids that age bury a lot. He might be traumatized. You may have to take him to a counselor."

Jessica didn't know what to say. She knew her sister-in-law meant well and what she said might be true. But the prediction wasn't exactly a comforting thought.

Emily suddenly stepped up beside Jessica. "Would you like some coffee, Molly? It's already made."

Jessica met her sister's eye and they shared a private glance.

Molly waved off the offer. "No, thanks. I've got to run. I just wanted to stop by and see how everyone was doing. You know, if you start feeling a little tight here, you're always welcome to stay at my place. We would love to have you and have loads of room."

Jessica forced another smile. "Thanks, Molly. It's nice of you to offer. We're a little . . . confused right now. But I'll keep it in mind."

There was loads of room at Molly and Matt's house, that was for sure. The vast, newly built minimansion was not at all to Jessica's taste, but now she suddenly envied it.

"Where's Sam? Did he go out?" Molly asked.

"He's around." Jessica pushed up the baggy sleeves of the borrowed sweater. "He was making some phone calls."

"He's in Dan's office," Emily added. "I'm sure he wants to say hello. I don't think he even knows you're here," Emily went on as she led Molly out of the kitchen.

Jessica wasn't sure how Sam could miss his sister's arrival. Unless the fire had made him deaf. But Molly was Molly. She had a heart of gold, and her effusive personality did grow on you—once you got to know her. She and Jessica had not gotten along when Jessica first met Sam, but now they were good friends.

The phone in the kitchen rang. Jessica listened to the message coming into the answering machine, expecting to hear her mother calling back. It was Reverend Ben, trying to get in touch with her and Sam. She stepped over to the phone and picked it up.

"Hello, Reverend Ben. It's Jessica," she answered.

"Jessica, I just heard the news about your house from Tucker Tulley. He told me your family got out in time, and you were all fine. Is that true?"

"Yes, we're fine. Except for our dog, Reilly. He inhaled a lot of smoke. Tucker brought him to a veterinary hospital."

"That's too bad. But at least you were all spared. I'm very thankful for that."

"We are, too," she replied quietly.

"So, you're staying with Emily and Dan for the time being?"

"At the moment, yes, we are. Everything is very . . . up in the air right now."

"I'm sure it is. This has got to be very disorienting for all of you. You're probably still in shock."

"We are. We still can't believe it," she admitted. "I keep thinking I'll just go out to my car and drive home . . . and put on my own clothes."

Ben didn't answer for a moment. "I expect you'll feel that way for a while, Jessica. It's only natural. Be patient with yourself. And your family. It's going to take some time to get your life sorted out again. This is a major challenge, for all of you. It will take time to get back to normal. The main thing now is that you're all okay."

"Yes, that's true. That's what we keep telling ourselves." Jessica nodded, tempted to ask him how long he thought it would take for their lives to get back to normal. He had seen families hit by this situation before, she imagined. He must have some idea. But finally, she didn't ask. It seemed too blunt or rude.

"Sam is with his sister right now. I'll tell him you called," she added.

"Yes, please let him know I'm thinking of you and praying for you, too."

Jessica smiled. She already knew that. "I will," she promised. "Thank you."

After Molly's visit, Emily and Jessica got ready for their shopping trip. The boys were content to stay behind with Dan and Sam, who promised to take them out to the park and play touch football in the snow. The plan seemed to cheer the kids up, Jessica noticed, especially Tyler. Darrell was willing, but more subdued. He was still distracted and worried about his dog, she knew. Before she left, she mentioned to Sam that Darrell wanted to visit Reilly.

"Sure. I'll take him. No problem," Sam promised.

"We won't be too long," Jessica said as she pulled on one of Emily's jackets and a scarf.

Darrell nodded. "Could you get me a dark blue sweatshirt? Like that one we found on vacation?"

Jessica kissed him on the cheek. All he wore these days were big sweatshirts and jeans. It wouldn't be too hard to replenish his wardrobe, she realized.

"I absolutely will. I might get you a gray one or a brown one, too, while I'm at it."

On the way to the mall, Jessica made a list of things she needed. It seemed overwhelming. Why not just write "Everything" and keep it short and sweet, she thought.

Emily kept the conversation light and bright, as if they were going out on a normal shopping trip. Her sister's temperament was the opposite of Molly's, which Jessica appreciated right now.

"Now just get the basics for the boys. It's so close to Christmas. We're all going to get them lots of presents. I've already bought them both the heavy fleece pullovers you said they wanted. And video games. But now I suppose they need the game player thingy again," she added, as if making a mental note to herself.

"Thanks, Emily. You don't need to get anything more. We'll manage," Jessica said, despite the way she felt inside.

Emily glanced at her as she parked the car. "We'll see. You can't possibly buy everything you need today, so let's just concentrate on the essentials."

Good plan, Jessica thought. Though everything on her list so far seemed important and essential.

The mall was decorated for Christmas, every window of every store. The wide promenade was filled with white and gold angels and huge Christmas trees. Generic-sounding carols piped through the sound system.

"Where do you want to start?" Emily asked.

"Good question." Jessica looked down at her list and then up and down the row of the stores. "Oh . . . let's just start walking this way and see what we find."

"Sounds good to me," Emily said agreeably.

"Thanks for coming, Em. I feel a little . . . overwhelmed."

"Of course you do. But it's probably better to get out today and do something practical. Even just to distract yourself."

"Yes, it is." Jessica felt odd in the mall, almost light-headed. But she knew it was better than staying in Emily's tiny house all day, rerunning the horror film of last night in her head.

They stopped in a shop with clothes for men and boys. Jessica's thoughts were so scattered, it was hard to concentrate. She hardly knew what she was buying but soon picked out an armful of T-shirts and sweatshirts, pants and underwear for all, and a good sweater for Sam.

Emily helped her carry the pile of clothes to the register then paid with a card. Jessica knew she would do the same for her sister any day, but it still made her feel self-conscious to accept Emily's help. They walked out of the store, carrying two big bags each.

It seemed like a lot, but Jessica knew it hardly made a dent.

"Well, that was fast," Emily said. "Where else would you like to go? How about a store for yourself now?"

"Oh, I don't know. I think I need to sit down." Jessica spotted a bench and sat with a long sigh. All the Christmas decorations and cheerful music closed in on her. The sheer abundance all around, the stores packed with goods and shoppers toting bags stuffed to the brim only reminded her of all her family had lost. She suddenly felt as if she could hardly breathe.

"Emily, I don't know how we're going to do it. I just don't know. How are we going to have Christmas for the boys? How are we ever going to replace everything?" She turned to her sister and swallowed back a lump in her throat. "The insurance company asked us to list everything we lost. Clothes, books, jewelry, china. All of Sam's tools and all the furniture. Some of those pieces came from Lilac Hall," she reminded her sister.

Lilac Hall, with its great house and gardens, had been the Warwick family estate, the place where Jessica and Emily grew up. Their father had been forced to give it up during a family scandal, and it was now a town historical site. Though most of its treasures had been sold at auction, a few precious pieces had been saved.

"So many things are simply . . . irreplaceable."

Emily squeezed her hand. "I know, honey. I know."

Jessica covered her face with her hand. She hated having a meltdown right in the middle of the mall like this. People were staring at her, but she couldn't stop.

Emily put her arm around her sister's shoulder. "I know it's hard, Jess. But try to calm down. You can't solve everything in one day. You have to take it slowly, one day at a time, one hour at a time. I know you must be terribly frightened, but you're not alone.

Everyone wants to help you and Sam get through this. And you will get through it, I'm sure of it. We're all here to help you."

Jessica took a deep breath and nodded. She wiped her eyes with a tissue and tried to center herself. Emily was right. She couldn't solve all their problems at once, especially not today. That was the one thing she knew.

"All right, let's get back to work." Jessica rose from the bench and picked up her shopping bags. "I need a few things for myself, I guess. I can't keep walking around in your bathrobe."

"Well, you could try," Emily countered with a small smile. "It would be very comfortable."

"Probably," Jessica agreed, trying to match her sister's light-hearted tone. "But I might get tired of all the attention."

As they strolled into the next store, Jessica glanced at her watch. She wouldn't shop too much longer. She hoped that by the time she returned to Emily's house, Sam would have some good news for them. About the dog and the insurance. About anything.

CHAPTER FOUR

$\sim$

$\mathcal{I}$T HAD BEEN A LONG AFTERNOON IN MEDICAL OFFICES. Jack's patience—the scrap that he possessed—was worn thin. He hobbled back up to the house as fast as his new set of crutches would carry him. He cursed softly under his breath, slipping on the snow, just about to tear the ligaments of his other leg.

Julie and Kate followed a few steps behind. He sensed them warily watching him, as if he were a volcano about to blow.

That's what he felt like. His right leg was encased in a fresh plaster cast to the knee. It should have felt better, but it hurt even worse, his ankle throbbing horribly.

It was so stupid to have injured himself like this, and it was his own fault. Trying to swoop in like Superman to impress that woman, to help her save a few dollars on a tow truck. What was it to him if she was down on her luck? Now, here he was, stuck wearing a cast until the ligaments healed. Which could take three weeks, the doctor had told him.

Unable to walk, to drive, to see straight from the sheer pain. Just because Julie Newton smiled at him with those big brown eyes.

He was just a darn fool.

And he was sure Julie knew it. What else could she think?

He reached the front steps, breathless and frustrated. The leg in the cast hurt too much to put any weight on it yet, though the orthopedist in Essex had called it a walking cast.

"I think you need to go up on your bottom. It will be easier," Julie gently suggested. "I'll bring the crutches for you."

He turned toward her with a scowl. What did she think he was, a two-year-old?

He threw the metal crutches up the steps. They landed on the porch with a clatter. Then he grabbed the railing with one hand and hoisted himself up step-by-step. It hurt something awful when he had to balance on his bad leg, but he gritted his teeth and finally made it to the top. Huffing and puffing, he leaned over and managed to scoop up one crutch before he lost his balance. Then he unlocked the door and stomped inside.

He staggered toward the couch. Just getting into the house was exhausting. How would he last three whole weeks with this chunk of cement on his leg? He would bust it off with a sledgehammer by tomorrow.

Now he really felt like an old man. Every muscle in his body ached as he shucked off his jacket and flopped down on the couch. The fall was catching up with him. It always hurt more later.

Moments later, Julie and Kate came in.

Julie sent Kate into the kitchen. "Why don't you color awhile," she suggested. "I'll be right in to make you a snack."

Jack watched Kate meekly leave the room. He knew he'd scared her but didn't know what to say.

Julie turned back to him and gently set the other crutch by the side of the couch.

"The doctor said you could have some ibuprofen. It will help the swelling inside the cast go down. You must be in a lot of pain," she added quietly.

"I don't need anything, thank you," he nearly shouted at her.

She looked shocked, even hurt for a moment. He stared at her, about to apologize, then turned his head away.

"We never stopped at the service station," he reminded her in a more reasonable tone. "The number's on the wall. They can still get the tow truck over here. It's not that late."

He hoped she would take the hint. He wanted her to go. He didn't need her here, hovering. He didn't need anyone.

When he looked back at her, she seemed confused. "What will you do? You can't even drive. It's not safe for you to be out here alone."

"I've been taking care of myself a long time. I'll manage fine. Don't worry about it."

She did look concerned. She wasn't just being polite. Why should she care about him? She didn't even know him. He stared out the window and took a deep breath just to keep from shouting at her. Why wouldn't she take a hint and go? How blunt did he have to be?

"You've got to get back on the road. You've got your family waiting," he reminded her.

"They're not in any rush to entertain us, believe me," she said quietly. She picked up the other crutch and then took his jacket from the back of a chair.

So maybe that was it, he thought. *It's easier to linger with a grumpy old coot like me than crawl back to her relatives for help.*

"I'll call for the tow truck," she said finally, "if I know there's someone who will stop by at least once a day to look in on you. Bring you groceries and whatever."

"Sure. I'll call someone. I have lots of neighbors who'll help me. No problem."

Not that one single name comes to mind at the moment, Jack added silently.

Friends had been his wife's department. After Claire died, Jack had let all his ties lapse. People called for a while then just stopped trying. He was what you might call a recluse, he realized. The nearest house down the road had been sold a few months ago, and he had never bothered to meet the new owners. He didn't even know what his closest neighbor looked like anymore.

Julie folded her arms across her chest. "Okay, I'll get the phone. You call a friend and tell them what happened," she said in a reasonable tone. "I don't feel comfortable leaving until I'm sure there's someone around to look in on you."

Jack took a breath and struggled to sit higher against the cushions. He needed a plan and didn't have one. He peered into the kitchen. Kate sat at the table coloring in a picture book.

Julie soon returned with the phone. Her expression was neutral, but he thought he detected a certain amused light in her eyes.

Jack took the phone then punched in some numbers. He listened for a moment. "Busy," he reported, glancing at her. "I'll try again later."

He forced a smile, but she didn't smile back.

"And what is the time and temperature right now, Jack?" She glanced at her watch. "I have . . . half past three."

Blast. She had caught him. Okay, one for her side.

Before Jack could muster up an answer, the brass bell at the Christmas tree stand rang madly. Saved by the bell, he thought.

Julie peered out the window. "What in the world is that?"

"Some customers for a tree. Just ignore it. They'll go away."

"Ignore your customers? Don't you want to sell your trees?"

He shook his head. "I don't care. Let them take one for free. Let them take two." The bell stopped. "See? They're giving up."

Then, a second later, it started again, even louder.

Julie looked down at him, her head tilted to one side. "Let me go out there. I can help them."

"You? How can you sell a Christmas tree?" He sat upright suddenly. His leg with the cast swung down and landed with a thump on the floor. "Ugh . . ."

She had already slipped back into her boots and was pulling on his big green parka, which swam around her slim body. She paused and bent over near him. "Are you all right, Jack?"

He waved her away, feeling a little queasy from the pain. "Just go on. Tell them to go away. They can come back some other time. I'm not going anywhere," he mumbled to himself.

He heard the door open and shut. Then Julie's light tread, hopping down the porch steps. He sat up slowly and watched her from the window. She trotted toward the tree stand and waved, her colorful scarf flying out behind her like a flag.

The customers, who were heading for their car, turned and smiled back at her.

Who wouldn't smile back at her? You'd have to be blind, Jack thought.

He watched a moment longer as Julie and the couple disappeared among the trees. Then he lay back and closed his eyes.

It was growing dark outside. The lights for the tree lot had gone on automatically.

Too late to call for the tow truck. And now she was out there, selling his trees.

She could be out there all night, he realized. It was the busy season, after all.

What next with this woman?

Jack closed his eyes. He shuddered to imagine it.

SAM HEARD JESSICA AND EMILY RETURN FROM THEIR SHOPPING trip and went to the door to meet them. Jessica was smiling, chatting with her sister, her cheeks ruddy from the cold, her eyes bright. Several shopping bags dangled from each hand.

For a moment it seemed as if she had just been out with Emily, shopping for Christmas; he completely forgot the real reason for their excursion.

Then he remembered. And remembered all he had to report to her.

"Hey, honey." He leaned over and kissed her cheek. "Did you guys buy out the mall?"

"Just about," Jessica replied with a laugh.

"How is Jane doing?" Emily put down her packages and slipped off her jacket.

"Still down for her nap," Sam reported.

"Oh dear. I'd better wake up her up. She won't sleep tonight."

Emily trotted up the stairs. Jessica had also dropped her bags at her feet and now shrugged off her jacket. "There's more in the car. I picked up some sneakers and boots for the boys. I hope they fit. I got you some work boots. You'll have to find your own sneakers though."

She peered into a bag and started to sort things out.

Sam touched her shoulder. "That's okay. I don't need to try them on right now." She looked up at him. He could tell she had sensed his serious tone, the expression on her face suddenly growing tense.

"Why don't we sit down a minute. I haven't seen you all day."

Sam led Jessica over to the couch, and they sat down side by side. Dan had made a fire and the room looked cozy, Sam thought. It was very different from their house, but it still had the same comfortable feeling. The comparison made him feel sad.

"Did you take Darrell to see Reilly?" she asked.

Sam nodded. "We went over right after you left. The dog was sedated. But Darrell got to pet him awhile."

"What did the vet say?" Jessica straightened her shoulders; he could see that she was trying to brace herself against more bad news.

Sam shrugged. "They really don't know. It could go either way, but it doesn't look good."

"How's Darrell? He must be so upset."

"He's still hoping the dog will pull through. I think he may be in denial. It's going to be hard if the dog doesn't make it."

Jessica nodded. "Did you speak to the fire department? When can we go back to the house?"

Sam knew she expected to find many possessions that had survived the blaze. He knew now that wouldn't be the case.

"We can go back tomorrow," he said evenly. "The fire department and the insurance company have finished their investigation. They seem to think the fire started in the family room. A light fixture that had some frayed wiring. The one that hung over the painted cabinet."

Jessica looked shocked. "One stupid light fixture burned our entire house down?"

"That's what they say." Sam paused. "There was no way for us to know it had worn out inside. I thought the lightbulb needed to be changed, but that wasn't quite it. It was really the wiring. I never saw it flicker or give any warning."

She swallowed hard and looked down at her hands. "Neither did I. I mean, I don't remember noticing anything odd with it."

"That's what they call the heart of the fire, the epicenter. Where it started. That's where the fire got the hottest and where they found the most damage." His mouth felt suddenly dry. It was harder than he had expected to relay this information to her.

"It was the worst there," she repeated. "How about the rest of the house? Was it any better toward the front rooms—or the upstairs?"

Sam took a breath. "Actually, the fire department described the damage as . . . extensive. But I'm thinking they have to tell you that," he quickly added, "to prepare you. It probably isn't that bad. But they don't want us to get our hopes up."

He saw her face go pale and her chin begin to tremble. She struggled to blink back tears. He took her hands in his, but she didn't even seem to notice. Her fingers were ice cold. He covered them with his own.

"Right," she said finally. "Maybe it's not that bad."

"You know me, Jess. I can do a lot with a little," he reminded her. "They're going to see that place from a different perspective entirely. I'm sure we can rebuild, honey. It will just take time and care. Like the first time we renovated."

She nodded again, still looking shocked. "When can we go back?"

"Tomorrow. Dan said he would come along to help, and Emily will come, too, I'm sure. Chief Rhinehardt wants to meet us there, to answer any questions."

"Oh, that's good of him," Jessica said politely.

"Yes, he's a good man. He's doing his best for us."

"How are the boys?" she asked, suddenly changing the subject. "Did you take them to play in the snow?"

Sam nodded and smiled. "They got soaking wet, of course. I think they could use some of those new clothes now."

Jessica rose. "I'll find their things and make them change upstairs. I don't want them to catch colds on top of everything else."

The phone rang and they looked at each other. Even though it was Emily and Dan's house, 99 percent of the calls today had been for Sam or Jessica.

Emily called down from the top of the stairs. "It's the veterinarian, Sam. I think you ought to pick it up," she added quietly.

Sam met her halfway on the staircase and took the phone.

"Hello? This is Sam Morgan."

"This is Doctor Curtis. I've been taking care of your dog, Reilly," a young woman explained.

"Yes, we met this afternoon," Sam reminded her. "How's he doing? Any news?"

He heard the young woman release a long breath, and his gut twisted with nerves.

"I'm sorry, Mr. Morgan. Reilly didn't make it. His lungs were badly damaged by the smoke, and there wasn't much we could do." The doctor said more about how they had tried to save Reilly, but Sam didn't hear a word. He nodded numbly. "Would you like to claim the body, or have us dispose of him?"

"Dispose of him? He's not a bag of trash. He's our dog!" He knew he was shouting. He couldn't stop himself. Something in her calm, smooth tone made him snap.

Why did they have to lose Reilly? That poor dog. Poor Darrell, he thought.

"I'm so sorry, Mr. Morgan. I didn't mean to offend you. We can arrange to have the dog's remains cremated and you can pick up the ashes," the doctor said.

Sam sensed Jessica at his side, but he didn't even glance at her. He felt his body shaking. "I'm not sure. . . . I have to speak to my family, to my boy, Darrell. Reilly was his dog," he explained. He knew he was going on too long, telling this woman more than she wanted to know. He stopped himself, his voice choked with tears.

"Of course. No rush. You can call tomorrow and leave a message."

Dr. Curtis apologized again and offered her condolences. Sam abruptly said good-bye and hung up.

He turned to Jessica. From her wide-eyed expression and the way she gripped his arm, he knew she understood what had happened.

"How will we tell Darrell? He'll be crushed."

He didn't know what to say.

"Maybe we should wait?" she suggested. "At least until tomorrow. It's been such a hard day for everyone."

It had indeed. The hardest day of his life.

He gazed down at her. He knew she meant well, but they had to tell Darrell. They couldn't keep something like this from him. It wouldn't be right to shield him from the truth.

"He's growing up, Jess. He's a teenager. He's going to feel awful. It's going to be hard, but he'll handle it. Loss is part of life. He's going to learn that sooner or later."

"Tell me about it," she said tartly. "I think our kids got a crash course on loss this week."

Sam sighed. "We have to tell him. There's no other way."

"Yes, I guess you're right." Jessica gripped his arm tightly. "Let's just call him in here and get it over with. Is he watching TV?"

He turned to see their son standing in the kitchen doorway.

"Was that the phone? Did the clinic call back?" Darrell asked, walking toward them.

Sam touched his son's arm. "Darrell, the doctor at the clinic did call. She had something important to tell us. . . ." He could hear his voice trembling and saw the look of fear drop down over the boy's face like a dark curtain. "Reilly is gone, son. He didn't make it."

Darrell stared in disbelief. His face looked fierce. "What do you mean, he didn't make it? I just saw him this afternoon. He looked fine. Is he dead? You said he would be okay." Darrell blinked hard. "How could he just . . . just die like that? That's not right. That's not fair. . . ."

Sam pulled his son close and wrapped his arms around the boy's trembling body. "I know it's not fair. It's not fair at all."

Jessica took a step closer and rubbed Darrell's tense shoulders. "We all loved Reilly. But we knew he loved you the most, honey. You took such good care of him. He was the happiest, most loved dog I ever saw. . . ."

Her voice trailed off. Sam knew how she felt. He didn't know what to say either. Darrell's heart was broken. What could you say?

"It's tough. I know it's tough, son," Sam said quietly. "But we all just have to accept this. It must have been Reilly's time. He had a good life, a long life. He gave us so much love. And you gave him so much love. That's the way it should be. But he had to pass on someday and . . . this was it. We'll get another dog soon, Darrell. A puppy, who will live a good, long time," he added.

Darrell stood with his head bowed then abruptly pulled away from his father. "I don't want another dog. I want Reilly. I want to see him. I don't care if he's dead. I want to say good-bye," he insisted.

He glared at Sam then his face crumpled with tears again. He covered his eyes with his hands, sobbing quietly. When Jessica tried to touch him, he shook her off.

Sam raised his hands in a calming motion. "Okay. If that's what you want, I understand." He touched Darrell gently on his shoulder. "Go get your jacket. We'll go see him and say good-bye."

Jessica stared at Sam as Darrell left the room. "It's good for him to have some closure, Jess. He needs to say good-bye to his dog."

She stepped back, hugging her arms around her body. "I guess that's the least we can do for him right now. I'll call the clinic and tell them that you're coming."

Darrell appeared, wearing a huge coat he had borrowed from his uncle. His expression was devastatingly sad.

He had been through so much in the last twenty-four hours. This entire ordeal had forced the boy to grow up in leaps and bounds, Sam reflected.

It was hardly the way he wanted his children to learn and mature. But parents don't get to choose the circumstances of these important life lessons. Sam had already figured that out. Parents don't get to choose at all.

CHAPTER FIVE

~~

O N TUESDAY MORNING, JESSICA WOKE TYLER AND DARRELL
at the usual time. They quickly ate some cereal then dressed
in their new clothes. They both wore brand-new shoes and carried
brand-new backpacks. It was something like the first day of school,
Jessica thought as she saw them off. But not quite.

Sam drove them both to school in Emily's car while Dan
dropped Jane off at preschool. Both Sam and Jessica's cars had been
damaged by the fire and were now in the shop, being steam-cleaned
and spray-painted.

By the time the two men returned, Emily and Jessica were ready
to head out to the house. Jessica carried some supplies—rubber
pails, gloves, heavy-duty trash bags. She pulled open the tailgate
and tossed the stuff into the back of Emily's Jeep.

"I wonder if Dan should take his own car," she said to Sam.

"What if we have a lot of things to bring back? It might not all fit in the Jeep."

"I can go back later. Let's just get over there. Rhinehardt said nine," Sam reminded her.

Jessica nodded and the four of them climbed into the Jeep.

"The temperature's dropped. We may have to chip through some ice to look for things," Sam said.

The house—what remained of it—would be filled with water. Jessica knew that, but it was still hard to picture.

"Then we'll be archaeologists," Emily said from the front seat.

"You can make anything sound positive," Jessica marveled.

"That's because I've had lots of practice as mayor," Emily joked. "Politicians specialize in positive."

"Well, I appreciate it," Jessica said.

Emily and Dan had been so kind and generous. Jessica really did feel very grateful. She had told Emily she didn't need to come this morning, but her sister had insisted. Jessica was glad now that Emily was there. As they drew closer to the house, Jessica felt nerves jump in her stomach. She could tell Sam felt nervous, too. He reached out and gripped her hand.

She spotted their mailbox which she had painted with flowers. At least it looked the same, untouched by the fire, covered with a bit of snow.

We need to collect the mail on the way home, she realized. *I need to have it held at the post office until we find a permanent place to stay.* She could already see that Emily and Dan's little gray cottage was not big enough for both of their families, despite her sister and brother-in-law's warm hospitality.

"Well, here we are." Emily pulled up the drive slowly. The Jeep bounced on the frozen ground and patches of ice. The drive was rutted from the heavy fire trucks and so was the front of the property.

"I see Chief Rhinehardt's car," Emily said. "He got here early."

Jessica saw the car up ahead, too. The fire chief stood nearby and waved to them. Distracted by his greeting, she didn't immediately focus on the house.

It was only when the Jeep came to a stop that she finally turned and saw it. She gasped out loud and pressed her hand over her mouth. She couldn't help it. For a moment, she thought she might be sick to her stomach.

Sam leaned toward her and put his arm around her shoulder. Emily glanced back at them, then, without a word, got out of the Jeep. Dan did the same.

"Sam . . . there's nothing left . . ." Jessica managed.

"Let's get out and take a look around," Sam said quietly. "I know it looks bad. But we have to see what's what, Jess."

Jessica nodded and wiped her tears. Then she climbed out of her side of the Jeep and hopped onto the snow.

She could barely stand to look up at the house. The once-beautiful structure was a charred shell. She could hardly tell that the house had been painted blue. Everything was scorched and burnt looking, like a pile of burnt toast.

The front wall was mostly intact, the windows smashed and the porch caved in. A shred of lace curtain blew out from an upstairs window, like a lone survivor, signaling for help.

Both sides of the house were eaten away by the fire and the back nearly a blank spot, like the back of a dollhouse. The roof was caved in, looking as though some fierce monster had taken a bite out of the peak.

Jessica took a few steps forward. Emily came to her side. "Are you all right?" she asked quietly.

"How could I be? There's nothing left, Em. Look at it."

Emily sighed and touched Jessica's shoulder. She didn't try to offer any false hopes or empty comforts, and for that, Jessica was grateful.

Sam and Dan were standing with Chief Rhinehardt, by the chief's car. Sam turned to her. "Chief says we can go inside, through the front. But not too far. He's going to come in with us."

Emily turned to her. "Are you up to doing this, Jessica? You don't have to go in if you don't want to."

Jessica swallowed back a lump in her throat. "I can do it. I don't want Sam to go in alone," she added.

They walked up to the front of the house and followed Chief Rhinehardt through the door. Sam waited for her and held her hand. Emily and Dan waited outside on the lawn. Jessica could see her sister was crying, her face pressed against her husband's chest. Emily had waited, not wanting her little sister to see her tears, Jessica guessed.

She blinked at the sight before her. It was their living room. But then again, it was not. More of a phantom of the room that had been so familiar and cozy. Everything was coated with black soot—the walls, floors, and ceilings, even the windows. Pieces of burned drapery hung in tatters, framing the shards of jagged glass that had once been windows.

The antique love seats were charred black, the oval coffee table burned completely and collapsed in on itself. Objects were melted, strange puddles that had once been radios or clocks.

Jessica took a step or two forward and felt as if she were walking in mud. The floor was covered with a wet pasty mix of soot, ash, and water—a black mud that coated every surface.

She stopped in her tracks. What was the point? It was hopeless. There was nothing here to save or salvage.

Sam stepped forward and picked up a chair that was tipped on its side, half burned. "I could fix this," he said quietly, putting it aside.

Jessica glanced at him. She didn't have the heart to argue.

"Listen folks, this house is unstable now. I can't let you go any farther than this room," Chief Rhinehardt told them. "The floor is gone past that point," he said, pointing to a spot in the arched doorway. "You could fall through into the basement and get hurt. Same goes for upstairs."

"So we can't really look for belongings that we might save?" Jessica asked.

"Sorry, not yet. If you have the house knocked down, the wreckers might be able to help you with that."

"Knocked down?" Sam stared at the fire chief. "Who says we're going to knock it down? I'm going to fix it, rebuild."

Jessica could see the fire chief struggle to hold his tongue. He stared down at the floor a moment. When he looked up, his expression was sympathetic. "That's up to you, folks. And the insurance company, I guess."

"Is that true?" Jessica asked. "Is the insurance company going to tell us what to do? I thought it was our decision to make."

Chief Rhinehardt looked sorry that he had spoken. "Hard to say. Every case is different." He avoided her gaze, Jessica noticed, and she knew he was trying to be diplomatic.

Jessica took a step toward Sam. She heard a crunch and looked down at her feet. She saw a piece of broken china and picked it up. It took a moment for her to recognize what the fragment had once belonged to, like a piece from a jigsaw puzzle.

Finally, she got it. "The Lenox vase your sister gave us when we got engaged."

Sam nodded. "Oh. Right."

Jessica tucked the china fragment in her pocket. With a sinking feeling deep in her chest, she turned to the door, ready to leave. There was nothing more to do.

As she gingerly walked to the door, the fire chief glanced at her. He looked relieved, she thought, to see her giving up. Sam took a moment longer, walking around the room, checking all the charred furniture. He picked out two more pieces and carried them to the door, where Chief Rhinehardt had placed the chair.

Jessica stepped outside and took a deep breath of the cold air. The pungent smell of smoke filled her head again, bringing back memories of their terrifying night.

She felt Sam walk up behind her and put his arm around her shoulders. "It's pretty bad," she said. "Worse than I thought. Much worse."

Sam didn't answer. "I'm going to take a walk around back with the Chief."

"I think I'll stay with Emily. I've seen enough for one day," she admitted.

While Sam walked off with the fire chief, Jessica headed toward her sister and Dan, who stood by the Jeep.

"So . . ." Emily started to speak, but didn't finish her sentence.

"Everything is ruined. There's nothing worth saving," Jessica managed. "We can't even walk more than a few feet into the parlor. The floor might cave in."

"A house like that is dangerous," Dan said. "I'm surprised he let you in at all."

"Chief Rhinehardt seems to think we should just knock it down. Well, he assumes we will," Jessica added.

"Oh no . . . really?" Emily looked distressed.

"Maybe you can restore it," Dan said. "If anyone can do it, Sam can."

"That's what he thinks," Jessica replied quietly.

She felt tears building again, but she was so tired of crying. She shook her head, feeling frustrated and angry. She had woken up this morning with a small spark of hope in her heart. She had truly believed they were going to spend a few hours here, sifting through the rubble and muck, finding bits and pieces of their belongings and putting their life back together again.

But that was not to be. Not today, anyway. She jammed her hands into her jacket pockets, feeling like she might scream.

Emily and Dan cast her sympathetic looks but didn't say anything. "I'm going to walk down to the pond," Jessica said, heading off toward the back of the property.

"Want some company?" Emily offered.

"No. I'm okay, thanks. I just want to be alone for a few minutes."

Emily nodded. She understood.

Jessica turned and tromped through the snow, heading down the gentle slope behind the house that led to a small pond. She found the path and began walking around the pond. Everything was still and quiet. One bird floated slowly on the water without making a sound. The trees and bushes around the pond were bare and the tall marsh grass, dried to a golden color, swayed in the cold breeze.

Jessica remembered the first time Sam had taken her here. It had been a beautiful summer day. Everything was lush and green. The pond was covered with flowering lily pads. It might have started raining—a sun shower? She wasn't entirely sure.

He brought her into the house first. He had bought it two years earlier but had just started the renovations. It looked a bit of a wreck to her but even then, she could see the potential. They weren't engaged at that point or even sure they would stay together. She had walked through the house, imagining how it would feel to live there. With him.

When they walked around the pond afterward, Sam had kissed her. Was it the first time? She wasn't sure now. Silly not to remember something so important. She did remember that kiss, though, and wondering if she was falling in love with him. She had probably already been in love with him, she realized. And fighting it every step of the way.

As if her thoughts had conjured him, her husband suddenly appeared behind her on the path that circled the pond.

"There you are." Sam caught up to her.

She turned and faced him. "Ready to go?"

He nodded. "I guess."

"What do you think now? Do you think we'll have to knock the house down?" she asked bluntly.

Sam looked surprised by her question. "I don't think so," he replied in a definite tone. "Rhinehardt's a good guy, but he doesn't know that much about building."

"I was just thinking about the first time you took me here. Do you remember?"

"Sure, I do." He smiled. "I wanted to show off my house, see if you liked it, show you I could be a responsible guy."

"Oh, I was very impressed." He put his hands on her shoulders and she smiled at him.

"Admit it. You married me for the house, Jess," he teased her.

"I married you in spite of the house. It was a run-down heap," she reminded him. "But we made it beautiful together."

Sam's expression grew thoughtful again. "Yes, we did."

He pulled her close and she rested her head on his shoulder and hugged him close. It wasn't the exciting, provocative kiss they had shared here so long ago. A kiss full of passion and questions. It was the familiar embrace of longtime lovers, married partners, sharing the load of their crisis.

Sam comforted her again as she quietly wept in his arms.

"We'll rebuild the house, Jess. We'll fix it again, just like it was. I know I can do it."

Jessica nodded. As they stood at the bottom of the hill and stared up at the charred ruins, she knew in her heart she didn't believe him. They would never have their house back.

"Why did this happen? Why us, Sam?"

Sam shook his head. "I don't know, hon. Just a bad break, I guess. Bad things happen sometimes. That's part of life."

"It seems so unfair. What did we do to deserve this? It makes me so angry," she admitted.

Angry at the world, at life in general. Angry at God, she wanted to tell him. But it was hard to say that out loud, even to her husband. Especially to her husband.

"I understand. I'm angry, too, but we have to get through this, Jessica. Being angry doesn't help. Wringing our hands and saying, 'poor me' isn't going to get us back to normal again. It just makes things worse."

Jessica didn't answer. She didn't feel he really understood what she had meant. That's the way Sam was. She knew that by now. Her husband had little tolerance for negativity. He swallowed his anger and pushed on. When they had arguments—not often, but all couples did—Sam would usually go outside and chop firewood or stomp off to his workshop and start pounding nails. By the time the disagreement was settled, he would be presenting her with some new piece of furniture.

It was a quality she admired in him most of the time. But just this once, she wished he would rant and rave. She wished he would get mad and let her do the same. She didn't want to wallow. She just wanted to vent. But she didn't want to make a scene in front of Emily and Dan, who were already sitting inside the Jeep, waiting for them.

She walked to the car beside Sam, staring down into the snow, matching his step. She felt foolish now, seeing all the rubber buckets and gloves she had thought they would need to salvage their belongings. There was nothing here for her. She wasn't sure when she'd come back. It wouldn't be any time soon.

JULIE POURED SOME MORE COFFEE IN JACK'S MUG AND TOOK AWAY a plate full of toast crumbs. "You don't have many friends, do you?"

"No, I don't," Jack admitted. He put aside the phone and the phone book and sipped the hot coffee. "I've just sort of . . . lost touch."

Julie had finally called for a tow truck and packed up her things. The car would take a day or so to be repaired, and he wondered where she and Kate were going to stay. But he forced himself not to get into it with her. She would find someplace, he told himself. It wasn't any of his business or concern.

She was still insisting he find someone to help him in the house and with the tree lot. Just to compromise, he had made a few calls this morning—real ones, not fake—but he couldn't find anyone to stop by the house to help him out.

"I can call a service," he finally said. "I'll call the doctor and see who he recommends."

Jack didn't like the idea of a stranger coming to take care of him. He didn't even like the idea of someone he knew doing him a favor. But Julie was stubborn. She wasn't going to leave until she knew he was covered.

"A home health aide, you mean?" She stood at the sink and glanced at him over her shoulder. "They'll do housework," she noted. "But I don't think they'll sell Christmas trees."

Not like you, he silently shot back.

She had sold quite a few trees last night. Jack had been impressed but didn't admit it. He never thought she would last out in the cold, handling the heavy trees, but she'd done fine. She seemed to enjoy it. She was stronger than she looked and friendly to the customers.

"I don't care about the trees," Jack insisted. "Let them rot. I'm going to give this place up."

"You don't really mean that." She stood by the sink, drying dishes.

"I do. I shouldn't have even opened up this year. See what it's got me?"

She sat down at the table across from him. Kate sat at the far end, working on a picture with her crayons and some sheets of colored paper. Julie picked up a stray crayon and twisted it in her fingers.

"All those beautiful trees. It's such a waste."

Jack waved his hand at her. "People can take them for free. I'll put an ad in the newspaper. 'Free Christmas Tree Day.'"

She smiled at him a little. The first smile he had coaxed from her all morning. "That would be interesting. I bet you'll be on the six-o'clock news."

He laughed. "I hope not. I certainly don't want to be."

"You just want to be left alone, right?"

She put it so bluntly, it caught him by surprise. He had been trying to tell her that for the past twenty-four hours, ever since he injured his leg. But now that she put it right out on the table, he wasn't sure how to answer.

You want us to leave, was what she was really saying. All he had to do was answer yes.

Why did it suddenly seem so hard to say that simple word?

He rubbed his cheek. "I'm not a very easy person to be around right now. That's just the way it is. The truth."

She didn't answer, just looked at him. He felt she understood what he couldn't explain. He still hurt so badly from the loss of his wife and son. It had twisted him somehow. Made him not quite himself anymore. Not quite right.

"You're not so bad, Jack," she said finally. "I mean, when you snap out of your Grinch act."

He glanced at her. He could see she was teasing him.

"I've been on my best behavior. I'm not sure how much longer I can keep it up," he warned her. "You ought to take that into consideration."

"In consideration of . . . what?" She tilted her head, her soft curly hair swinging to one side. "Are you asking me to stay on, to help you?"

He cleared his throat. "I—I'm not sure."

Was he? Well . . . maybe. How had that happened?

Julie took a deep breath and flattened both hands against the table. "Look, here's what we can try. I can stay here with Kate. Do the housework and help you outside with the trees. In exchange for room and board, and a small salary. You wouldn't have to pay me much."

She paused and checked his reaction. When he didn't start arguing with her, she added, "We can try it for a few days—say, until the car is fixed. Either of us can pull the plug at any time, no hard feelings."

"What about your family in New York?"

"I'll call my brother and tell him we'll be a few days late."

He had to ask. "And your ex? He won't care?" Jack regretted the question at once. What a dumb, clumsy thing to say.

But Julie looked at him evenly and said, "My ex-husband is no longer part of my life or Kate's. And that's the way it's going to remain. So—" Her mouth quirked up in a smile. "I can stay or go. It's your call."

Jack nodded, taking in her offer. He held his mug of coffee with both hands, nervously drumming his fingers on the smooth sides.

He had exaggerated when he said he didn't care about the trees. The lot was a big investment. If he didn't sell the trees, or at least most of them, he would be out a pile of money. He wasn't lacking financially, but it didn't make sense to take that loss when he didn't have to.

Still, having her here, day after day . . . He wasn't sure he could handle that. He wasn't used to any kind of company at all. Not even a dog. And a little girl and a pretty woman like Julie . . .

Jack rubbed the back of his neck. "Let's get something straight. Don't expect me to talk all the time and be real . . . social. It's not that I have anything against you. I think you're . . . you're fine. But I'm not used to talking much. I'm used to just . . ."

"—I know," she finished for him with a slight smile. "You're used to being by yourself. Talking to yourself," she added playfully.

He had to smile. It was true. He had started talking to himself. "That's right."

"Don't worry. I won't talk to you. Too much," she added. "Anything else? Don't you think I can do it?" She leaned forward in her chair. "I'm strong enough, I don't mind the cold, and I've worked in stores, so I know how to handle customers."

"I know you can do it. That's not what I'm worried about."

She stared at him, her eyes pressing him to explain.

He couldn't explain. He wasn't going to even try.

But he did need her help. Around the house, at least until he didn't see stars every time he tried to put weight on his leg. And with the tree lot. At least for now.

"Listen, a trial period. A few days, to see how it goes. I guess you're stuck around here anyway, until your car gets fixed. You might as well earn some money . . . and it will help me out, too," he finally admitted.

"Yes. It will help both of us."

She stuck out her hand. He realized she wanted to shake on their deal. He hesitantly took her hand in his. It felt smooth and cool; her skin was so soft. His hand looked large and calloused around hers, lined with sap stains so deep in his skin that he could never get them out. He quickly pulled his hand back, feeling embarrassed.

"Mommy, can you help me?" Kate called from the other end of the table. Julie turned and walked toward her. "Of course I can, sweetie. What's up?"

Jack thought Kate was having some trouble with her drawing, but then he saw Kate pull her mother down and whisper in her ear. He knew from the child's expression and from Julie's that they were talking about him. Katie had heard the grown-up conversation and understood that she and her mother would be staying at this house. With him. Indefinitely.

Jack thought she looked wary. Kate probably didn't like the idea of being around such a scary ogre. She had looked terrified yesterday when he tossed the crutches and had a fit. She had shied away from him ever since.

He tried to catch her eye and smile. But she looked back up at her mother then slipped off her chair and ran upstairs.

Jack suddenly regretted agreeing to this arrangement. That was just what he didn't want, feeling bad because the little girl didn't like him. Didn't he already have enough troubles weighing on his mind?

He wasn't sure what he was getting himself into here. He wasn't sure at all.

Chapter Six

***

$\mathcal{M}$OLLY AND MATT'S HOUSE WAS BIG. VERY BIG, WITH SIX bedrooms and several full bathrooms. But Fenway Park would not have been big enough to contain the energy of Tyler and Darrell, and their cousins, Noah and Nick.

At least, that's how it seemed to Jessica on Saturday morning when all the children were home from school and rainy sleet fell, making it impossible to get them outside.

A few days ago, it seemed like a good idea to move from Emily's snug cottage to Molly's spacious minimansion. Molly had four children of her own, but the older girls, Amanda and Lauren, were away at their first year of college, and her middle child, Jillian, was the perfect babysitting age. Betty, their four-month-old baby, was still in arms and no trouble at all.

But Molly had also opened her doors to her younger sister

Laurie, who was going through a difficult divorce and needed a place to stay with her twin sons.

The three younger boys were close in age and would start off together all right. But before very long, there would be shouting and name calling and inevitably, someone furiously telling on someone else.

No matter how hard the parents tried to negotiate, the kids just didn't get along.

"There's a lot of hormones flying around in there," Molly had observed the night before as the adults heard shouts from the family room. "That's what it is."

Jessica didn't entirely agree with that analysis, though she was sure the hormone level didn't help. She thought Laurie's boys were spoiled and rude. And she knew Laurie thought the same about her children.

It had been suspiciously quiet all morning, but just as she was taking a load of laundry out of Molly's dryer, Jessica heard a fight break out in a bedroom upstairs. She grabbed the laundry basket and ran upstairs to investigate.

"It's my turn!" she heard Noah shout.

"No, it's not. It's my turn. You just had a turn," she heard her son Tyler shout back. "You said I could use it now."

"I changed my mind. I'm not done yet. Get lost."

When Jessica reached the doorway, Tyler was staring at Noah, looking as if he might explode. "That's not fair!"

"Big deal. It's my game," Noah snapped back.

Tyler stared at him angrily, then grabbed for the controls of a video game that Noah was holding high above his head, beyond Tyler's reach.

"Tyler—" Jessica called to him from the doorway, but he didn't seem to hear her. Before she could stop him, he jumped on his cousin, grabbing him around the neck and pulling him down.

"Tyler! Stop that right now!"

Jessica dropped the laundry basket and ran into the room. After a brief struggle, she managed to pull Tyler off his cousin. Noah lay flat on the carpet, holding his nose. It looked as though it might start bleeding. She hoped not. Laurie got hysterical whenever her children so much as sneezed. She might go over the edge at the sight of blood.

"You sit right there, young man," Jessica sternly ordered Tyler as she crouched down and tended to Noah. "Noah, try to sit up, honey. Let me see your nose."

He took his hand off his face and Jessica checked the injury. No blood, thank goodness. Then he looked down at his game controls and saw that a handle had been cracked off.

His face crumpled like a ball of paper, and he let out an ear-piercing shriek.

Sam and Laurie ran into the room. Jessica turned, holding the broken video controls. She didn't know why she felt so guilty all of a sudden. But she did.

"They had a fight over the game controls. Over whose turn it was," she explained as she stood up.

Sam stared down at Tyler, who looked very repentant, sitting on the bed with his gaze down, hands folded in his lap.

"Who started it?" Sam asked.

"He did!" both boys answered simultaneously, pointing at each other.

Laurie stepped forward and knelt down next to Noah. "Your nose! Look at it! It might be broken!"

"I don't think it's broken, Laurie. It's not even bleeding," Jessica said calmly.

"It doesn't have to bleed. It could still be broken," Sam said helpfully. "Here, let me have a look."

He also knelt down near Noah and checked the boy's nose.

Laurie had recently had professional photographs taken of both her children and had sent the headshots around to modeling agencies. Though Laurie talked a lot about the auditions, as far Jessica knew, the boys had not been called for any jobs yet. Jessica sighed, wondering if Sam's sister was now going to hold them accountable for the ruin of Noah's modeling career.

"I don't think it's broken," Sam said finally. "It might swell up a little. You ought to get him some ice."

"I will," Jessica said quickly.

Laurie glanced at her but didn't say anything. She turned Noah's head to the side and critically examined his profile. "I see a bump," she announced. "He didn't have that before."

Jessica left the room, relieved at having an excuse to escape.

When she returned with the ice pack, Tyler was out in the hall, leaning against the wall. "Dad said to wait outside until he's ready to talk to me."

He looked very mournful. Jessica knew the confrontation wasn't entirely his fault, but she tried not to give him any sympathy. "Yes, you wait right there. We need to have a talk."

Jessica went into the bedroom. Noah was seated on the bed and Laurie sat next to him.

She handed Noah the pack. "Hold this on your nose awhile. You'll feel better soon."

"Here, honey. Let me help you." Laurie fussed over her son.

Sam looked up at Jessica. "Tyler broke the controls for the game. I told Laurie we would buy him a new one."

Jessica felt her mouth twist in a sour expression. Just what they wanted to spend their money on right now. And right before Christmas.

"Maybe it could be fixed?" she asked.

And maybe it wasn't entirely Tyler's fault the toy is broken, she wanted to add. *If Noah learned to share a little bit and not to taunt his younger cousin, this wouldn't have happened.*

But she didn't want to get into a fight with Laurie, who was, more often than not, emotional and irrational, even in normal conversation.

They were guests here. She didn't want to embarrass Sam in front of his family.

"You can't fix these things. We already tried that once," Sam reminded her. "You have to ship it to the moon, and it never comes back right."

Jessica sighed. She knew he was right. "I was just wondering."

Noah tugged on his mother's sleeve. "Can I watch TV now?"

Laurie nodded and stroked his head. "Sure, honey. Just keep that pack on and let Mommy know right away if you see any blood." She fixed Sam and Jessica with an accusing frown. "It must be very painful. He's being very good about it."

Noah slipped off the bed and ran out of the room. Jessica saw him make a gloating face at Tyler as he skipped past.

"Sam, Tyler's waiting for you. Why don't you talk to him in here? I'm going to fold some laundry."

Jessica knew if she stayed any longer, talking about the kids with Laurie, she might end up popping her sister-in-law in the nose.

Sam seemed to sense this and quickly nodded. "Okay, honey. I'll be right in to help."

Jessica carried the overflowing basket into the bedroom she shared with Sam. It was a large room with its own private full bath. It was Amanda's room, Molly's stepdaughter. She would be home soon for winter break, but Molly promised when the older girls got home, they would share the small maid's room that was in the basement.

Jessica didn't like the idea of putting her niece out of her own bedroom. The girls wouldn't be back until mid-December, but Jessica didn't think she could last that long around here. Not with Laurie and her children under the same roof. She just hadn't found the right time to talk to Sam about it.

Sam walked in as she was matching up socks.

He sat on the bed and started to help her. "I had a talk with Tyler. He said he was sorry for starting the fight, and he understands he has to be nicer to Noah."

Jessica's jaw dropped. "I heard the whole thing, Sam. Noah was taunting him. He promised Tyler he would give him a turn on the game, then he went back on his word and teased him with the toy, holding it over his head. Tyler felt frustrated. It wasn't entirely his fault."

Sam's mouth set in a tight line. "I'm sure there was blame on both sides, Jess. Tyler has to learn you can't just jump on somebody and knock them down if you feel angry. He broke the toy and we're responsible."

Jessica sighed and grabbed up another pair of socks, rolling them in a tight ball. "Well, if we stay here much longer, we'd better open a charge account at the toy store. I'm not sure we can afford it."

"What's that supposed to mean?"

"It means that we're not comfortable here. The boys don't get along at all with Laurie's kids. And I don't blame them. If the boys aren't fighting, then the baby is crying. Amanda and Lauren will be home soon and we'll be taking up their bedrooms."

"It's a big house. It's as big as an airplane hangar, for goodness sake. I'm sure we can all find a place to sleep here."

It was a big house, and that was part of the problem, too. But it was hard for Jessica to admit that part to Sam. It wasn't so very long ago that Molly was a struggling single mother, living in a tiny apartment above a store. She and Sam were always taking care of Molly's girls so Molly could pursue her many part-time jobs to make ends meet.

Then she met Matt Harding, a successful doctor. They married and Molly started a catering business, Willoughby Fine Foods, which was now wildly successful. They had this house custom-built, Molly's dream house, and then had another baby.

The tables had turned. Molly's life was a fairy tale with a happy ending. Now they were the needy ones and Molly was helping them. Jessica didn't begrudge Molly one bit of her good fortune or happiness. That wasn't it at all. It was just hard to be surrounded by all this conspicuous luxury in the light of all they had just lost. It was hard to be the ones in need.

It was just . . . hard.

She glanced at Sam. She didn't think he would understand, and she didn't want to start another argument.

"Sam," she began quietly, "we're all under a lot of stress right now. Especially the kids. I don't think these living arrangements are good for them. Tyler is still sleeping in his clothes, afraid he might need to run out of the house in the middle of the night, and Darrell is having nightmares. All this fighting with their cousins, all this noise and activity—it's making things even more stressful for us."

"I know, Jess. I know what the boys are going through. And

you," he added. Sam sat on the edge of the bed, his elbows resting on his knees. "We really need to have some patience. It's only been a week. I think it was very generous of Molly and Matt to have us here. We're not in a position to be choosy."

"What about the insurance? Won't they cover a stay in a motel for us?"

They had put in claims for rebuilding the house, for their belongings, and for their living expenses. Jessica thought they could ask for an allowance toward a hotel, though she didn't know for sure since Sam had been handling all the paperwork.

She could tell from Sam's expression that Sam didn't like that idea. "I don't want to bring the kids to some drafty, drab motel. We'll definitely be on top of each other in a place like that. We won't even be able to cook our own meals. Or wash clothes."

What he said was true. It would be inconvenient, and the atmosphere would probably be depressing. Maybe a motel was not the answer, Jessica realized.

"How about staying with my mother? Even with Sara and Luke, there's still plenty of room."

Jessica's mother lived in a large Victorian house in the best section of town. Emily's older daughter, Sara, and her husband, Luke McAllister, had been living with Lillian for the past two years, ever since Lillian had taken a fall on the attic stairs, making it clear that she needed more help and company than she'd ever admit.

"Your mother's house?" She could tell from Sam's expression that he hated the idea. He shook his head. "I don't think so. Did she even invite us?"

Jessica had been over to visit her mother a few days after the fire. Lillian had been sympathetic, most of the time. But she hadn't mentioned housing them.

"Um, no. But I'm sure if I asked her, she would agree. She's not totally heartless." Jessica wished she didn't sound so defensive. Her mother was difficult, no question. Sam, though, never cut Lillian any slack.

"No, not *totally* heartless," he conceded, and Jessica could hear the unsaid words: *Just mostly heartless.*

Jessica ignored his reply, sinking her head into her hands. Tyler and Noah's conflicts were nothing compared to the lousy chemistry between her mother and Sam. Maybe that match wouldn't be such a good idea either. But any place seemed better than Molly's right now.

"My mother invited us for lunch after church tomorrow. I'll ask her if we can stay a little while."

"I guess we'll just have to see how she feels about it," Sam said tactfully. She could tell he hoped her mother would say no.

She folded a T-shirt and placed it on the top of the pile. "I guess so."

It had been a busy day at the tree farm. Julie had been a whirlwind, helping customers choose the trees and get them loaded onto their vehicles. After a while, Jack just tried to stay out of her way. He had been outside, too, hobbling about on his crutches and helping where he could, spelling Julie when she needed to take care of Kate.

Kate was an easy child. She was content to play in the snow or "help" her mother with the customers. Julie also had her play in the Christmas shop, making decorations with the craft supplies she found there. That distraction had amused the little girl for quite a while, though the sight of activity in the deserted shop had brought a pang to Jack's heart.

Julie had talked about making dinner, but Jack insisted on taking care of the meal. He had been feeding himself for a long time and didn't need her to wait on him. He also felt obliged to do his share, since she had been working hard outside all day.

He found a store-bought lasagna in the freezer and heated it up in the oven then added a bowl of salad on the side. Not much, he thought, calling them both to dinner.

"Wow, this looks great." Julie smiled as she took her place. "I'm starved," she admitted.

"The cold makes you hungry." Jack dished out the portions as she passed the plates. "I hope Kate likes this stuff. If she doesn't want it, I can fix her something else."

"Kate loves pasta, don't worry. She'll eat as much as you," Julie warned him.

The little girl dug in hungrily. They were both so easy to please, making him feel like Superman. He had to remind himself to keep some perspective.

"Katie made some beautiful decorations today," Julie remarked. She touched Katie's hair. "We ought to show Jack."

Jack stiffened; it was a touchy subject for him. "Sure. You can show me later," he said. "When you're done with dinner."

"You can keep them. For your Christmas tree," Kate offered.

Jack glanced at her. "I don't have a Christmas tree. But thanks anyway."

Kate looked puzzled. "Why not?"

Jack shrugged. He couldn't find an answer that wasn't too curt. "I don't know. I just don't need one anymore. Okay?"

Kate's eyes widened. She looked as if she might cry. Jack realized his tone had been too harsh and was instantly sorry. But he didn't know what to do.

Julie spoke up, her tone soothing. "You can bring the decorations to school, Katie. You can give them to Mrs. Jensen for a Christmas present. I bet she'd love that."

Julie had enrolled Kate in a preschool at a church in town. It was good for Kate to be with children her own age, to be learning and playing. It gave her a sense of structure and kept her from thinking too much about the divorce, Julie had explained. It sounded to him like the child had been through a lot this past year.

"Hey, great idea," Jack said, with a little too much enthusiasm. "I bet your teacher will love that. I bet she has a great Christmas tree. No sense wasting them on me," he added.

Kate didn't answer. She stared at him a moment then looked up at her mother. "Can I get up now? I'm finished."

Julie nodded. "Why don't you go upstairs and play? You're going to have a bath soon."

They both watched Katie leave the room. Jack glanced at Julie. He didn't feel like eating any more either.

"I'm sorry. I didn't mean to scare her."

"I know." Julie sighed. He guessed she might be angry at him but didn't want to start an argument.

"I just . . . don't want a Christmas tree anymore. I didn't know how to explain it." When she didn't reply, he added, "it's hard to talk to children if you aren't used to them. I was never much good at it."

He thought of David, the way they had butted heads time and again once his son became a teenager. Claire had always been a buffer between them, forcing them to talk things out and reconcile. But once she was gone, Jack didn't know how to keep the peace anymore. It wasn't long after his wife's death that he and his son had their final blowup and then David was gone.

"I think you talk to her pretty well," Julie remarked. "Most of the time."

He shrugged. That last bit hadn't been one of his better moments, for sure.

"She hasn't really been the same since the divorce. Her father, my ex-husband, had a terrible temper. He scared her. Now she's afraid of men. Especially angry ones," Julie carefully explained.

Jack wasn't exactly surprised by Julie's admission. He could see the child was withdrawn and skittish. But the sudden realization that Julie and her daughter had been at the mercy of some angry, even abusive husband was disturbing.

Maybe that's why Julie is practically oblivious to my foul moods, he thought. *She was used to far worse.*

"I don't mean to pry but—what you said before—your ex really doesn't see Kate?" It was hard to imagine anyone having a kid like that and abandoning her.

"No." Julie's voice was tense. "He doesn't have any interest in us, and frankly, that's the best possible outcome." She shrugged, as if shaking off memories.

Jack stood, picked up some dirty dishes, and limped over to the sink. "I'm sorry," he said quietly.

He glanced over his shoulder. He wasn't sure if she had even heard him.

When she didn't answer he said, "I'm real sorry if I scared her. And if I asked you about something you would rather not discuss . . . well, it won't happen again."

Julie turned. "It's okay. And as for Katie, I'm not blaming you, Jack. I just wanted you to understand."

He nodded and scraped off the plates. He should have guessed.

He should have been more aware of the kid and thinking less about himself. It made him feel small and selfish. Julie probably thought he was, too.

After cleaning up the kitchen, Jack went into his room to read. He heard Julie and Katie upstairs. Katie was getting her bath, and he heard them laughing and felt relieved. Kids could bounce back so easily. Not like adults.

A while later, he heard them down in the kitchen. He felt trapped in his bedroom and tried to focus on his book, a history book about World War II. He liked to read and would sometimes go through several books a month, especially in the winter. But tonight, he couldn't seem to concentrate.

He had only gotten through a few pages when the scent of something baking tantalized his senses.

He heard Julie call to him. "Jack? Would you like some cookies?"

He sighed and put the book down. Fresh-baked cookies. When was the last time he'd had one of those?

"What kind?" he yelled back, sounding choosy. Just to delay the inevitable, he knew.

He heard Julie laugh. "Picky, picky."

Then Katie laughed, too.

"I'm not going to tell you," Julie said. "You'll have to come out and see. . . ."

He put down his book, got off the bed, and put a slipper on the foot without a cast. Then he smoothed out his flannel shirt and pushed back his hair. He still needed a haircut, but he had trimmed his beard a little shorter, which helped him look less like a homeless person. He hoped.

He limped into the kitchen and saw Kate sitting at the table, fresh from her bath, wearing her pajamas and a robe. She looked like a little flower in a garden, he thought.

There was a dish of cookies on the table, chocolate chip. Kate was eating one with a glass of milk and Julie was at the stove, taking out another cookie sheet.

"Do they meet with your approval?" she asked.

He smiled at her. "My favorite kind. How did you guess?"

He sat at the table near Kate but not too close. She did seem afraid of him and he felt a little pang.

He reached out, took the entire plate of cookies and set it in front of his place. "These are all for me, right?" He rubbed his hands together in anticipation.

Kate looked surprised but didn't say anything.

"They call me Cookie Monster around here, did you know that?"

She shook her head.

"Oh, well it's true. I could eat ten dishes of cookies like this. No problem."

"You'd get a tummy ache," Katie warned him.

Jack shook his head. "Cookie monsters don't get tummy aches."

"That's lucky," Kate said.

He nodded. "Sure is."

Julie walked over, smiling at him. She looked pleased that he was making an effort with Kate. It made him feel good inside to please her. Real good.

"Sorry, Monster, these cookies are for Kate's class. You can only have one. Or maybe two," Julie said, playing along with his game. "If you're a good monster, I mean."

He made a mock sad face that made Kate smile again. "Okay. I understand."

"I'll make you ten plates another time," Julie promised.

"I'm going to remember that. You don't want to go back on a promise to a monster, believe me."

She laughed in earnest and he felt the same glow.

"You want some milk, Monster?" Kate offered him her cup.

He smiled at her. "Thanks. I'll get my own. You drink that up. It will make you grow tall and pretty . . . like your mother."

Whoops. How did that slip out? Jack didn't dare look at Julie. He wasn't sure she had even heard him.

"Want to see my book?" Kate drew closer, showing the picture book she had at the table.

"Sure, let's take a look." Jack was pleased by the invitation—and eager for any distraction.

"Why don't you read it to her? It's getting close to bedtime," Julie said.

"Me?" Jack blinked.

"Sure. You can read. I've seen you," Julie teased him. "It's written for preschoolers. I think you can handle it."

Kate stared at him with an expectant expression, and Jack knew he was stuck. But maybe that was okay. This was the moment to prove he wasn't such a bad, scary guy after all, wasn't it?

He looked down at the book again. The cover showed a little rabbit standing off by himself in a playground, looking rather apprehensive while a lot of other rabbits were busy playing.

"Okay, here we go. *Lester Makes a Friend . . .*" *Well, so far I can relate,* Jack thought.

The story was, as Jack expected, about a lonely rabbit named Lester who moves to a new neighborhood and doesn't have a friend. He couldn't remember the last time he had read a children's book aloud. At first, he felt self-conscious and read the text in a flat, matter-of-fact tone. But Kate was quite involved in the story, though she had doubtless heard it a million times before. He found that out when he tried to skip a few lines.

She pulled her chair closer so she could see the pictures. The gesture pleased him for some inexplicable reason.

He soon got involved in the story, too. Lester was quite a likable little fellow with a number of traits that Jack couldn't help but identify with. He found himself feeling sorry for Lester because the little bunny was so shy.

Before he knew it, Jack was reading Lester's dialogue in a rabbit voice. This seemed to please Katie even more, so of course, he continued.

When the story was done, he saw that she wore a very thoughtful expression.

"Did you like that?"

She nodded, taking her book back. "Lester looks sad sometimes. But I like the ending."

In the end, Lester learns that in order to have a friend, you have to be a friend. Though that was something Claire used to tell David, it made Jack think more about the present than the past.

"Me, too," Jack said. "It was a good ending."

"Okay, Kate. Bedtime," Julie said. Kate nodded and slipped off the chair, carrying her book under her arm.

Julie glanced at Jack as they left the room. She didn't say anything, but the look in her warm brown eyes reached right down and almost set his battered heart ticking again.

Almost, he thought.

He cleared his throat and picked up his own book again.

A short time later, Julie returned to the kitchen and began cleaning up the cookie sheets and ingredients. Jack sat with a cup of tea and his book, caught red-handed eating more cookies.

He glanced at her, his mouth full of crumbs. "Never get between a monster and a plate of cookies."

She smiled at him. "I wouldn't even try."

She sat down across the table from him. Her cheeks were flushed from baking, and little curls had sprung out around her face from her ponytail. She never wore any makeup, he noticed. She didn't need any.

She rested her chin in her hand, watching him read. He tried to ignore her, but it was impossible.

"Kate get off to sleep okay?" He knew she must have but couldn't think of anything else to say.

"As soon as her head hit the pillow. She had a long day."

"Didn't we all."

"It was nice of you to read to her. She enjoyed it."

"I liked it, too. It was a good story," he said honestly.

For some reason, that comment made Julie smile. Then she looked serious again. "Do you have any children, Jack? You've never said."

The question stole his breath away. He shook his head, his gaze fixed on the page he had been reading, though the type suddenly blurred.

"We had a son," he said quietly. "I lost him, too."

"Oh . . . I'm sorry." Julie sat back. She stared down at the table a moment then rose and walked to the counter and began putting things away.

He realized his reply had given the impression that David was dead. He hadn't really meant to do that. He considered saying more, explaining what had happened. But then he felt he just couldn't get into it. He didn't want to.

What did it matter? He didn't have to tell her his whole life story. It was better to keep some distance. A lot better.

Finally, the kitchen was tidy with everything in place and the counters spotless. Julie was very organized, Jack had noticed. In just a few days, she had cleared up his mess and made the entire house neat and clean.

"Well, I'm going up to bed. See you tomorrow." Julie paused in the doorway. "I'm taking Kate to church tomorrow morning. Would you like to come with us?"

"Uh . . . no. Thanks. I'll stick around here. There'll be a lot of early customers tomorrow."

"Oh, right. I almost forgot. I'll be home a little after eleven, and I'll work in the afternoon," she said quickly.

"That's all right. You take your time. You don't have to work around the clock. That's not what I expect."

She nodded, suddenly looking self-conscious. Both of them seemed to forget that he was her employer now, paying for her help. It wasn't a personal relationship, even though it often felt that way.

"Sure. Well, good night," she said quickly.

"Good night, Julie."

Jack listened to her footsteps, climbing the stairs to the second floor. He let out a long sigh. He had to keep her at a distance. That was for sure.

But it wasn't easy. And it was getting harder every day.

CHAPTER SEVEN

$\sim$

IT WAS A CHALLENGE TO GET EVERYONE READY FOR CHURCH on time, but somehow Jessica managed. She always made the boys wear good clothes on Sunday—dress pants and nice sweaters—especially when they were invited to her mother's house afterward. She also knew that today her family would be the center of attention in their close-knit congregation. She didn't want her children to look shabby, but jeans and sweatshirts were all that they had right now, so it would just have to do.

She would have been wearing the same if Emily had not insisted Jessica take some of her best outfits, including a beautiful navy blue suit. Emily claimed the skirt was too snug on her hips these days. Jessica knew that was just a gracious fib. Emily jogged nearly every morning and rarely gained a pound.

Her sister did have a closet packed with beautiful clothes and probably would never miss the suit. But it had been generous of her, Jessica thought, as she slipped on the finely tailored skirt and jacket.

Still, Jessica couldn't help thinking about her own closet, all the items she'd enjoyed choosing in the stores and wearing, the special ones that made her feel attractive and stylish. She had to start from scratch with a wardrobe now—a project that might have been fun if she and Sam weren't so worried about money.

"Jess, are you ready?" Sam called from the bottom of the staircase.

If she kept the boys waiting much longer, they would look a complete mess by the time they got in the car.

"I'll be down in one minute," she called back. She surveyed her reflection as she swiped on some lipstick. The sleeves of the jacket were too long and the shoulders too wide. *But this is as good as it gets, pal,* she told herself.

Jessica turned away from the mirror, far from satisfied but more or less resigned.

They arrived at church with a few minutes to spare before the service began. There were still many people milling about in the narthex and corridors.

Jessica felt everyone turn to look at them as they entered. Sam stopped to speak with Tucker Tulley and his wife, Fran. Jessica smiled and nodded a greeting but kept walking toward the sanctuary, her hand on Tyler's shoulder. Darrell followed a few steps behind.

She spotted Emily and Dan already seated in a pew near the front. Jane sat between them, and on Emily's other side sat their mother. Jessica headed for the empty row just behind them.

"Jessica, you poor dear." Sophie Potter seemed to pop out of nowhere. Her hand rested on Jessica's arm, detaining her.

"Hello, Sophie. How are you?" Jessica smiled mechanically.

"How are *you*?" the older woman said pointedly. "We were all so sorry to hear the news about your house. What a tragedy. You must still be in shock."

"Yes, it has been a shock."

It was hard to talk about the house. Even with people she had known since childhood, like Sophie. Jessica wasn't sure why. She just didn't want to discuss it, sift over the details, relive the horror over and over again.

Sophie nodded knowingly. "We had a fire once. It burned down the apple shed, but we caught it in time, before it spread to the house." She shook her head. "You were blessed that night, getting your family out safely. That's the main thing."

"Yes, it is. We were very lucky," Jessica said.

How many times had she repeated that phrase? She was beginning to feel hypocritical saying it lately. It wasn't that she was ungrateful; she was still thanking God every day for getting them all out safely. But what they'd been through that week—Reilly's death, moving from place to place, feeling the loss of their home and all their belongings, the boys' nightmares—none of that felt lucky.

Sophie put a hand on Jessica's arm. "We have tons of stuff out at the orchard, a house full of things I don't need anymore. If there's anything at all you want, you just let me know."

"Thank you, Sophie. That's very kind." Jessica knew the older woman meant well. But she could hardly imagine what Sophie Potter's castoffs would look like—afghans knitted in 1955? Pots and pans that dated back to World War II?

"I'll talk to Sam. See what you need. He can come by anytime." Sophie nodded, satisfied with that idea.

She patted Jessica's arm then headed for her seat. But several others now stood in line to offer their sympathies—Grace Hegmen and her father, Digger; Vera Plant and Carolyn, the minister's wife. Jessica nodded and smiled, thanking them each in turn for their concern.

Sam came down the aisle, and they walked to their seats together. The boys were already there, talking with their uncle Dan and amusing Jane over the back of the wooden pew.

"Good timing," Jessica murmured. "I was hoping you would come along and save me."

Sam gave her a puzzled look. "Save you? From what?"

She knew he didn't understand and she couldn't explain then and there. The chorus of well-wishers had made her feel as if she were on the receiving line at a funeral, and all the sympathy had sent her spirits plummeting again, reminding her of all they had lost.

She sat down and Emily whispered to her, "Nice suit. You have good taste."

"It was a gift. A very thoughtful one."

"I recognize that suit." Lillian cast a discerning eye over her youngest daughter. "Emily wore it during her last campaign. Are you trying to tell us something, Jessica? Planning on running for office?" That was her mother's idea of a joke.

"Not at all, Mother. I think Emily is doing a fine job. I wouldn't want to challenge her in this town."

The truth was, the way things were going, Jessica had been seriously thinking of returning to work full time. The suit would come in handy if the bank took her back. She hadn't spoken to Sam about it yet. They had both been so busy and there had been so little privacy while living at Emily's and then with Molly. But, the way things looked now, another salary seemed a necessity. Besides, Jessica couldn't imagine Sam objecting. He would probably feel relieved by her decision, she thought.

The chorus had begun singing the introit, and Reverend Ben

took his place at the pulpit. Jessica tried to focus her full attention on the service, hoping to get a spiritual boost this morning. She certainly felt she needed it.

Unfortunately, her cares and worries soon distracted her, and it was hard to concentrate, even on the sermon, which she usually found interesting. Reverend Ben was speaking about the hidden need in the community, the food pantries and agencies where struggling families came to get warm clothes and enough food to put on the table for their children.

"We live in a land of plenty. In a comfortable, if not outright affluent community. Yet within a few miles of this church people are struggling. People are choosing between turning up the heat and buying their children new shoes. People are choosing between buying medication and food to eat. . . ."

That was true, Jessica thought. Some people had so little. Her mind lurched. She had so little. She was now . . . one of those people. One of the needy. A charity case. It hurt to realize that, but she couldn't deny it. The simple idea made her nearly burst out in tears.

"This is the season for trading our Christmas wish lists," Reverend Ben continued. "Trying to choose between cell phones that play music and send out e-mail. Or gigantic TV screens that make our living rooms look like drive-in movie theaters. . . ."

That line drew a few chuckles, though not from Sam, she noticed. He would miss watching the weekly football game this afternoon in their family room. He would probably watch it with Matt, Molly's husband, on a TV even bigger than the one they used to have. But it wouldn't be the same.

Reverend Ben paused and pushed his wire-rimmed glasses a bit higher on his nose. "This is the season of giving, all the TV commercials tell us. But giving what, and to whom? More cell phones and iPods to those who already have so many high-tech toys?"

Jessica sighed. How would she do her holiday shopping this year? It was going to be difficult. The boys still wanted nice gifts, and it seemed more important than ever to try to make them happy this Christmas. Material things, yes. But if it made them feel better, was that so bad?

The sermon ended, and it was soon time for Joys and Concerns, the part of the service when the church members shared their happy moments and challenges. As Reverend Ben went around the sanctuary, people asked for prayers for the sick and announced anniversaries and birthdays or reunions with relatives.

Sam raised his hand and Jessica cringed. Didn't they already have enough attention? "Yes, Sam?" Ben said, recognizing him.

Sam stood up. "As most of you know, my family survived a terrifying experience last week when our house caught fire and burned down."

Jessica heard a few people murmur, and one person actually gasped. Apparently, the news had not reached everyone in town.

"But we're truly thankful that everyone escaped the house safely and we're able to join you here today. We're also very grateful for all the thoughtful calls and messages from our friends and the help of our family as we get reorganized."

Reorganized? That was a nice way of saying it. Jessica looked down at her hands, not daring to meet Sam's eye. Was he done yet? She felt everyone staring at them.

"Tucker Tulley just told me that a lot of people brought items to church today that they thought we might need to set up a new home," Sam continued. "Jessica and I want to thank all of you for your thoughtfulness and support."

Jessica forced a smile as Sam sat down. She had often volunteered at the church's annual rummage sale. She imagined the collection of donated goods would look much the same—plastic dishes, worn pieces of furniture, mugs with dopey sayings on them, and tacky seascapes. Nothing she would ever want to have in her home.

Maybe she was more like her mother than she had ever wanted to admit. Proud and very particular, even when it seemed completely irrational. Just like her mother, she had a strong sense of privacy and a need to present a certain face to the world. Why else would she be wearing this suit that didn't really fit her all that well?

It was hard for her to have everyone looking at her family now as if they were needy and homeless. Which, in fact, they were. But she just wasn't comfortable with that idea of herself. The fire, their neediness, all of it made her feel shame.

Apparently, Sam didn't feel that way at all. She glanced at him, sitting beside her, looking comfortable with himself. As he always did. They really were so different in so many ways. Sometimes she didn't notice it at all. But sometimes, that was all she saw.

AFTER THE SERVICE, EVERYONE DROVE OVER TO LILLIAN'S HOUSE for lunch, as they had planned. Sara and Luke had stayed home from church to get everything ready. Much like her mother, Emily, Sara was not very interested in cooking. She was a reporter and her schedule so scattered, she didn't get many chances to fix real dinners for herself and Luke.

Luke, however, was quite able in the kitchen, just like Sam. It was always fun to hear the two "macho" guys trading recipes. Today the young couple had prepared a buffet, with bubbling hot quiche, cold shrimp salad, mesclun greens with vinaigrette dressing, and scones.

Luke even remembered to set Lillian's portions aside, free of any "exotic spices," which meant any seasoning beyond salt and pepper.

As usual, they ate in the formal dining room, the table set with one of Lillian's many sets of fine china and flatware, which she often spoke of passing on to her daughters and granddaughter. But somehow never did.

Dining at her mother's house had been a challenge ever since she and Sam had started a family. Jessica followed the conversation with one ear, listening for sounds of her children playing in the next room with the other.

"So when will you hear back from the insurance company?" Luke asked Sam.

"Not for a few weeks. They take their time."

"Insurance companies run the world, don't kid yourself," Dr. Ezra Elliot chimed in. Dr. Elliot had been part of the family circle for as long as Jessica could remember. He had been her father's friend, but was also a good friend and a great support to her mother, especially after her father had died. Ezra had a sweet spot for Lillian, Jessica knew, and it surprised her that his role had never moved beyond that of a loyal friend and companion. Jessica also realized she probably didn't know the entire story. Her mother still had some secrets, that was for certain.

"Insurance and drug companies," Lillian agreed, "they have us all over a barrel. And speaking of barrels, the oil companies are outright bandits. Did you see my oil bill this month? I thought I was having one of my spells and seeing double."

The conversation bounced from one topic to another, as usual. Jessica was relieved to be in the company of her family, who talked about things other than the fire, and who didn't ooze sympathy all over them.

That would never be the problem with her mother, she thought with a small smile.

She remembered her conversation with Sam, and how she had planned to ask her mother if they could stay in her house awhile. But so far, she hadn't found the right moment to bring it up.

"Did you hear that?" Lillian sat up sharply. She listened intently, like a hunting dog stalking prey. "Did something break in the living room? Where are those children?"

Sam traded a look with Jessica as he got up from the table. "I didn't hear anything. But I'll go check."

"Yes, go look, Sam. I didn't hear anything, Mother," Jessica said. "I'm sure it's okay."

Jessica remembered the first time they had brought Darrell here. How he had started playing under the table and nearly pulled down the tablecloth, almost breaking everything above. Then, for the second act, he had slid down the long stairway on an area rug, pretending it was a boogie board. Though an antique bean jar had been the only casualty, her mother had acted as if Darrell had swung a wrecking ball at the house.

The boys were older now but still full of energy. Jessica kept a watchful eye on them. She didn't want to find herself bidding on another antique bean jar on eBay this week.

Sam soon returned and took his seat again. "They're just playing a board game. Nothing to worry about."

Lillian looked at him suspiciously, as if she didn't entirely believe the report, but she didn't press the point.

"So, you're living at Molly's house now," Sara said, turning to Jessica and Sam. "How's that working out?"

"Couldn't ask for more," Sam replied. "She put us in a big bedroom with a private bath. The boys have the same setup. The place is as big as a hotel."

"Molly's been very generous. But Sam's sister Laurie is also living there now with her two children, and the four boys don't get along very well," Jessica confessed.

"Goodness me. Sounds like a madhouse." Her mother's eyes widened.

Perfect opening, Jessica thought. "It is very stressful, Mother. We were wondering if we could come and stay here awhile. You do have lots of spare rooms upstairs, and we would help with your bills. The food and utilities," she offered, remembering her mother's rant about the oil bill.

Jessica felt Sam staring at her, but she didn't meet his glance. Her gaze was fixed on her mother, who seemed to be considering the idea.

"Live here with me? I must be very popular. Everyone in the family wants to move in," she quipped, looking at Sara and Luke.

"We'd love to have you here," Sara said. Luke nodded. "Not that it's our decision," Sara added carefully.

"It most certainly is not," Lillian affirmed. She turned to Jessica. "How long do you think you would need to stay?"

"Oh, I don't know. A few . . . weeks?" That seemed the right answer, she thought. It would probably be six months or more before their own house was livable. Especially since it was the middle of winter, which meant it would be hard to get the house rebuilt quickly. But she couldn't tell her mother that and ruin their chances completely.

"A few weeks? Hmm . . . I don't know. Possibly . . ." Lillian wavered. She looked at Sam. "What do you think?" she asked bluntly.

Sam was taken by surprise. Jessica knew what he thought. She just hoped he wouldn't be honest with her mother.

"About staying here?" he asked.

"Isn't that what we've been talking about?" Lillian replied sharply, and Jessica saw Sam's typically relaxed expression grow tense.

"If you'll have us, I would be grateful. It seems to be what Jessica wants," he answered in an even voice.

Her mother sniffed. She seemed disappointed she hadn't caught him in her trap. Maybe this wasn't such a good idea after all, Jessica thought.

Suddenly, they all heard a crash from the living room. A real crash, not an imagined one. Then the sound of Tyler crying. Sam jumped up from the table and jogged into the next room.

Jessica saw the expression on her mother's face and knew the delicate balance had not tipped in her favor.

Lillian shook her head. "That's just what I mean. I can't have all these disruptions. It's not good for my blood pressure. I had a bad report from the doctor on my last visit. I can't risk another stroke, Jessica. These boys and all their activity—it would be too much for me. Too much," she repeated, shaking her head.

"I understand, Mother. I just thought I would ask."

Across the table, Emily cast her a sympathetic look.

Sam returned again. "Tyler and Darrell were fooling around. Tyler fell and knocked over a lamp, but it didn't break."

"Miraculously," Lillian murmured. She didn't ask how Tyler was, Jessica noticed.

"He isn't hurt?" she asked.

Sam shook his head. "He's fine." He pulled his chair up to the table again. "Did I miss anything?"

"Mother has decided she's not able to have us here, after all.

It would be too much for her. Her blood pressure is acting up again."

Jessica heard Sam's sigh of relief. "That's too bad. Thanks for considering it, Lillian," he said cheerfully. "I guess we'll stay at Molly's and see if we can work things out."

"I've got an idea," Luke cut in. "What if you took a cabin at New Horizons? It's almost time for the winter break. I can move around a few of the teachers. They're going to leave soon anyway. There's a very nice cabin with two bedrooms and a fireplace. It's not as luxurious as Molly's house. But you'll have your privacy."

"Hey, that's a great idea." Sam grinned at her, and Jessica could tell he loved the idea.

Luke, who had been a police officer in Boston, had founded the center and now ran it. Offering the cabin was his call. A good thing and a bad thing, Jessica thought. It was a thoughtful gesture, she knew.

Except that she didn't want to live there. The cabins, which were originally summer cottages, weren't so bad. They had been renovated and winterized a few years ago when the center opened. But they were definitely rustic, with a sleepaway camp atmosphere. Jessica could see spending a weekend in the country at such a place. But live there? Indefinitely?

"Thank you, Luke. It's nice of you to offer," Jessica said. "Sam and I will talk it over."

She cast Sam a look that said, *Slow down, pal. I have a say, too. Remember?*

Sam sat back in his seat. "Sure, Jess and I need to talk. But it's a great idea and very generous of you. Thanks, Luke."

Luke and Sam exchanged a glance. Jessica felt as if the entire situation was already decided and nothing she said would make the slightest difference.

CHAPTER EIGHT

"I T'S JUST TEMPORARY, JESS. YOU'RE RIGHT ABOUT LEAVING
Molly's house," Sam added. "We need our own place, our
privacy. Staying with our relatives isn't working out."

Despite Jessica's insistence that they could see the cabin another
day, Sam made them stop at the New Horizons campus with Luke
right after their visit to Lillian's.

Now she and Sam stood outside the cabin while the boys ran
over to the basketball court. They had found a ball in the back of
Luke's SUV and began to play, ignoring the patches of snow on the
blacktop.

Luke had gone to the main building for a set of keys so he could
take them inside. Jessica didn't really need a tour. She could already
tell what the place was like from peering through the low windows.

Rustic would be a nice way of putting it. More like cramped and
depressing, she thought. Sure, they would have privacy, especially

once the center was closed for the winter break. But it was nothing like a real house. Certainly nothing like the home they had lost.

"Sam . . . I don't know if I can live here. I mean, it's just a shack. It looks cold and damp inside."

"Luke winterized everything. New windows and insulation. I did some of this work myself," he reminded her. "Look, there's a wood-burning stove in the living room. It gives off plenty of heat."

She looked at the stove through the window. It terrified her. The fireplace hadn't started the blaze that had devoured their house. Still, she couldn't imagine purposely lighting a fire indoors ever again.

She took a deep breath and stepped back from the window. "It's not really a living room," she pointed out. "I'd call it the *only* room."

Sam forced a smile. She could see he was losing patience but trying hard to convince her. "Good point. Open floor plan. That makes the place feel more spacious. Think of it this way, it will take five minutes to clean up here, not all day."

Jessica couldn't argue with that. She'd had a sign in her old kitchen that read, "It's a small world . . . unless you have to clean it."

She realized now she should have been more grateful that they'd had a house so large it took all weekend to clean up.

"Jess, please." Sam rested his hands on her shoulders. "Trust me on this. It's a good solution. We can stay here, rent free, as long as we need to. Not that it will be that long," he hastily added. "We'll have our privacy. The boys have plenty of space to run around and play. We won't have to put them in straitjackets, the way we would have to at your mother's. Look at them—" He made her turn and follow his gaze. "This is kid paradise. Luke already said they can use the gym and the library, any time."

"Just what I had in mind. Moving to a sports complex." Jessica let out a long breath and crossed her arms over her chest. He had her beat. She couldn't win this and decided to stop trying.

They would have their privacy and maybe it wouldn't be for that long. Though Sam had repeatedly offered to pay some rent, Luke wouldn't hear of it. That was important, too. This was a challenging time for them. They all had to sacrifice and compromise. Sam hadn't said that exactly, but she knew that's what he was thinking.

She looked down and sighed. "Okay. Let's try it. It can't be worse than breaking up fights between Tyler and Noah every five minutes."

Sam smiled and his brown eyes sparkled. "That's my girl." He slung his arm around her shoulder. "It's going to be fun having Christmas here. You'll see."

THEY MOVED IN ON WEDNESDAY AFTERNOON, THEIR FEW BELONGINGS packed into Sam's newly repainted SUV. They picked the boys up at school and all went over to New Horizons together. Sam and Jessica both thought it was important to keep the kids part of the process. The boys had been through so many changes during the past two weeks, she worried about how it was affecting them. But they seemed to be rolling with the waves, Jessica noted. Which was more than she could say for herself. She felt pulled under and wasn't sure she would surface anytime soon.

Luke and Sara were both at the cabin to help them move their things inside. "Here, let me take that." Sara stepped over to help as Jessica walked toward the cabin with a big black trash bag filled with bedding.

They had borrowed a few duffel bags for clothes from Molly,

but the rest of their things were packed in black trash bags and boxes. Like real vagabonds, she thought.

"I'm okay. There isn't much," Jessica replied.

"At least we didn't need any furniture," Sam said, holding the door open for her. "There's a load of stuff over at the church, though. I asked Reverend Ben to bring us a few things that looked good."

Jessica glanced at him. Lately, her idea of what looked good and Sam's seemed worlds apart.

In just a few minutes, their bags and a few cartons were inside the cabin, piled in the middle of the "only" room.

It really wasn't so bad, she told herself. Luke had thoughtfully arranged for the cabin to be cleaned before their arrival. Even the windows sparkled, Jessica noticed. Though the shelter was basic, it was freshly painted. The kitchen was tiny, but the small appliances were not too old or run-down looking.

"Where do you want to start?" Sara asked helpfully.

"I guess we can make up the beds," Jessica said.

The two women picked up the bedding and headed for the smaller bedroom. The room had camp-style bunk beds with wooden frames. The mattresses were thin, Jessica thought, making a mental note to buy some foam mattress pads.

The boys ran in and followed them. "Is this going to be our room?" Tyler was already climbing up to the top bunk bed, without using the ladder.

Sara nodded. "Sure is."

"I call top!" He pounced on the mattress and bounced around. "This is awesome! How come we never had these in our old house?"

Jessica opened a sheet with a snap. "Because you each had your own bedroom. You didn't need to sleep together in one room."

"I like this better." He peered over the edge of the bed and looked at his brother who was now sitting on the lower bunk.

"Hey, Darrell," Tyler said, smiling upside down at him.

Darrell ignored him. "Mom, can I put a poster under here?" He pointed to the bottom of Tyler's mattress. "That would look cool."

"Sure, that would be fine." Jessica pulled out the pillows and handed one to Sara.

Sara glanced at her. "I think they like the bunk beds."

Jessica nodded. Kids were so easily satisfied sometimes. Tyler thought the room was a big improvement over his old one.

She couldn't help but think of how she had carefully decorated each of their bedrooms in the old house. Tyler's room had been dark blue with a Curious George monkey theme. Darrell's room was more suited for a teenager, with two walls a pumpkin color and the others electric green. He had put up his own posters of sports heroes and music celebrities and photos of his friends and family. And Reilly, of course.

Darrell had been so subdued since Reilly's death. He had been mourning, Jessica knew. It was good to see him a bit more animated today, excited about the cabin.

Even if she hated it.

"Okay, boys, scoot. We have to make up the beds now," Jessica told them.

Tyler quickly scrambled down from his perch. "Can we play basketball, Darrell? Luke gave me a ball and said we can keep it."

The perfect housewarming gift for the boys. And Sam, Jessica thought.

Darrell nodded. "Okay, Ty. Let's go."

Tyler could barely carry the ball, much less get it through the hoop. But Darrell was usually patient and tried to teach his little brother. He had been even more patient since the fire, Jessica noticed. As if in some way, he appreciated Tyler more.

They ran out of the room and Jessica heard the door slam.

"At least you'll know where they are when they go out to play," Sara said.

Jessica nodded and forced a smile. Everyone was trying so hard to convince her of the upside of this place. Did she look that glum? Probably. And she shouldn't be, she reminded herself.

"We really appreciate everything you and Luke are doing for us," she told Sara. "This place is awfully sweet. I'm sure we can make it cozy." She didn't fully believe any of that but thought that maybe if she said these things aloud, she would convince herself.

It wasn't long before the beds were made, their box of hand-me-down dishes and glasses was unpacked, and their clothing and other housewares were put away.

"I hope you guys are comfortable here," Luke said as he and Sara pulled on their jackets and got ready to leave. "If you need anything else, just let me know."

Sara leaned over and gave Jessica a hug. "I would have loved having you at Grandmother's house, Aunt Jess. But I think this might be a better solution, after all. You know how Lillian gets."

"I do," Jessica agreed. Considering Sam's relationship with his mother-in-law and the way Lillian reacted to her energetic grandsons, they wouldn't have lasted there very long.

"It was best to skip that stop. We probably would have ended up here anyway," she had to admit.

She and Sam stood at the door and waved as Sara and Luke drove off. It was not even five o'clock, but it was already growing dark outside. "Maybe we should call the boys in. They could get hurt playing in the dark."

"I'll get them," Sam said. "It's still early, though. I thought we could go buy a tree."

"A Christmas tree?"

"Sure, why not? It will cheer up the place," he added. "We'll just have to make some decorations. Or pick some up."

The thought of decorating a Christmas tree tonight was overwhelming. "Not tonight, Sam. . . . We're still unpacking."

"No, we're not," he pointed out.

"I still have organizing to do," she insisted. "Can't it wait?"

Sam leaned back, staring at her. "Did you really say that? The woman who runs out to get her Christmas tree the minute Jack Sawyer puts his sign up?"

Jessica knew that was true. "This is different."

His teasing expression disappeared. His tone was warm and tender. "I know you're blue tonight, honey. I know this isn't your idea of a great place to settle. But we can fix it up a little, make it more our own. A tree would definitely help. I'll get some pizza for dinner, and the kids will have some fun tonight."

When she didn't answer he added, "The boys have to have Christmas, Jess. It's important that we try to keep things as normal as possible for them. We have to keep going. I know how you feel, but we have to show the kids that it's not the end of the world."

That did it. He didn't understand at all, did he?

She couldn't pretend things were fine for another second. "It does feel like the end of the world to me, Sam. Why can't you just admit how awful this situation really is? Is sticking a Christmas tree in this shabby little shack going to make anything better?"

He looked stung by her outburst but didn't answer.

"We lost everything. Why can't you just admit that?"

Sam stared at her for a long, cold moment. Then he grabbed

his jacket and walked to the door. "I'm taking the kids to get a tree. We'll be back in a little while."

Suddenly left alone, Jessica sank down onto the small couch and cried. She put her hands up to her face, disgusted with herself. Why couldn't she just make the best of it, the way Sam did? Why did she feel so broken? And why did she keep dissolving into these ridiculous tears? She was sick of crying, but she couldn't seem to stop. She stared around the strange, nearly bare room and felt so empty. So bereft.

How had she ended up here? It felt like a nightmare that just wouldn't end.

She heard a knock on the door and wondered if it was Sam, coming back to apologize. She quickly wiped her eyes with the back of her hand. She didn't want him to see that she had been crying again.

She stepped to the door and saw Reverend Ben through the window. He stood on the front step, holding a brass pole lamp.

He smiled at her as she pulled open the door. "Reverend Ben. Sam said you might drop by. I hope it wasn't out of your way."

Ben and Carolyn Lewis lived in the village, in the opposite direction. And yet he had come all this way to bring them a lamp. It was kind of him, also typical. Reverend Ben was one of the kindest people she had ever known.

"I wanted to see how you were doing. Sam said you could use this lamp, and I also have a very nice area rug on the front step out there."

He set the lamp down and Jessica looked it over. It needed to be polished but it wasn't so bad. In fact, it was a little like one in their old family room.

"The wiring is all new," Reverend Ben told her. "I checked it myself."

She glanced at him, feeling he had read her mind. "It's very nice. Thank you. Can I help you get the rug?"

"I'll bring it in later when I go."

It appeared he expected to stay and talk. Jessica wasn't in the mood for visitors. Even Reverend Ben. But she didn't want to seem rude. "Would you like some coffee or tea?"

She wasn't even sure where the coffee and tea bags had ended up. Or the cups. She half-hoped he would refuse.

"I wouldn't mind some tea, thank you," he said. "If you're having some."

"I was just going to put on some water." She couldn't forget her manners, no matter where she wound up. Her mother had drummed good etiquette into her and Emily so thoroughly. *Never let your guests feel uncomfortable* was the first rule. Though Lillian herself seemed to follow the opposite of that credo most of the time.

Jessica opened a few cupboards and found a small pot. She filled it with water and set it on the tiny stove to boil. Then she looked around for the tea, sugar, and cups.

"Sam took the kids to get a Christmas tree," she explained. "He'll be sorry he missed you."

"That's all right. I'll catch him at his shop sometime." Ben sat on a stool at the counter that separated the tiny kitchen from the "only" room.

"It must be hard on your family, all this moving around. On top of everything you've been through."

Jessica glanced at him. She wasn't going to lie and act as if the last week or so had been a snap. A big, fun family adventure. The way Sam might have answered.

"It is hard. *I* think it is, anyway." She located two cups and put tea bags inside. "It was bad enough to lose our house. But wandering around and ending up here for who knows how long . . . It doesn't seem fair."

He nodded. "You feel angry. I understand."

"Yes, I feel angry." She looked at him with an unexpected sense of relief. Finally, somebody was willing to acknowledge her true feelings. "Mostly, I just can't understand. Why us? Why did this have to happen to my family? I know we aren't perfect, but we try to do right. We try more than some people, I'd say. Is this the reward we get?"

When Ben didn't answer, she added, "Sometimes I feel as if we're being punished. I really do."

"By God, you mean?" he clarified.

She thought he would be shocked by the idea stated so plainly. But he didn't look shocked at all. She realized he had probably heard this before. She couldn't be the first person to have vented to him about a tragic loss, to be boiling over with all these feelings of confusion, frustration, and even anger.

She swallowed hard and nodded. "Yes. By God."

Reverend Ben nodded. He didn't answer for a moment.

"I wish I could explain it to you," he said at last. "But nobody can, of course. I'm not going to try to tell you that it could be worse. Or that something good can come out of all this tragedy, either. It might," he added. "But that's not the point, is it?"

She was relieved that he wasn't trying to smooth over the truth with a bunch of easy clichés—or trying to make her feel guilty and ungrateful for thinking this way.

"No, it's not the point," she agreed bleakly. "I don't believe that anyway. I can't see what possible good can come from any of this."

"I don't know why bad things happen to good people," the Reverend admitted. "Can you blame God for the fire? I have to tell you, Jessica, I just don't know about that either. Maybe it's just chance. A random accident. Maybe we can't hold God accountable for such things, but we can turn to him for help. For comfort, when bad things do happen."

Jessica noticed the water for their tea was boiling, and poured it into the cups. But her mind was on what Reverend Ben had just said.

Had she tried turning to God for help and comfort in the midst of this mess? Is that what Ben was asking her? She had prayed. Immediately after the fire and in the days that followed, she had offered heartfelt prayers of thanks for her family coming out alive. But other than that? She couldn't really remember. She had felt too drained to turn to God. Too empty.

And mad.

She set out the sugar and milk then sat on the stool across from him. "Sam says it's not the end of the world, but it feels as if it were to me. It feels as if our life will never be the same. It will never get back to normal."

Reverend Ben nodded. "I'm sure it feels that way. You've suffered an overwhelming loss. But things will get better. Some days, it might seem the situation really isn't improving. It might look even worse."

Like moving into this cabin? she wanted to say.

"But as time passes, you and Sam will gain a foothold again and keep going. I know you will." He looked across the counter and met her gaze. "I think you have to accept the fact that things will never be exactly the same, Jessica. That's just not how life works. Change is inevitable, even in the best of times. Good experiences and bad ones, they come to us all, and they change us, especially an event this momentous. You know that," he reminded her.

Jessica nodded and sipped her tea. She did know what he said was true. But it wasn't her favorite life lesson. She had always felt she was a good-hearted person, but at her core, she knew she wasn't that flexible. She liked her life settled and predictable.

Perhaps it all went back to her childhood, when her father had been involved in a scandal and brought to trial. The Warwick family had been among the wealthiest and most respected in town back then. Her father narrowly escaped a jail sentence but had died shortly after the trial, a relatively young man. Her mother had to sell the family estate, Lilac Hall, and they lost nearly all their wealth. Jessica had only been in elementary school, so she hadn't fully understood what was going on. She knew it was something awful, though, and the events had shaped her. She was not a risk taker. She was the very opposite—a conservative person who appreciated routine and stability. There was nothing so wrong with that, she believed. That's just who she was. But now, her security-loving temperament made these unforeseen changes all the more painful.

"I know the way I am," she said slowly. "I don't like change. I don't think I ever did. When my father got in trouble and we had to leave Lilac Hall, it frightened me. It frightened us all. And now, it's different but the same. It feels as if I'm losing everything all over again."

Reverend Ben looked up from his tea. "Do you know, I was just thinking about that same thing. I wasn't in Cape Light then. But of course, I eventually heard the story. From your mother mostly," he added. "That must have been a terrible loss for all of you. But look at your mother," he went on. "Maybe you were too young to realize all she went through, all the challenges she faced. She held your family together and created a new life for all of you. A lot of people would have left town, but not Lillian. She stayed and fought and did what she had to do. And she never let despair overpower her."

"She was very brave," Jessica agreed, "but she also grew so hard and bitter. . . . Is that what I have to look forward to? Is that the cost of making it through?"

"Not if you don't want it to be." Ben met her gaze and held it. "You don't have to deny your anger or your frustration. I'm not saying that, believe me. But don't let the fire take more than its toll, Jessica. Don't lose your courage and your trust in yourself, or in Sam and your marriage. Don't let the fire take all that and your faith, too," he added quietly.

Jessica knew what he said was true. But it was cold comfort to her. She was trying her best not to give in to despair. Didn't he see that? It was very hard for her. Maybe even impossible.

Ben sighed and sat back. He looked around the small cabin.

"There are a lot of nice things in the storeroom people have donated. You ought to stop by the church one day and take a look."

Jessica nodded, relieved he had changed the subject. "I will, Ben. I'll come this week."

"Good. Well, I'd better go. Carolyn is waiting for me."

Jessica walked him to the door, and he brought in the small rug and set it by the couch. "You're in luck. I think the colors might even match," he remarked as they rolled it out.

"It does match," she agreed. "And it makes the room look warmer. Thanks for all your help."

"It was nothing, really." He smiled at her and gave her a quick hug. "Take care of yourself, Jessica. Your family needs you. Now, more than ever."

She nodded, knowing what he meant. *Don't slip away from them into a tunnel of self-pity.*

She watched Reverend Ben's car pull away and just as she was closing the door, she saw Sam pull up, a Christmas tree tied to the roof of his car. The boys tumbled out, Tyler carefully carrying a box of pizza.

Darrell helped Sam take the tree off the car and then took one end. Sam carried the other and also an armful of pine garland and a wreath that was almost as big as the cabin.

Jessica ran out to meet them. She could tell from Sam's expression, he knew she was concerned about spending so much money. It now seemed an extravagance to buy such a big tree, and the wreath and garlands—

"Guess what? Jack Sawyer heard about the fire and made me take all this stuff for free."

"That was nice of him," Jessica said, genuinely surprised.

"He gave us a stand and a box of ornaments, too. I'll bring them in later."

"Can we eat the pizza?" Tyler asked, popping his head out the door. "I'm so hungry, Mommy."

"Absolutely. I think we all must be hungry." Jessica held the door open for Sam and Darrell as they carried the tree inside. They left the wreath and garland out front.

The boys gobbled up their pizza quickly, eager to get started on the tree. Tyler found some plain white paper and scissors and showed everyone how to make snowflake ornaments, a skill he had just learned in preschool. Jessica was surprised at how pretty the lacy white designs looked against the dark green branches.

Sam had been right. The tree did make the cabin feel more homey. Maybe, she thought, at least for tonight, things were getting a little better for them.

WEDNESDAY HAD BEEN SLOW AT THE TREE LOT. FEW CUSTOMERS came out in the middle of the week. Julie had stayed in the Christmas shop most of the morning, making ornaments and decorating wreaths. It disturbed Jack to see her doing the same exact craft work his wife had loved, but he made an effort and held his tongue. It wasn't Julie's fault. She was an art teacher, for goodness sake, he reminded himself. She was very creative and definitely had a knack for it. The ornaments and wreaths she decorated sold well. He thought she should keep all the money from the shop for herself, but hadn't gotten around to telling her that yet.

When it was time for Julie to pick up Kate at preschool, Jack asked her to drop him off in town. He pointed to a corner and asked her to pick him up there in half an hour. He didn't explain where he was going or what he had to do.

But when she picked him up later, it was pretty obvious. Jack had finally gone to the barbershop for a haircut and straight-edge close shave. No more long straggly hair, no more beard. When he finally sat upright and took a long look at himself in the barber's mirror, he felt shocked. He felt as if he were looking at another man.

Julie seemed to feel the same way. She nearly passed him on the street corner, and he had to wave her down to get her to pull over. He opened the passenger side door, and she gaped at him open-mouthed as he climbed into the car. He sat stiffly, staring straight ahead.

"I had a haircut," he grumbled.

"Yes, I noticed." She started the car and pulled away from the curb.

Jack smoothed his hand over his head. His hair was still thick, dark brown with strands of silver at his temples. He felt the back of his neck, where the hair abruptly ended. "The barber went a little too far. I don't generally wear it this short."

"Really?" Julie glanced at him briefly. "You ought to start then."

He looked at her, but she turned back to the road as she steered the truck down Main Street. What did that mean? Did she like the way he looked? Anything would have been an improvement, he told himself. If he had shaved his head and had it buffed with car wax, she would have said she liked it better.

His face felt cold, no longer covered by the beard, and his head felt oddly light. Missing the weight of all that hair, he decided. Or just light-headed from Julie's subtle compliment.

THAT AFTERNOON JULIE WAS IN AND OUT BETWEEN THE CHRIST-mas shop and taking care of Kate. Despite his crutches, Jack managed to handle the few customers who came in at the end of the day.

When he walked into the kitchen that night, the room was steaming, filled with a rich, tantalizing scent.

"Something smells good." He stepped to the sink and washed his hands.

"Beef stew and noodles. I hope you like that." Julie turned from the stove and gave him that look again, as if she almost didn't recognize him, her gaze lingering. Haircut shock, he had to call it.

"Beef stew. My favorite," he replied.

"You always say that, Jack," Kate remarked. "Whatever's for dinner, you say it's your favorite."

"I have a lot of favorites, I guess." Anything Julie cooked seemed to make the list. He sat down at the table and smiled at Katie.

"Mine is mac and cheese," Kate told him. "That's what a favorite is. Just one."

"It's better to have a few, like I do. Then you don't always have to eat the same thing to be happy, see?"

Kate considered this line of reasoning carefully. "I guess," she said.

Julie laughed as she dished out the stew. "You must be freezing, Jack. It was cold out there this afternoon."

"It wasn't so bad. There were hardly any customers. I was in the shed most of the time."

"It was nice of you to give Sam Morgan and his boys that tree and all those decorations."

"I didn't just give it to him. I knocked a few dollars off the price, that's all. Sales were slow today."

She met his glance and laughed. "I know you gave it to him for free. Why is that such a big secret? Are you afraid it might get around that you have a kind side?"

Jack wanted to smile but bravely fought it off. She had caught him. Again. "Just keep it quiet, okay? You'll ruin my reputation. I felt sorry for the guy. His house burned down."

"I heard about it in church. How awful. They seem like such a nice family." She looked down at her plate and shook her head. "I wonder if there is anything I could do for them."

She was a rare one, Jack thought. Julie had so little of her own but was thinking of how she could help the Morgans. She had such a good heart.

Dinner passed quickly, too quickly. It was one of the few times during the day when he had the chance to sit and talk to Julie. He helped her clean up, and then Kate arrived with her book, so he knew it was getting close to her bedtime.

That had become the routine every evening. Kate didn't even ask anymore. She just presented the book and sat at the table, waiting for him.

Jack came over and sat down next to her. "What have we here . . . *Lester Saves Christmas*?" Jack read the title then peered at her, his eyebrows comically raised. "That Lester, he has a lot of adventures, doesn't he?"

He heard Julie laugh. But it was true. Every night was another adventure for Lester the rabbit. He had his first sleepover, got in trouble at school, took a plane ride to visit his grandmother, had a birthday party. Now he was saving Christmas.

"Okay, let's start . . ." Jack began reading the story. Kate's lovely little face quickly assumed a thoughtful expression, the way she always looked when he read aloud to her. She leaned closer, listening.

Then she suddenly tugged at his sleeve. "I can't see the pictures."

"Oh, sorry." He moved his chair closer to hers then put his arm gently around her shoulder, with the book propped in front of them. "How's that?" he asked.

She nodded. "That's good."

He began reading again then felt her squirming around. She was suddenly sitting in his lap. He felt a lurch in his heart. But he sat very still and kept reading. He didn't want to make a big deal out of it and scare her away again.

"Make the rabbit's voice," Kate reminded him.

"Oh, yes. I forgot." He looked at Julie. Her brown eyes were glowing. He didn't dare hold her glance for long.

A short time later, Lester had saved Christmas and the entire rabbit family was pictured in their bunny hole, cuddling under their Christmas tree. Piles of gift-wrapped packages were visible underneath the tree, the shapes looking suspiciously like carrots.

"I wonder what's in there?" Jack pointed to the picture.

"Maybe it's umbrellas," Kate guessed.

"Maybe. I didn't even think of that."

"They have a pretty tree," she remarked.

"Yes, they do." He closed the book, trying to avoid this touchy topic.

"You should have a Christmas tree, Jack," Kate said.

"I have loads of them. They're all outside. Didn't you ever notice?"

His joke made her giggle. He was proud of himself for fielding the question so deftly. And keeping his promise to Julie—not getting touchy and scaring Kate again. Julie had looked nervous at the start of Kate's questions, but now her expression looked relaxed again.

"I meant inside. The dressed-up kind of tree," Kate persisted.

"Oh . . . well . . ."

He didn't know what to say. How could he say that he didn't like to celebrate Christmas anymore, all alone. It was too painful. Too many memories.

"I like to keep my trees outside. If I chose one to come in, I think the other ones would feel bad," he said finally.

He caught Julie's eye. She lifted one eyebrow, looking surprised and pleased by his answer.

Kate wasn't buying it. "But if you don't have a dressed-up tree inside, with lights on it and everything, Santa Claus can't find you," she informed him. "You won't get any presents. Right, Mommy?"

Now he and Kate both looked at Julie.

Jack silently asked her to help him out, but she wouldn't meet his eye. "That's right, honey. Jack doesn't have a decorated tree inside, and Santa probably won't come here. Which is too bad, because Jack is really a very nice man, and he deserves a few presents."

Jack felt himself flush. Was he actually blushing? Could she possibly like him, he wondered?

He brushed the thought aside. *She's just trying to be nice, to say nice things in front of her daughter. She isn't flirting with me or sending some secret message.*

He forced a smile. "Santa hasn't stopped here in a long time, Kate. I think he's forgotten where I live."

He spoke in a joking tone then saw her crestfallen face. He suddenly realized Kate thought she wouldn't get any presents for Christmas either if Santa couldn't find this house.

"But he knows where *you* are," Jack said quickly. "He knows where all the really nice kids are and what they want for Christmas. He has a big map, with stickers with kids' names on them all over it," he elaborated. "I'm sure your name is on there. In big letters, too."

Kate looked comforted by this explanation. "My favorite present that I asked him for is a Webkinz dog. And I want a ballet skirt . . . and my other favorite is a pink bike. . . ."

She continued, item by item, with Jack nodding thoughtfully.

"I wrote it down in a letter. Well, Mommy wrote it for me," she told Jack. "And we put it in the mailbox."

"But you know Santa can't bring you all those presents," Julie reminded her.

"Yes, I know." Kate sighed. "Too many favorites," she explained to Jack.

Jack nodded. He felt his heart melting. He knew Julie would struggle just to get a few of those gifts.

"Santa has the letter," Jack promised her. "Don't worry, he'll find you wherever you are."

"At Uncle Peter's house, on Long Island," Kate said.

"Yes, that's right. You won't be here for Christmas. So you don't have to worry. I'm sure your aunt and uncle have a very nice tree," he assured her.

Jack felt bad instantly. With all this talk about Christmas, he had almost forgotten that Julie and Kate would be on their way again and he would be alone. He met Julie's gaze, and the soft light there seemed to signal that she was thinking the same thing.

"Time for bed, Miss Kate," Julie said. She walked over to Kate's seat, and the little girl jumped into her arms. Kate was probably too big for Julie to carry, but she was too sweet and cute to resist.

Jack sat and read the newspaper. He turned the pages slowly, listening to Julie put Kate to bed. The soft murmur of their voices, then quiet.

He waited. Would she come downstairs again, as she sometimes did, and work at the table on her decorations? Or should he just give up and go to bed? He got up and began emptying the dishwasher, dragging around his cast. He was too nervous to sit still and read.

Finally, he heard her light step on the stairway, coming toward the kitchen again. She walked in and picked up the kettle and filled it with water.

"Want some tea?" she asked.

"No thanks." He took a mug from the cupboard and handed it to her. "That Lester. What's next? I suppose in the next book, he'll be the first rabbit in outer space."

Julie laughed then looked at him, tilting her head to one side. "I'm sorry if Kate asks too many questions and puts you on the spot."

"Oh, I don't mind. At least she's not afraid of me anymore."

"No, she's not afraid of you. Now she's worried about you. She said you need a dressed-up tree, even if we go to Long Island. She's positive Santa won't find you otherwise."

Jack smiled and shrugged. "Maybe she's right. Maybe that's just my trouble."

Julie stepped closer to him. Uncomfortably close.

"Jack, the trouble with you is—"

She stopped herself before finishing the sentence.

"Is what?" he coaxed her. He wasn't sure he really wanted to hear what she had to say. But he couldn't resist. She was standing so close he could smell her perfume. Or maybe it was just the scent of the flowery soap she used.

Her warm brown eyes sparkled at him. "Never mind." She shook her head, looking suddenly self-conscious. She shut off the stove and put the cup away. "I'm sort of tired. I think I'll just say good night."

He nodded at her, without saying anything, his mouth suddenly dry as sand.

She left the room and he was left wondering what she had been about to say. Was she really thinking about him? He knew he was thinking about kissing her when she got so close. He hadn't felt like that in a very long time.

The impulse was both exciting and scary. But he couldn't let himself go off the deep end and act like a fool.

She's had some problems and is pulling her life together, he reminded himself. *But it won't be long before she's ready to get out in the world again. She'll catch some guy's eye in a heartbeat. Some younger guy,* he told himself.

There was no use getting involved with her. No sense complicating matters, he reminded himself.

No sense at all.

CHAPTER NINE

*J*ESSICA COULDN'T UNDERSTAND HOW SHE AND SAM HAD brought home a huge load of food from the supermarket on Saturday, but by Monday, the refrigerator looked bare. It seemed impossible.

Not if you have two growing boys and a large, hungry husband, she reminded herself.

She grabbed up the plastic grocery bags from the backseat of her car, two in each hand, and walked toward the cabin. Her high heels poked into the soft ground, making her steps shaky. She wasn't used to wearing heels and panty hose and being all dressed up this way. But she was going to get used to it. In a hurry.

She saw the lights inside the cabin and saw Sam and the boys through the front window. Sam ran to the door and opened it, then stepped outside.

"Need some help?" he asked, taking the bags from her.

"Sure, thanks."

He stood in front of the door, blocking her way.

"Aren't we going inside?" she asked.

"Not yet. . . . We have a surprise for you."

"A surprise? What is it?" Jessica couldn't help smiling. She had hinted all week about so many conveniences she missed. She wondered what Sam had bought for her. A vacuum cleaner? A blender?

Sam smiled back. He looked positively happy.

Then, before he was able to say anything more, she heard an odd sound.

It sounded like a . . . bark.

"Sam, you didn't." She stared at him. "Is there a dog in there?"

"It's not a dog. . . . It's a puppy."

"A puppy? You didn't really bring home a puppy, did you?"

"The boys are thrilled. Darrell was practically crying."

Jessica sighed. That made two of them.

"Just come in and see her. She's adorable."

Jessica was sure the puppy was adorable. What puppy wasn't?

Reluctantly, she walked inside. Tyler ran over to her and pulled her by the hand before she could even get her coat off. "Come and see our new dog, Mom. Isn't she so cute?"

Darrell sat on the floor near the Christmas tree, with the puppy in his lap. The dog was crawling all over him, flopping and falling on her shaky legs.

The puppy appeared to be a yellow Lab mix, very much like poor Reilly. But her fur was a little shaggier. She probably had some Golden Retriever mixed in. She was going to get big, Jessica thought, looking at her paws. Too big for the cabin.

"She's really smart, Mom," Tyler reported. "She already knows her name."

"You named her already?"

The boys nodded together. "We're going to call her Sunny. Because of her fur," Tyler explained.

"Oh . . . nice." She knelt down and petted Sunny's head. The little dog eagerly licked Jessica's hand with her sandpapery tongue.

Sam stood beside her. "She's cute, isn't she?"

Jessica stood up again. "Yes, she really is," she had to admit.

Then the puppy got up on her hind legs and clawed Jessica's dress and stockings, making a wide run.

"Oh dear, grab her, will you? I don't want her to tear Emily's dress." The panty hose was no problem, but the dress had been borrowed from her sister.

"Why are you all dressed up today?" Sam asked.

"I had an appointment." She looked down at the puppy, who was now chewing Darrell's shoelace. "Where did you get the dog?"

"I was working at a house in town, and they had all these puppies to give away. She was the smartest, I thought."

Jessica wondered how Sam could tell that, but she didn't want to get off track. She watched the boys play with the dog a few moments then she pulled on her husband's sleeve. "Let's go outside. I want to talk to you. Privately."

Jessica felt so angry she could hardly keep her thoughts straight, but she waited until they were a good distance from the cabin. "How could you go out and get a dog without asking me? How could you put me in this position with the boys?" she demanded.

"What position?"

"Well, now I have to be the bad guy and say the dog can't stay, don't I? Couldn't we have discussed this first?"

"I tried to call you, Jess. You weren't around. If I didn't take her tonight, someone else was going to snatch her up."

She dug her hands in her coat pockets. "You shouldn't have done this without asking me, Sam. It wasn't right."

"It's an early Christmas present. The kids needed something to cheer them up. Did you see Darrell? This is so good for him. He needs to get over Reilly. They already asked if Sunny can sleep in their bedroom."

Jessica wasn't sure she was ready to get over Reilly. Why should Darrell be? "I know they like the dog. They would like any dog you brought in here. That's not the point. We're not ready to get a new dog yet. This cabin is too small. There's barely room for the four of us."

"A puppy doesn't take up much room, Jess."

"Not right now. But she's going to grow. She has big paws," Jessica added, citing one of the few things she knew for sure about dogs. "Who knows how long we'll be living like this? And who's going to train her? You and the boys are out all day."

"You're home. Dogs aren't hard to train. She already whines when she wants to go out. She'll be good company for you. You're alone all day out here." Sam crossed his arms over his chest but his tone was very reasonable. Too reasonable, she thought. He clearly wasn't taking her objections seriously.

"I'm going back to work," she told him. "I heard there was an opening at the bank. That appointment I had today—I went in and met with my old boss, Mr. Dwyer. It's not at my level, but he expects something better to open up soon. It's just about at my former salary, too."

The shocked look on Sam's face made Jessica feel a pang of guilt. But he had surprised her with the dog, so maybe they were even, she thought.

"We never talked about you going back to work," Sam said.

"What happened to staying home with the boys and trying for another baby?"

She shook her head, feeling impatient with him. He could be so unrealistic at times. So . . . illogical.

"Things have changed, Sam. I don't want to get pregnant now—not until we're settled again. And we definitely need the money. I doubt the insurance company is going to pay us much, considering our coverage."

Sam looked grim. She knew he couldn't argue with that. He had been working with the insurance agent, calling almost every day to track the progress of their claim. They still didn't know how much they would be reimbursed, but it didn't look good. The agent had already explained that since Sam bought the house at an auction and did most of the work himself, they would never get back the full value.

"We should have talked about this, Jessica, and decided together. It's an important decision that affects the whole family. You shouldn't have just gone off and taken this job without talking it over with me."

She knew what he said was true, but she had been afraid that if they got into a big discussion about it, Sam would try to talk her out of going back to work, saying they didn't need the money that badly, or he would tell her to wait awhile. Or maybe say the boys needed her now.

The boys did need her. She felt sad about giving up time with them. She loved to share their day after school, to hear their stories and take them to their various activities. She just liked to be around for them and felt guilty about leaving the house all day, especially now. But another part of her insisted that she needed to return to work for the family. For everyone's well-being. Nothing was perfect. Maybe after they got back on their feet, she would work fewer hours or stay home again. She had to take one step at a time, and this one, she believed, was the next step for her.

"You keep telling me to move on," she told Sam. "Well, I'm trying. Going backward, maybe. But, I'm trying to deal with things as they really are. I am going to miss being home with the boys. That goes without saying. But it's for their welfare, too. We need the extra salary and to tell the truth, I can't hang around this cabin every day. It . . . depresses me."

"Are you sure about this?"

"Yes, I've thought it through." The bank could seem a bit dismal, too, she knew. But it meant she would be getting out of the house and at least acting as if she were okay.

Sam crossed his arms over his chest and shook his head. "Okay, I give up. I don't want to argue with you. Of course, more money coming in is a good idea. But I just wish you had said something to me first, Jessica. We used to talk about these things, not keep big secrets."

She nodded, feeling suddenly upset and teary-eyed. She was so emotional lately, that was another struggle.

She hadn't meant to hurt Sam. But talking to him was so hard these days. She just couldn't be honest. Sam didn't want to hear about her anger and her worries. He always managed to hip-hop right over those ugly feelings and point to some distant rainbow, far off in the future somewhere.

Of course, he couldn't see that. He believed in focusing on the positive, no matter what. That was just his personality and part of the reason she had fallen in love with him in the first place. But now they just weren't in sync, and she felt distant from him.

"So when do you start?" His question jogged her from rambling thoughts.

"Wednesday. I know it's soon, but they need someone right away. I couldn't argue about it."

"What about the boys?" he asked curtly. "What will they do after school?"

"There's an after-care program at both schools, where they can do their homework and play sports. But that won't start for a few weeks. I guess for now, you'll have to pick them up."

She glanced at him, wondering if this request would make him even angrier. But he seemed to accept the situation. Sam was flexible that way and always put his children first when they needed him.

"So, what about the dog?" she asked. "Do you understand now why I was so upset? There won't be anyone home to take care of her. Sam, I'm sorry, but I think you should return her. We'll explain to the boys it's not the right time yet, not until we get our own house again. They'll understand."

Sam stared at her. "Are you kidding? I can't do that. Now you sound just like your mother, Jessica."

So he was mad. Really mad, she realized. He knew the one thing she hated in an argument was to be compared to her mother.

"This cabin is so run-down, I can't think of a better place to train a puppy," he added.

Jessica tried to hold on to her temper, but it was difficult. "It's not fair for the dog to be alone all day. She'll get lonely and destructive. Do you want her chewing everything in sight?"

Not that they had that much anymore to destroy. But what they did have seemed all the more valuable.

"I'll take her to my shop. I'll keep Sunny there during the day and bring her home at night. The boys will be there after school now anyway. They can take her out for walks and play with her,"

Sam added, looking rather smug that he had solved the problem. "See, it all works out."

The dog and the boys after school, all in his shop—well, he was the one who had offered. To Jessica, it sounded like a recipe for total chaos.

Tyler came to the door and peeked outside. "Dad? I think Sunny needs to go out."

That meant it was already too late, Jessica knew.

"I'll be right in, just hold on a second. Put Sunny down on those newspapers we spread out," Sam called back as he hurried inside to help them.

Jessica slowly followed, regretting that she hadn't bought more paper towels.

ON TUESDAY MORNING JACK SPRANG OUT OF BED. IT WAS A SPECIAL day. The horrible chunk of plaster that was stuck to his leg was finally coming off. He couldn't wait. He had been marking the days on his calendar. Three entire weeks, which somehow felt as if they had passed both slowly and quickly.

He showered and dressed in a hurry, pulling on one of the new shirts and a pair of khaki pants he had ordered on the Internet. He told himself he wasn't trying to look good for Julie, that he had to look decent to go into town. He didn't want to embarrass her and Katie.

The haircut and loss of his beard still threw him off, but Julie seemed to like it. He had caught her looking at him a few times when she thought he wouldn't notice. He even kept up with the shaving now, every morning. Kate liked to sit close to him at story time, and he didn't want to scratch her with his beard. That's all it was.

He splashed on some aftershave and checked himself quickly

in the bathroom mirror. He didn't look that old, did he? He was forty-two years old. To hear people on TV talking, you would think hitting forty was being a teenager again. Forty was the new thirty, that's what they said.

Jack knew he had been through too much to ever feel that young again. Maybe that was it. He wasn't old by current standards; he had just been through a lot in his life. That made him feel . . . mature.

Lately, though, he had felt as if the clock was going backward a bit. That was a good thing, right?

For as long as it lasted.

Kate and Julie were already at the breakfast table. He took a mug of coffee and sat down with them. "New shirt?" Julie asked.

He nodded and opened the newspaper, focusing on the sports section.

"It's nice. You look good in blue, Jack," she said.

He nodded again, but didn't look up. "Thanks. Anybody want that toast?" he asked, changing the subject.

She liked him in blue? He would be back online tonight, he decided, ordering a lot of blue stuff.

After breakfast, they climbed into Jack's truck. Julie drove and Kate sat between them. "I bet you're tired of chauffeuring me around," Jack said. "You won't have to do that anymore once the cast is off."

"I don't mind. But maybe you're not so crazy about my driving," Julie added with a grin.

Jack had squeezed his eyes shut a few times with Julie behind the wheel. But he didn't want to criticize.

"You've been handling the truck better," he said in an encouraging tone. "Another year or so, and you'll be fine."

She laughed. She wasn't the type to take offense; that's why he felt comfortable teasing her. She teased him, too. He never thought of himself as the kind of guy who could laugh at himself, but Julie could make him do that.

They dropped Kate off at her preschool, which was at the church on the green. Julie walked her in and Jack waited in the truck. His wife used to attend this church. She was very active in all kinds of committees—the community outreach, the Christmas fair. You name it, Claire signed up. She had David in Sunday school and the youth group until he was nearly a teen. Jack used to go to church with her sometimes, mostly on holidays. Claire knew the minister well and when it came time for her funeral service, just about the entire congregation turned out. Everyone here liked her. The reverend had given a fine eulogy. He had said all the right things, Jack thought.

That had been some comfort. It was just the way Claire would have liked it.

Jack had never visited her grave in the cemetery on Beach Road. He never thought of her there, but somewhere, up above. But now that he would be able to drive again and the holidays were coming, he thought maybe he should put some flowers on the headstone. Claire had always loved flowers. She had loved Christmas, too. He still missed her so, especially at this time of year.

"So, ready to get that chunk of plaster off your leg?" Julie hopped back into the truck and started the engine. "You've been very patient, I must say. All things considered."

He had been pretty awful sometimes, too, he knew. But it was nice of her not to mention that.

He nodded, still feeling melancholy from his reverie. He forced himself to snap out of it and focus on the present. "I can't wait. Let's go."

The orthopedist's office in Essex was crowded, and they had to wait longer than Jack expected. The nurses kept calling Julie "Mrs. Sawyer," and after the first time, she didn't bother to correct them, Jack noticed.

Finally, he was led in to see the doctor, who removed the hard cast and examined his ankle. Then Jack was sent somewhere else in the building to take an X-ray. Then back to the doctor again.

"You're healing well," the doctor told him. "We can move to the soft cast now. You can take this one on and off." The doctor showed him how the Velcro straps wrapped around the hard plastic. "Take it off to sleep and in the evenings, keep your leg elevated and use ice and ibuprofen if you still have pain."

"Great." Jack pushed down the leg of his pants and hopped off the table.

"You're looking well, Mr. Sawyer," the doctor said, writing some notes in a folder.

"Thanks. So are you," Jack replied, ignoring the doctor's meaning. He had cleaned up his act a bit the last few weeks; people were noticing.

Jack almost felt like skipping as he and Julie left the doctor's office. His leg felt about ten pounds lighter.

"How's your ankle?" Julie asked as they walked toward the truck. "Does it hurt to have the hard cast off?"

"A bit," he had to admit. "I'm just glad it's gone." He reached the driver's side door first and held out his hand. "Keys, please?"

Julie laughed and handed the keys over to him. "Never come between a man and his pickup truck."

"I'm glad you figured that out, Julie."

As they drove off, Jack checked his watch. "It's not too long before you need to get Kate. We could stop in town and get some lunch. No sense going all the way home and back again."

"Good idea." Julie, who had been staring out the window, now glanced at him curiously.

Jack deliberately looked back at the road. He was taking her out for a meal. By accident. It wasn't a date. So why did it suddenly feel like one?

"This is such a pretty town," Julie murmured.

"I suppose so," Jack agreed with a slight sense of surprise. He had been to town a few times since Thanksgiving, but today for some reason, he finally noticed all the Christmas decorations. From the harbor and village square at one end, all the way down the avenue, Main Street was decked with garlands of white lights swooping over the street. Pine wreaths with red bows adorned all the streetlights. Christmas shoppers thronged the streets, peering into windows filled with holiday displays, with golden ribbons, miniature trees, and miniature train sets circling them. The town looked bright and festive and welcoming.

Jack had not gone out to eat in the village for a long time. There was an attractive-looking café called the Beanery not far from the green, he noticed. Though it had been there awhile, he had never tried it. A glance through the windows showed a thick line of waiting customers snaking to the door.

He saw a parking spot on the other side of the street and pulled the truck in. They were right in front of the Clam Box diner, an old standby. The food wasn't anything to write home about, but it was reliable, and there was something cozy about the old place.

"How about the Clam Box?" he suggested. "It will probably be faster than the place across the street."

"This looks fine," Julie said. "I love clam chowder."

"They have plenty of that. Three kinds, if I recall correctly."

A little bell rang as he opened the door for her. He glanced around. The place wasn't very crowded.

Lucy Bates, the owner's wife, suddenly appeared and greeted him with a wide smile. "Jack Sawyer, how are you?"

"Hello, Lucy. Good to see you." It *was* good to see her. She had always been so sweet and friendly whenever he had brought his family here. She had been very kind when his wife was sick, too. He remembered her visiting Claire in the hospital.

"I'm not supposed to be working," she confided. "But I'll show you to a table."

She took two menus and led them to the table by the window. He let Julie sit first then slipped in the other side of the booth. "Lucy, this is Julie Newton. She's working at the tree farm this year."

He didn't know how to explain Julie. Was she his employee? Was she a friend? She was all of those things . . . and so much more, he thought. He had stumbled over his words but Lucy didn't seem to notice.

"Hello, Julie. Nice to meet you. Ever eat here before?"

Julie shook her head. "Jack says you serve good chowder."

"Not bad. Get the New England, though. And the clam rolls are our best dish."

"Thanks for the tip. That all sounds good to me."

"How's it going at the tree farm this year?" Lucy asked Jack. "We really need to get our tree. Maybe we'll get up there this weekend. The boys still like to go, though they're getting big now. They used to love coming to your place, Jack. That horse-drawn sleigh and visiting Santa Claus . . ."

Jack felt his cheeks grow red as Lucy described the way the tree farm had been in years past. Julie stared at him. What was she thinking? He had told her about the Christmas shop, but he had never mentioned the other activities.

"Yes, it was fun. A lot of work though. How are your boys, Lucy?" he asked, trying to change the subject.

"Growing up," she answered with a smile. "C.J. is into computer science—he's reprogrammed everything in the house—and Jamie wants to be the next Steve Nash. How is David? What's he up to these days?"

Now Julie was really staring at him, her brown eyes wide as saucers.

Jack looked down and ran his hand over his smooth hair. "I don't know what David's doing. We've lost touch," he answered honestly.

The pretty redhead stepped back, realizing she had asked too many questions. "Oh, I'm sorry. Well . . . I hope he gets back in touch with you soon. Teenagers go through all kinds of things, you know. Especially boys."

David wasn't a teenager anymore, Jack thought wistfully. He'd be almost twenty-one now, a grown man.

Lucy handed them two menus. "I'll send the waitress right over. I've got to get to work. I went back to school," she explained. "I'm a nurse now, can you believe that?" she asked Jack with a laugh.

"Wow, that's great. Charlie must be very proud."

"Sometimes he is. The rest of the time he's sort of annoyed I'm not working here anymore," she confided with a little smile. She glanced over her shoulder. "Too bad. I don't think he ever appreciated what a good waitress I am. Was, I mean."

"I'm sure he didn't," Jack agreed.

"So long. Nice to meet you, Julie," Lucy added as she left them.

"Nice to meet you, too," Julie said.

157

Jack watched Lucy go, knowing he had some 'splaining to do. He picked up his fork and fiddled with it nervously.

"I thought your son passed away, Jack. Isn't that what you told me?"

He sighed. Julie was so straightforward. He liked that about her. Most of the time.

"I said I lost him. That's the truth. David took off a few months after his mother died, and I haven't heard from him since."

"Oh . . . that must be hard for you," she said quietly.

"Yes, it is," he agreed.

The waitress appeared, and Julie ordered a cup of New England clam chowder and a clam roll. Jack ordered a Reuben sandwich.

He suddenly felt awkward, at a loss for conversation. Which was strange; talking always seemed so easy when they were at the house. Maybe taking her out wasn't such a good idea.

"Thank you for telling me the truth about your son," Julie said finally. "It must be very painful for you, not knowing where he is. I'm sure it's difficult to talk about."

He looked at her, feeling guilty. She was too easy on him.

"I need to apologize," he said. "I didn't mean to mislead you. But I never found a chance to explain."

"That's okay. Now I know. How long has it been?"

"Almost two years," Jack said sadly.

"And you haven't tried to find him?"

"I tried. I even hired a private investigator for a while, but I don't think David wants to be found. He would have gotten in touch by now if he wanted to."

"Why did he go? Did you have an argument?"

"We always had arguments, once he got into high school. The usual things. His mother used to smooth things over between us when she could and after she was gone, that was that. We argued one night. He left the house. I never saw him again."

Julie's gaze was sympathetic but she didn't say anything.

"I look back and think of all the things I should have done differently, you know? But you don't get second chances in life. That's not how it works."

"Oh, I don't know. Sounds like you would give your son another chance if he called. Maybe he feels the same way you do but just doesn't know what to say, doesn't know how to start things over again. Lots of us make bad decisions when we're young."

"Did you ever?" he asked. Something in her tone and the expression on her lovely face begged the question.

"Yes, I did. I married the wrong man. I just wanted to get married, I guess. And have a child. I felt like I was getting older and I wouldn't find anyone else."

He stared at her, amazed. How could she think she lacked for choices? Didn't she own a mirror?

"Life must be lived forward but can only be understood backward," she told him.

"Where did you learn that, in a philosophy class?"

She shook her head. "A fortune cookie, I think." He finally smiled again. "Did you get married young, Jack?"

He wasn't ready for that question, but she had been so open with him, he felt he owed her no less. "Yeah. I was only nineteen, but I felt very sure of what I was doing. And I never had any regrets," he added honestly. "Claire and I met in high school. We both grew up around here."

"Sounds like you were happy."

"We were. Until she got sick."

He didn't like to talk about Claire with anyone, and it felt odd being so frank with Julie. But it was so easy to talk to her, it was . . . uncanny. He just felt as if he had known her a long time. He even thought Claire would have liked her if they had ever had the chance to meet.

"Cape Light is such a beautiful town. I can see why you never wanted to leave."

"I like it. Still undiscovered, still very country. It's great in the summer. There's the beach, sailing. We get some tourists but not too many."

"What do you do the rest of the year, when you aren't selling Christmas trees?"

"I have the nursery and my landscaping business. I'm pretty busy." These last two years, his client list had dwindled. He had enough work to get by, though he knew he could be busier. "I used to have a big greenhouse, too, but I let that go."

He said that about a lot of things, didn't he? He hoped she didn't think he was lazy.

"I like living in a place like this, sort of hidden away. Carlisle was like that." She took a bite of her clam roll. "The town where my brother lives is a real suburb. He's in a condo. All the units look the same. I don't know how his family can find their way back when they go out somewhere."

Jack couldn't imagine Julie in a place like that. Something wasn't right about that picture. He had almost forgotten she planned on leaving soon. He didn't want to talk about her going away. Not today, anyway.

"Do you have any other close relatives, Julie? Another sister or brother?"

"It's just me and Peter. Our father died when I was in high school, and my mom passed away a few years ago."

So she really is alone. Just like me, Jack thought.

Julie drew in a breath and for the first time looked hesitant. "Now that the hard cast is off, do you want me to stay? I wasn't sure about that."

"Sure, I want you to stay," he said quickly. "I mean, if you want to," he added. "This is the busiest time for the tree lot, from now until Christmas. And you've started with those ornaments and trimming things. . . ."

She looked pleased. He knew he didn't have to say more and give his real feelings away.

"I would like to stay," Julie told him. "Until Christmas. Kate will be happy. She likes her new preschool."

He smiled. "I've been meaning to tell you, I want you to keep all the sales from the Christmas shop. It's all your work. It's only fair."

"Don't be silly. I've had stands at flea markets and craft fairs. It doesn't work like that, Jack."

"I don't care how it works at a flea market. This is my business. I run it as I like. You cleaned that place up, got it organized. You keep whatever you make in there and don't argue with me, okay?" His tone turned a bit gruff, but he knew she could tell it was only an act.

"That's very generous of you." She took a drink of her soda. "In that case, mind if we stop at a store on our way back? I saw a place in town where I can pick up some more art supplies."

"No problem. Let's get more ribbon for the wreaths, too. They're flying off the rack."

She nodded and took a bite of her clam roll. "Is it true what Lucy said about the tree farm? It sounds like it was a real Christmas village. That must have been fun," she said wistfully.

Although Jack felt relaxed and happy in her company, he wasn't ready to talk about the past. That was still too hard. "It was a lot of work and bother," he answered, his tone shorter than he meant. "It really wasn't worth the effort," he said more gently, "though the kids enjoyed it."

"I'm sure they did." Julie tried to catch his gaze but he purposely looked out the window. "So, who dressed up as Santa Claus?"

He pretended he didn't hear her for a moment.

"I did," he said quietly.

Now here was a moment when he really should have lied to her. At first her eyes widened in shock. Seconds later she looked as if she might laugh. She was smiling so broadly, he had to smile, too. Her dark eyes shone and a dimple creased her cheek.

"Why is that so funny?"

"It—it just is." She was laughing now, and he made a face, pretending to be insulted. "I'm sorry, Jack, You just don't strike me as the Santa type. . . . But I mean that in a good way," she added quickly.

Not the Santa type, in a good way? Should he take that as a compliment? He couldn't say. All he knew at that moment was that he liked her. Liked her a lot. He felt better just being around her, happy and hopeful. And he hadn't felt happy or hopeful for a very long time.

He looked down at her slender hand on the table, close to his. He had an impulse to reach over and cover it with his own. What would she do? Would she be upset with him? Surprised? Tell him she was sorry, she was only trying to be friendly and he had totally misunderstood?

The bell on the door jingled, announcing the arrival of a new customer. Jack looked up to see the minister from the church on the green. Julie turned her head and smiled.

"It's Reverend Ben," Julie said quietly. "Do you know him?"

"Yeah." When she raised an eyebrow in interest, he just shrugged and said, "It's a small town."

Jack saw the minister coming over to their table. Great. He hadn't been to church since Claire's funeral and had never been that keen on it before then, either. He just wasn't the churchgoing type.

Julie greeted the pastor happily. Jack nodded stiffly.

"Hello, Julie, nice to see you." Then Reverend Ben looked at Jack. "Hello, Jack. How are you? It's been a while."

"Oh, I'm all right. Getting along okay, I guess."

"That's good. Must be busy at the nursery now."

"We're picking up speed every day." Jack glanced at Julie. "I hurt my ankle. It's better now, but Julie's been working with me. She's a big help."

"I'm sure she is." Ben smiled at both of them. "Carolyn and I will be along soon to get our tree. Save a good one for us."

"I'll find a perfect tree for you, Reverend," Julie promised.

Ben smiled. "It doesn't have to be perfect, as long as it has lots of character."

He nodded, taking them both in with a sweeping glance. He looked very satisfied by what he saw, Jack noticed.

After Reverend Ben had left, Julie turned back to Jack. "I like him. He's very easy to talk to, not like most ministers I've met."

"Yes, he is different. More like a regular guy. I mean that in a good way," he added, making her smile again.

The waitress came by and took their empty dishes. Julie ordered coffee and looked over the dessert list. Jack found his gaze drawn back to Reverend Ben, who was sitting alone at a table on the other side of the diner.

He recalled how the minister had called and even visited a few times after Claire's death, but he never responded. He wondered now if he should have allowed Ben to get closer. Maybe it would have helped, especially when it came to dealing with David.

Thoughts of his son weighed heavily on his heart lately. Jack wondered if he should try to talk to Ben now. He had heard that Ben had trouble with his own son, Mark, who abruptly dropped out of college in his first year, wandered around the country, and barely kept in touch with his family for several years after. Mark had finally come home and everyone had reconciled. Maybe the minister would have some advice to offer?

No, Jack decided, he couldn't do that. He didn't go to church. Not even on Christmas. It wouldn't be right to ask for help now, he decided.

SAM WALKED INTO THE CLAM BOX, HEADING FOR A SEAT AT THE counter. He didn't like Charlie Bates very much, or the soap-box philosophy the diner owner offered his patrons as he worked at the grill. But he did enjoy Tucker Tulley, Charlie's best friend, who often stopped in for lunch at this time. Sam didn't see either today, but he heard someone call out to him.

He turned and spotted Reverend Ben, seated alone at his favorite table. "Join me for lunch, Sam? You know how I hate to eat alone."

As far as Sam could see, Reverend Ben relished his solitary moments whenever he could find them and was probably just saying that to be polite. But Sam could use some company today. It had not been an easy morning.

"So, what's new?" Ben asked. "How are things working out with the cabin? Is Jessica feeling better about it?"

Sam bowed his head a moment then looked up at Ben. "Jessica finds the cabin small. I think her exact word was *dismal*. She doesn't want to have to stay there all day long, so she's going back to work at the bank. Well, that's not the only reason she's taken a job," he added. "But it's part of it."

"When does she start?" Ben asked.

"Tomorrow." Sam picked up his menu then put it aside without opening it.

"You don't look too happy about that," Ben noted.

"I know we need the extra salary. It's the logical thing to do. But she just went out and committed to the job. Never said a word to me. It's like she didn't even care what I thought."

"Did she ever explain why she didn't talk it over with you first?" Ben asked.

Sam sighed and sat back. "She said she was afraid I would try to talk her out of it. That I would ask her to put it off, or something. She doesn't think I'm facing up to our problems." Sam shook his head, feeling angry. "That's rich. I feel as if I'm the one carrying this whole load on my back, protecting her and the kids from how bad it really is."

Ben suddenly looked concerned. "How bad is it, Sam?"

Sam stared down at the table. "I've been the one dealing with the insurance company. I started to think our claim wasn't looking that good after a few things the agent told me. I spoke to the insurance company again this morning, and they gave me a final figure." He paused. "It's bad, Ben. It's . . . pathetic. It won't even cover partly restoring the building, much less replacing our belongings."

Sam passed his hand over his eyes a moment, trying to control his emotions. He thought he might feel better, confiding this disaster to someone, especially to Reverend Ben. But saying the words aloud made the truth sound even harsher and even harder to accept.

Ben leaned forward, looking surprised and upset. "But why, Sam? How are they able to do that? It doesn't seem right."

"We didn't have the greatest coverage," Sam admitted. "We were trying to save a few dollars and who ever thinks something really horrible is going to happen to them, right? And you know insurance companies. They have a million ways of figuring out how to pay less than they really should."

"That's for sure." Ben sighed.

A waitress appeared. "What can I get for you?" she asked.

Neither Sam nor Ben needed to look at the menu. They both knew it by heart. Sam ordered a burger and Ben ordered a bowl of Rhode Island chowder.

"Is there any recourse for you?" Ben asked after the waitress had left them. "Any appeal you can make?"

"I asked about that. They're sending me some paperwork." Sam rolled his eyes. "If I have to fill out one more form, I'm going to scream. But that's one of their tricks, too. They try to wear you down, meeting all these endless requirements, burying you under mountains of red tape." He sighed. "I guess deep down I expected it would go this way, but I was really hoping for better."

"Of course you were. And you deserve better. Much better," Ben agreed.

"The payout won't be nearly enough to restore the house, not even if I do all the work by myself. Which, of course, I can't. Tyler would be in college by the time it was finished."

The waitress came by and dropped off their food and filled both cups with coffee. Sam stared at his burger but didn't touch it. Ben tasted his soup and added a sprinkle of pepper.

"If you don't restore the house, what are the other alternatives?"

Now Sam really lost his appetite. He felt his stomach twist in a knot. "We would have to knock it down and build something much more modest. Or just put the property up for sale."

Just thinking about either of those choices pained Sam deeply. It was traumatic enough to watch his beloved house go up in flames, the house he had brought back to life with his own two hands, with his own sweat and blood and imagination. The fire was an accident. An act of nature . . . or even of God. But to purposely, intentionally put a wrecking ball to that house . . . He couldn't do it.

"Sam, you've had some very difficult news and you have a lot to think about now. You don't have to figure it all out this morning. New choices you didn't even know about might open up for you," Ben reminded him.

"Maybe. But I have to tell you, Reverend, I'm not feeling that hopeful right now. And you know me," he added. "That's saying a lot."

Ben forced a small smile. "Yes, it is."

"You would think that after all we've been through, we could at least get a fair settlement from the insurance company. We could at least get that," Sam said. "I feel so cheated and robbed. Twice in a row. What is this all about, Reverend? When does it end?"

"You feel like you're being tested? Is that what you mean?"

Sam nodded. "Sure. If you want to put it that way, yes. That is how I feel. Like Job, in the Bible. I never could quite believe that story. How he just . . . sucks it up, you know?"

Ben didn't even try to explain it. "It is hard to identify with that one. It is pretty . . . extreme," he agreed. "I've sometimes wondered if that story is more about not holding God accountable for such catastrophic acts, but keeping hold of your faith and having the faith to turn to God in times of need."

Sam nodded. "Since the night of the fire, I don't think I've stopped praying," he admitted. "First just for feeling blessed we all got out alive. Then, asking for help as we wandered around town, not knowing where we would live. I did pray that we would get a fair settlement on the claim. . . . I guess God either didn't hear that one or that even He doesn't have much sway with the insurance companies.

"You know what the hardest part of all this is to me?" Sam went on. "I don't know how to tell Jessica. That's what I'm most worried about right now. Not even the thought of knocking down the house seems as bad."

"You have to tell her, Sam, as soon as possible. She might take it better than you think," Ben added quietly.

"I don't think so." Sam shook his head. "I've kept promising her and the boys that we'll rebuild the house just the way it was. I guess that was unrealistic of me, but I didn't know what else to say. I really believed we could. But now . . . they'll think I was lying to them. Or that I was some naïve fool. Jessica will. She already says I'm too optimistic."

"Maybe you are optimistic. But by and large, that's a good thing," Ben assured him. "They know you're trying your best. It's hardly your fault the claim came in low. Don't take this all on your shoulders, Sam. The fire wasn't your fault. You can't make it all better for everyone overnight, either."

Sam glanced at Ben. Behind his wire-rimmed glasses, the reverend's sharp blue eyes were bright with emotion. Ben was, above all things, a real friend.

Sam rubbed his forehead and sighed. "Yes, I know. It's hard not to try though."

Ben smiled gently. "Everyone has to do their part, Sam, to pull together as a family now. Even if that means changing their expectations."

Sam knew that was true, especially for himself. "Tell me about it. I had a crash course in the subject this morning. But it will still be hard to tell Jessica."

"Of course it will. But couples have to talk about difficult subjects. You're in it together and you have to share this with her. It's only fair. To both of you," he added.

Ben paused and caught Sam's gaze. "Don't make that house the measure of everything," he warned. "It was a beautiful house, but only because you and your wife created it with love and caring. Only because of the family inside. 'For where your treasure is, there will your heart be also.' The Book of Luke," he reminded Sam.

Sam nodded, considering the familiar bit of Scripture that he now heard differently than ever before.

His family was his treasure, Jessica and his boys. Not the house, the wood, the plaster, and the pipes. All that had been destroyed. The love that they shared, that bound them; the path on which they had come so far together; their future, still a story to be told—all that was what mattered.

He had to remember that. And remind Jessica, too.

CHAPTER TEN

◠

*A*FTER HIS LUNCH WITH REVEREND BEN, IT WAS difficult for Sam to concentrate on the work in his shop. An outside job would have been better, he thought, one where he could have just hammered away mindlessly. But he was in the middle of repairing a very delicate set of antique chairs for a very fussy client.

The work required concentration with the jigsaw and other cutting tools. After a while, he put it all aside, afraid he might have an accident.

The forms to contest the insurance claim began to print out from the fax machine in his tiny office. The pages seemed to be coming and coming. He picked up the pile and dropped them on his desk. More paperwork to fill out. He couldn't deal with it right now.

Reverend Ben had been right. He couldn't blame himself, and he couldn't make it right in one night all on his own. He had to tell

Jessica. Tonight. She would be upset, he was sure. But once she got past that, they could put their heads together and try to figure out the next step.

It was barely four o'clock when Sam closed up his shop and headed back to the cabin. He thought he would shoot some basketball with the boys while it was still light outside. That would cheer him up.

When he pulled up, he didn't see Jessica's car. The cabin was dark. So the boys were not home either. He went inside and looked around. Even the dog crate was empty. The silent, vacant space gave him a bad feeling.

Was she so unhappy that she had just taken the boys and left him?

He was panicking. Just his state of mind today. An unusual mood for him, that was for sure.

He had to laugh at his paranoia when he realized that if Jessica had left, she never would have taken the dog. She must have just gone out somewhere—to the grocery store?

Then he saw a note on the countertop, propped against the salt shaker. Jessica's handwriting, he could tell before he even picked it up. It said she had taken the boys to their old house to go ice skating at the pond.

He put the note down as a wave of sadness washed over him. Of all places for her to go today. He sighed and stared around. He didn't feel like waiting for them to come back. He went out, locked the front door, and climbed back into his SUV. Then he headed down Beach Road to their old house.

It was a short ride. Too short, Sam thought.

He pulled in the drive and parked next to Jessica's car. The sun was beginning to set, streaking the sky with rose and purple clouds on the horizon. He glanced up at the burned ruins of his house, the sunset colors reminding him of the fire. A blue tarp flapped over the gaping roof and back wall. A bird flew out one of the windows.

The structure looked even more pathetic and hopeless now than it had that first day when they returned with Chief Rhinehardt. *Maybe it's me,* Sam thought. *Maybe it's what I know now that I didn't know then.*

He sighed and dug his hands in his pockets. He heard Tyler and Darrell at the pond, shouting and laughing. He saw Jessica standing at the edge of the pond, holding Sunny's leash.

Her back was turned and she didn't see him as he walked toward them. Tyler did and he waved. "Daddy's here. Hey, Daddy! Want to skate with us?" he shouted, scrambling across the ice.

Normally, Sam loved to do anything with the boys. Jessica always said that was the real reason he had wanted kids—so that he had a legitimate excuse to run out and play all day. The way Sam looked at it, that's what dads were for.

He came to the edge of the pond and waved back. "Let me see you skate, Ty," he said.

"I'm good now. I didn't fall at all," Tyler bragged, lurching backward but catching his balance. "Why don't you skate with us, Dad?"

"I don't have my skates with me, Ty. And it's getting dark. Next time," he promised.

His skates had been destroyed in the fire. That was the real reason. He guessed Jessica had borrowed a few pairs from Luke for the boys. At least the kids were not lacking for equipment, living at New Horizons.

Jessica walked over to him, the puppy leaping around on her leash then trying to bite it. "They wanted to come out here, so I said okay."

It was her last afternoon with them before she started working.

"What did they say when they saw the house?" Sam asked quietly.

The boys had asked a few times to come and see their old house, but Sam and Jessica kept putting it off. Partly because they didn't want to see it again themselves, Sam knew.

"I tried to prepare them for what it looked like. Darrell just got very quiet. Tyler said it looks ugly. But otherwise he seems fine. . . . I didn't know what to do," she confessed. "They had to see it sooner or later, didn't they?"

Sam nodded. Another missed opportunity for her to have talked something over with him, he thought.

But maybe that wasn't fair. Situations like this happened so spontaneously. They couldn't be consulting with each other every moment. He had been in the same position over other decisions concerning the boys.

She glanced at him. "Do you think I shouldn't have brought them over here? Was it too soon?"

Sam shook his head. "No, you did the right thing. They had to see it."

He felt the puppy climb up his leg and he absentmindedly patted her head. He stared out at the pond. Darkness was falling quickly now, but he could not mistake the outlines of his two children. Darrell, making large circles and figure eights with smooth, athletic grace. Sam remembered the first time he got Darrell up on skates when he was just working with him as a mentor at New Horizons.

Tyler was far from steady on the ice, but as the younger brother, pushed himself to keep up. And did a good job, Sam thought.

"Watch this, Daddy. I can turn really fast, see?" Tyler picked up speed then made a fast circle.

"Whoa, very good. That was great." Sam clapped his hands.

Darrell swooped by. Using a branch as a hockey stick, he smacked a chunk of ice across the pond. "Can we play hockey out here sometime?" he asked Sam.

"Absolutely. I'll get Luke to loan us some gear. Maybe he'll even come," Sam added. His buddy Luke was always up for a game of any kind.

Tyler swung an imaginary hockey stick. "Goal!" he shouted, and pumped one small fist.

"Okay, boys. It's getting dark. Come on in, we have to go . . ." *Home,* Sam nearly said.

They were home. But they were not. It was a sad, confusing feeling.

"Yeah, come on guys, you must be cold," Jessica called out. "Besides, I still have to fix dinner."

For once, the boys skated in without needing to be nagged. The puppy started barking as soon as Darrell stepped onto the bank. Once he changed back into his boots, he took the leash from Jessica, kneeling to hug the excited dog.

Sam gathered up the skates and abandoned helmets. With Darrell and Sunny leading the way, they headed back to the cars.

They were all very quiet as they passed by the house. It was now almost dark, and the burnt-out shell of their once-beautiful home loomed up in the shadows, seeming almost ominous.

Sam looked over at Jessica, trying to catch her eye, to share his feelings, even with a glance. But she was staring down at the snow as she walked along, her shoulders bowed as if under a heavy weight.

Just the way he felt.

Tyler walked beside him. "Our house looks so ugly now. It's scary. It looks like a haunted house or something."

"Yes, I know," Sam said quietly.

"You're going to fix it for us again, right, Daddy?"

Sam glanced down at his son, his bright eyes and trusting expression. He felt so choked up, he could hardly answer.

He knew now he couldn't do that. He couldn't make it the way it had been. He couldn't turn back the clock to the day before the fire.

He nodded quickly. "Sure, Ty. I'm going to fix it," he promised. "We'll have a great house again, don't worry."

Jessica was looking at him now. It was hard to read her expression in the shadowy light. He thought she tried to smile a little, but he wasn't sure.

Sam's step slowed. Everyone else had reached the cars and was waiting for him. He had walked past the house but felt it looming over his shoulder, like a big black bird that had swooped down and stolen his happiness, his very sense of well-being.

Stolen his trust in himself.

His family was homeless. That was the truth of the matter. He couldn't lie to himself anymore.

He felt the weight of what had happened crash down, as if the entire burnt hulk of the building had suddenly collapsed on top of him.

He knew he had to tell Jessica the truth about the insurance claim. Tell her tonight, as he had planned.

But for all his good intentions, he knew he would not follow through. Not tonight. Somewhere out here he had lost his nerve. And now he didn't have the strength or the energy to do what he had to do.

JACK WOKE UP ABRUPTLY FROM A SOUND SLEEP. HE SAT UP AND listened. He heard Katie crying and Julie's quick footsteps in the hallway above, running to the bathroom and back again.

What was going on? Maybe Katie had had a nightmare. She didn't seem herself tonight, quiet and out of sorts. Julie had put her to bed early. The little girl didn't even want to hear a Lester story, so Jack guessed she didn't feel well.

He got up, pulled on his jeans and a sweatshirt, and walked to the bottom of the stairway. A light was on upstairs. He heard Julie rummaging through the hall closet.

"Is everything okay?" he called softly.

She came to the top of the stairs and looked down at him. "Jack? I'm sorry we woke you."

"That's all right. Did Katie have a nightmare?"

Julie shook her head. Her long curly hair was hanging loose around her shoulders. He had never seen it like that before.

"I think she has a fever. But the thermometer I had with me isn't working, and I can't seem to find one up here."

Jack started up the stairs. He saw her step back and quickly tighten the belt on her bathrobe.

It was hard not to look at her. But he tried his best.

When he reached the top of the stairs, he went into the bathroom. He opened the medicine cabinet and poked around inside, moving bottles and tubes about. Finally he found a thermometer and a bottle of rubbing alcohol.

"The old-fashioned kind, sorry."

Julie took it quickly. "Those digital ones break right away. These are more reliable."

She walked back to the bedroom. Jack hesitated then followed. He stood in the doorway and watched as she cleaned the thermometer, shook it, then placed it in Katie's little mouth.

Katie looked so pale and sleepy, barely lifting her head from the pillow. Julie looked tense, sitting on the edge of the bed as she watched the clock on the nightstand.

After a few minutes, she took the thermometer out, held it up to the lamp, and read it.

"Oh dear, this can't be right." She glanced up at Jack, looking alarmed.

"What does it say?" He walked in without asking.

She handed it up to him and he read it. It was almost a hundred and three.

"Try again. Maybe the mercury didn't go down far enough when you started."

"Yes, that might be it." She shook the thermometer again, checked it under the lamp, then offered it to Katie. "I'm sorry, baby. I have to do this over."

Kate murmured something and tossed her head but finally took the thermometer and kept very still, Julie's hand on her flushed cheek.

Jack watched the clock this time. "Three minutes, right?"

Julie nodded. He felt worried now himself. Katie shouldn't have a fever that high. It was dangerous.

Finally, the minutes ticked past. "Okay, it's time."

Julie took the thermometer out and carefully read it.

"The same." She handed it up. Jack looked at it again, too. The silver line had hit just about the same exact mark. These old-fashioned things were accurate. You couldn't fool them.

"You ought to call Dr. Harding. He has an emergency number on the office recording."

"Good idea. I'll go down and get the number." She jumped up and started toward the door. "Can you stay here with Kate?" she asked, glancing over her shoulder.

"Absolutely."

Julie turned and disappeared. In the midst of the emergency, he couldn't help thinking how beautiful she was. Maybe that wasn't right, but he couldn't help it.

He turned to Kate. She lay back on her pillows with her eyes closed, but he wasn't sure she was asleep. He touched her little hand. It felt dry and hot. He remembered when David had high fevers. It was always scary for him and Claire.

"Hey, Kate," he said softly. "Are you asleep?"

She opened her eyes slowly and stared at him. Her blue eyes were glassy and wide, her cheeks flushed. "A little bit."

"How do you feel?"

"Hot. And my ear hurts." She rubbed her left ear.

"Wow, that's not so good." He sighed. "I knew you didn't feel good when you didn't even want to read about Lester tonight."

She almost smiled. "I have a book where Lester gets sick. He gets a bad cold."

"Well, maybe we can read that one next—when you feel a little better."

"I don't have it now. It's in a box that Mommy sent to my uncle's house."

"Oh . . . I see." Jack nodded. The information, stated so plainly, made Jack's heart lurch. It was easy to forget that Julie and Kate would be leaving soon. Sometimes it hit him smack between the eyes.

"Maybe I can find that one in the library," he suggested.

She nodded, closing her eyes again. "Good idea, Jack."

Her adult tone almost made him laugh. He would have, if she hadn't looked so sick.

Julie came upstairs. "I spoke to Dr. Harding. He said it sounds like an ear infection. He said to give her a bath to bring the fever down, and some children's Motrin. I don't have any of that with me, though," she added, looking concerned.

Jack jumped up. "I'll get it. There's a convenience store near the entrance to the highway. It's open twenty-four hours."

Julie looked surprised. "It's the middle of the night, and it's a long ride to the highway."

"It's okay," he insisted. "You need any help with the bath?"

"We'll be all right."

"Okay. See you in a little while." Jack stopped and turned to her. She was looking up at him, her lovely face amazed and very grateful.

He knew if he stared any longer, he might just lean over and kiss her. That wouldn't help Kate any, he reminded himself.

Or Julie.

Jack grabbed his jacket and hat then drove his old truck as fast as he dared, up Beach Road to the highway. He ran into the store, got the medicine and some other items he thought Kate might need, like juice and tissues, and practically threw his money at the clerk.

He was back in record time and ran upstairs with the bag, still wearing his hat and jacket.

"I got the stuff," he said, breathless. "How is she?"

"Her fever went down a tiny bit after the bath. Not that much. This should help though."

Julie opened the Motrin bottle, measured out the dosage in a tiny plastic cup, then coaxed Kate to sit up. "You need to take some medicine, honey. This will make you feel better."

Kate took one look at the cup of orange liquid and twisted her head away. "I hate that. It sticks in my throat and makes me all choky."

Choky? Was that even a word? Jack knew just what she meant though.

"Come on, honey. Jack drove a long way to get it for you. The doctor said you need it."

Julie glanced over her shoulder at Jack, silently imploring him for help.

Jack smiled at Katie and stepped over to the bed. "I bet Lester doesn't like medicine either," he said.

Kate shook her head. "No, he doesn't."

Julie looked surprised at the conversation but didn't interrupt.

"Well, you just told me he gets sick sometimes, too," Jack improvised. "So how does his mom get him to take his medicine?"

Kate thought for a moment. "She sings a song."

"What song?" he asked curiously. "A special song?"

Kate shrugged. "Just any old song. It doesn't matter. Something nice."

"If I sing, will you drink that?"

Julie looked up at him, shocked, but struggling not to smile. Okay, so he had lost his mind. Officially. He had lost his mind for this little girl and her beautiful mom.

"I guess I'd drink it then," Katie said thoughtfully.

"Okay . . . well . . . here goes."

He saw Katie smile in anticipation but didn't dare look at Julie. He stood up straight and took his hat off. Then he looked down at Kate, holding his knit cap to his chest.

He didn't know what song to sing. The only one that came to mind was the "Star-Spangled Banner." Which he occasionally sang at ballgames. But he didn't think Kate would consider that one "nice."

The only other song he knew all the lyrics to was "You Are My Sunshine." He decided that one would have to do.

He cleared his throat and began to sing the familiar song. To his surprise, he didn't feel the least bit corny telling Kate she was his sunshine.

By the time he reached the last verse, his voice was thin and strained. Somehow he kept his face fixed in a serious expression, as if singing a silly song in the middle of the night at a child's bedside was nothing unusual.

When he was finally done, Kate clapped her hands. "Nice song, Jack."

"Glad you liked it. Now down the hatch, miss," he reminded her.

Julie held out the cup again. This time, Kate took it and drank it to the bottom. "Good job," Julie said.

"Jack did a good job, too," Kate pointed out.

"He sure did." Julie glanced at him. The look in her eyes would keep him happy for a week, he thought.

He watched Julie tuck Kate in and kiss her cheek. He wanted to do the same but didn't feel he had the right.

He smiled at her before she closed her eyes. "Sleep well, Kate. See you tomorrow."

Julie gathered the medicine and the water glass and turned off the light. "I've got to put these things in the kitchen," she said. "I think I'll have some tea. I'm too awake now to sleep."

"Me, too," Jack agreed. Racing out in the frigid cold and driving like a maniac had given him a rush of adrenaline.

"I think I'll make some coffee and just head out to the tree lot," he said when they reached the kitchen.

The suggestion made her laugh. "It's half past three. It will just be you and the raccoons."

"I guess you're right. I'm better off in here with you."

"So, my company is preferable to a pack of raccoons. What a compliment."

He smiled at her. He knew she was teasing him. "I could do better than that, believe me."

He caught her eye and realized he had slipped. Julie's eyes flashed but she quickly busied herself, filling the kettle with water.

She sat down at the table near him and hugged her pale blue robe around her body. "It frightens me when Kate gets sick. I know kids are always catching things, but I hate to see her with such a high fever and . . . you never know. If anything happened to her, I don't know what I'd do. She's all I've got," she added wistfully.

Jack reached out and took her hand. "Don't worry. She's going to be fine. You can take her to Harding tomorrow. I'll drive you."

Julie smiled at him. She hadn't pulled away from his touch, he noticed. Her hand seemed relaxed, holding his. As if it were always this way. . . .

"You helped me a lot tonight, Jack. I'm really grateful. I don't know what I would have done otherwise."

"Oh, you would have been all right. But the Motrin will help her," he agreed.

"I don't mean just that. Though it was a heroic gesture," she said with a grin. "But just being there. And your singing. Whatever gave you that idea?"

Jack smiled. "Didn't you ever notice that your daughter is willing to do anything Lester does? That didn't take much brainpower to figure out."

Julie nodded. "I guess I was too worried to think creatively. Well, thanks for that, too. You have a nice voice, Jack. The performance was very memorable."

He felt himself blushing and didn't know what to say. He liked just sitting here, holding her hand, looking into her beautiful face.

If he could freeze a moment in his recent life, a moment to return to any time he felt blue or lonely, this would be it.

"What are you thinking about, Jack? You look so . . . thoughtful."

He sighed. "I'm thinking . . . I'd like to kiss you."

Then he leaned over, cupped her cheek with his hand and did just that. When his lips met hers, he paused. The sensation was almost shocking. Her mouth was so soft and sweet. He kissed her slowly, amazed for a moment that she didn't pull away but instead kissed him back. He felt her hand on his face and in his hair. His hand slipped around her waist and pulled her closer, though the table was definitely a barrier to their closeness.

When he finally pulled away, he took a long, shaky breath. He leaned his face against her hair. It felt like silk on his cheek and smelled like flowers.

She seemed moved, too. He heard a long sigh as she slipped her hand from around his neck.

He stared into her eyes a long moment, wanting to tell her how he felt about her. How he really felt and everything she had come to mean to him. She and Katie.

The shrill whistle of the kettle filled the silence. It sounded to Jack like an emergency alarm going off, warning that he was heading in a dangerous direction.

Julie pushed her hair back from her face. "I'd better get that."

She rose and walked to the stove. She poured some tea into a mug and was about to pour a second cup.

Jack came to his feet, too. "That's okay. I guess I'll skip the tea and just turn in."

"Right." Had disappointment just flashed through her eyes?

"I'd better get upstairs anyway. I need to check on Kate, make sure the medicine is working. Good night, Jack."

"Good night." He nodded his head as she walked past him.

He headed back to bed, knowing he wouldn't sleep a wink.

EVERYONE WOKE UP LATE THE NEXT MORNING.

Jack was the first one in the kitchen and made coffee. Julie walked in, dressed in a sweater and jeans, her hair still wet from the shower.

"Coffee, great. I can also use some toothpicks with that to keep my eyes open."

"Don't worry. I make it strong." She made good coffee, too, he had noticed. Just the way he liked it.

He handed her a cup and then the milk. She didn't take sugar. He knew that now. He stood by the counter and drank his own. All he could think about was how he had kissed her last night. He wondered what she was thinking now. If she would say anything. He wondered if he should say something.

"How is Katie doing? Is she awake yet?"

"She woke up at about six and I gave her something to drink. Then she went back to sleep again. Her temperature is down, but she's still running a fever."

So Julie didn't get much sleep last night either, he realized. He felt bad for her. She looked worn out, too. Just as lovely, of course, but tired.

"I can drive you in to town to see Dr. Harding. Kate probably needs a visit."

"Yes, he said to come in this morning. But I can take care of it by myself. You don't have to go, too."

"I have a few things to do in town. The bank and stuff." He shrugged. There was no urgent need to go to the bank. He wasn't very good about money and would sometimes keep checks and piles of cash around the house for weeks. But Julie didn't know that.

"If you're going in anyway, I guess it would be helpful." She glanced at him over the edge of her coffee cup. "Are you getting another secret haircut?"

Her dark eyes sparkled. He thought she was joking with him, but wasn't sure.

He ran his hand self-consciously over his hair. "Do I need one?"

She took him in with an appraising look, and he felt himself melting like a pat of butter on a slice of warm toast.

She suddenly shook her head and looked away. "Not at all. You look fine just the way you are, Jack. You're a very handsome man."

Very handsome? Had she really said that?

Jack stared at her. He swallowed. He thought he should say thank you. But he couldn't speak.

"Mommy, can I come down now?" Kate called from the top of the stairway.

Julie ran into the living room to meet her. "If you feel up to it, honey. We're going to the doctor soon, so you might as well come eat something, if you can."

Jack turned and stared out the window over the sink, still reeling. Was she just trying to flatter him? She was always so honest—even blunt at times—he didn't think she was the type to offer false flattery.

He thought she was beautiful. But he doubted he would ever have the courage to tell her.

As he drove the three of them into town, Jack was glad he had offered to take Julie and Kate to the doctor. He could see that Julie was tired after her long night, and the usually easygoing little girl was a bit cranky and in need of attention.

Twenty minutes later, he dropped them off at the doctor then went to do his alleged errands. He bought a cup of coffee and walked down Main Street. Every shop was decorated for Christmas, of course. The toy shop window was particularly interesting to him this year. Since David had grown up, Jack had hardly been aware of children's toys. So many different varieties had sprung up recently; some looked very high-tech and intimidating.

But he knew that Kate still yearned for the classics, a baby doll and stuffed animals. A miniature tea set.

Suddenly, he couldn't believe his eyes. Right up front, with his head and paws poking out of a Christmas stocking, Jack spotted his new, lop-eared friend Lester. Holding a carrot, and wearing his signature baseball hat and backpack, the dear little guy was ready to go home with the first customer to claim him.

Jack dumped his coffee in a trash bin and ran inside the store. He could hardly believe his good luck today.

DR. HARDING HAD DETERMINED KATE HAD AN EAR INFECTION and prescribed antibiotics, which Julie needed to pick up at the drugstore on their way home. Jack walked into the store with her and stood by Kate while Julie talked to the pharmacist.

Kate felt tired, so he lifted her up and held her in his arms. She dropped her head on his shoulder and closed her eyes. He could tell from the sound of her deep breathing that she had fallen asleep in his arms. It was a very sweet feeling, he thought.

He was standing there a few moments, waiting for Julie and

trying to keep perfectly still so Kate could sleep, when he heard someone call to him.

"Mr. Sawyer?" A girl in her early twenties walked toward him. She was a pretty girl with blond hair and bright blue eyes, a powder-blue knit cap pulled low over her brow. "Remember me?"

"Christine . . . how are you?" Jack spoke softly trying not to wake Kate.

"I'm good. How are you?"

She looked at Kate with curiosity and then at Julie, who had just returned from the pharmacy counter holding a small white bag.

"I'm fine. I'm doing okay," he said evenly. He glanced at Julie. "This is my . . . my friend, Julie Newton, and her daughter, Kate. Kate isn't feeling well. We've just come from the doctor."

"Oh, I'm sorry." Christine peered at Kate's sleeping face. "She's so cute."

"Yes, she is. Very smart, too." Jack caught himself, bragging like a proud father. "How are you? What are you doing now?"

"I'm in school. I'm working on a degree in education. And I just got engaged," she added with a grin. "But we're not getting married for a while, at least not until we both finish school."

Jack nodded. "That makes good sense." Christine always was a levelheaded girl.

"So . . . how's David? Do you ever hear from him?"

Jack shook his head. "No, I don't. Nothing's changed on that score."

Christine's question meant she had not heard from him either, Jack realized.

When David had first disappeared, Jack thought if there was one person in the world he would get in touch with, it would be

Christine. She had been his steady girlfriend for two years during high school. David had been crazy about her. But the few times Jack had inquired, Christine always said she hadn't heard a word. Finally, about a year after David had left, she admitted they had been in touch a few times, after David first left town. But he had made her promise not to tell and was moving around a lot. The last place he had called her from was Florida. But she claimed she hadn't heard from him in several months and had no idea where he had gone.

At the time, Jack didn't believe her. Now he did.

"I'm sorry . . . I just thought I'd ask." She shrugged.

"That's okay. If I ever do hear, I'll let you know."

She might be married with children by then. Would she even care? She had already found someone else. She was engaged. But David still seemed to matter to her. Jack could just tell by the expression in her eyes when she said his name, the tone of her voice. Funny how those things are, the loose ends of relationships that never get tied up. This one might always remain a question mark, Jack thought. His son had not treated this sweet girl very well. David had hurt her, and Jack was sorry about that.

Jack smiled wistfully. "Well, we'd better get going. Nice to see you. Say hello to your folks for me."

"Nice to see you, too. And have a merry Christmas," she added, glancing at Julie and Kate.

"Same to you," he replied.

As they walked to the car, Jack turned to Julie. "That was my son's girlfriend. Well, former girlfriend. She told me she's engaged to be married. So she must have gotten over him."

"Maybe. She seemed very curious about him, though."

Jack glanced at her. "Yes, she was. I noticed that, too. But she has to go on with her life. She can't wait for David to come back, that's for sure."

"No, of course not. But if you really care for someone and they leave you, feelings don't just disappear. Unfortunately. Two years isn't long if she really loved him."

Jack didn't answer. He knew that was true. He would have feelings for Julie long after she left Cape Light. That's just the way it was. He was coming to accept the inevitable.

As Jack expected, as soon as they got home, Julie took Kate back up to bed and gave her the new prescription.

"She'll need about twenty-four hours on the medicine before she feels like herself again," Julie said when she came downstairs. "The doctor said the more she sleeps, the faster this will go away."

"I think you should catch a nap yourself. You look beat," Jack told her. He had heated up some soup for their lunch and made two turkey sandwiches while Julie was upstairs. Julie took a few bites, but he could tell she was more tired than hungry.

"I wanted to go out to the shop and work on the decorations," she said. "We'll probably get busy again."

Jack knew she was right. It was less than two weeks before Christmas Eve. Twelve days, exactly. The countdown had begun. The lot had been busy in the late afternoon and early evening—mothers coming with kids after school and entire families at night.

"I can handle it. I don't want you to get sick, too," he added, purposely avoiding her gaze.

She smiled at him. "Okay, maybe I could use a nap. If I went out there now, I might get in trouble with the glue gun."

Jack grinned at the idea. "We could wind up with some very weird wreaths."

She laughed, rested her hand lightly on his shoulder for a moment, then walked past his chair. "Don't let me sleep too long, okay?"

"Sure. I'll wake you in a little while," he promised.

He felt his heart skip a beat as she left the room, and couldn't for the life of him understand why. Then he realized. He and Julie had been treating each other with an easy intimacy. A romantic intimacy. He couldn't quite believe it, feeling that sweet connection that he had never expected to feel again.

After lunch, Jack went outside to the tree lot. His ankle hardly bothered him, even with the plastic brace on. He tossed some trees around, sorting out a fresh shipment, then cleaned up the place a bit. Then he looked through the most expensive trees he had for sale and picked out one he thought was just perfect.

It was over two hours later when he walked upstairs and knocked softly on the door to the room where Julie and Kate slept.

The door was partially open, and he saw Julie sitting on the edge of the bed. She looked as if she had just woken up. She blinked at him. "I thought you promised to wake me in a little while. I slept the whole afternoon."

"You needed the rest. Besides, I was busy," he explained.

"A lot of customers?" She sounded concerned.

"No, busy inside. Come on down with Katie. I have a surprise for you."

He waited in the living the room. It was late afternoon, nearly dark outside, and he turned off the lamp on the end table so that only the colored lights on the Christmas tree glowed.

He heard them coming and stepped back. He couldn't wait to see the look on Kate's face. Or Julie's.

Kate came first. She stopped on the stairway, her face pressed between the railings of the banister. "Look, Mommy! A Christmas tree. Jack made an inside tree!"

She ran down the rest of the steps and straight up to the tree. She stared at it, looking at every ornament.

Jack felt himself smiling. The expression on her face was priceless, full of wonder and innocent joy. He wished he could bottle it and save it for some gloomy day when he would be all alone here once more.

Kate turned to him. "Jack, did you do this all by yourself?"

"All by myself. Do you like it?"

"It's beautiful. It's a very nice tree." She reached out and stroked a branch, as if it were a dog. Jack nearly laughed out loud.

Julie stepped over and stood beside him. She rested her hand on his arm. Her touch lingered. "Jack . . ." She shook her head. Her eyes were glassy, as if she might cry.

Jack felt alarmed. He hadn't meant to upset her. "Is something wrong?"

"No, not at all." She smiled again. "It was just so sweet of you to go to all this trouble, so thoughtful."

"I just wanted to cheer Kate up. So she would feel better. I used a few ornaments from your shop. I hope that's okay."

"Of course it is," Julie replied.

Jack hadn't been able to use any of the ornaments still packed away in his basement. Those would bring back too many memories. Instead, he had found some ribbons and odds and ends in the Christmas shop and a bag of candy canes. Somehow, he had managed to fill the branches; the lights helped a lot.

"There's one more special touch. But I need Kate's help," he said, looking down at her. "I have a star for the top. Think you could put it on for me?"

Kate looked thrilled by the assignment. "I can do it," she promised.

He showed her the star with the holder that clipped to the tree-top. Then he picked her up and lifted her high enough to reach. Without much trouble, Kate did the job.

"Great." Jack held her in his arms and smiled at her. "Now the tree is perfect."

"It was very nice of Jack to decorate this tree for you, Kate. What do you say?" her mother coaxed.

"Thank you, Jack." She put her arms around his neck and hugged him.

"You are very welcome," he answered quietly.

Finally, he set her down again. Kate gazed up at the two adults. "The tree isn't just for me," she told them. "It's for Jack, too. Because now when Santa flies by, he can find Jack's house."

"That's right. I almost forgot. I know you were worried about that," Jack said.

"I was. Everyone should get presents. Even you, Jack."

"Well, thanks."

Julie made an apologetic face at the half-baked compliment, but he knew what Kate meant.

Besides, he didn't need Santa. He already had his gift: this time with Julie and Kate.

CHAPTER ELEVEN

$\mathcal{S}$ AM KNEW HE HAD TO TELL JESSICA THE BAD NEWS. BUT in the days that followed their visit to the old house, he just couldn't find the right moment. There was always some reason. Last week, Jessica had started her new job. She came home tired every night, overwhelmed by getting into a new routine—a full-time job added to all the shopping, cooking, laundry, and cleaning up. Sam helped her as much as he could, but he could see the tension and exhaustion in her eyes.

The weekend was almost worse. New Horizons had held its annual Christmas party on Sunday, and Sam and Jessica had spent all day Saturday helping Luke and Sara clean, decorate, and cook. It was the least they could do, since Luke had been so kind to them. The weekend vanished in the whirlwind of preparations and the party itself. Afterward, Sam was too tired and distracted to get into any heavy discussions at home.

The cabin was so small that private conversations with Jessica were few and far between. In order to talk out of the boys' earshot, Sam either had to find a time when the kids were outside playing, or coax Jessica to step outside into the cold. It was crazy. They were all on top of each other in the small space yet not nearly as emotionally close as they used to be. Especially him and Jess.

As he drove back to the cabin on Monday night, he was determined to tell her about the insurance claim. He didn't care what was going on. He had been holding the information back from her for a week now. He couldn't put it off any longer.

He walked in with Sunny and unhooked her leash. Jessica was in the kitchen cooking dinner, an apron over her fancy work clothes. Sam kissed her on the cheek.

"Where are the kids?" she asked.

"I dropped them off at the main building. They wanted to use the computer in the library for a few minutes. They claim they need it for homework."

"Or something," Jessica replied. "I guess we need to put at least one computer under the Christmas tree."

"Yeah, I guess that's unavoidable," Sam agreed. It was a week until Christmas Eve. They hadn't done any shopping yet, except for necessities. "I think the break from computers has been good for them. Last night, I actually found them playing Scrabble. How wild is that?"

Jessica laughed. "I don't believe you. You should have taken a picture."

If I still had a camera, I would have, Sam nearly answered. But he didn't want to remind her again of their losses. As if she needed any reminders.

Sam had picked up their mail at the post office and now

dropped it on the counter. Jessica began sifting through the envelopes, separating the bills from the junk mail.

"Oh, look. Something from my old friend, Marty Graham." She opened it up. It was a Christmas card with a handwritten note inside. "What a nice note. Marty heard about the fire. She invited us to stay with her for Christmas, at their house on Cape Cod. You remember Marty, don't you?"

"Yes, of course I do. Very nice of her to offer."

Marty was an old college friend of Jessica's. Sam didn't much like her, or her husband, Ted? Ken? Kevin? He had no intention of spending the holiday with them and couldn't imagine why Jessica would want to either. They were both snobs, he thought. Ted did something with money. A stockbroker or bonds trader. Investment counselor? Sam couldn't remember. He did remember Ted made loads of money. Which made Sam feel like . . . a bug.

Marty was very fussy, he recalled. She shared all of Jessica's worst traits and none of her redeeming graces. Their two boys were okay, but both were a lot quieter than his kids. The few times they had gotten together, the four boys planted themselves in front of a TV; it was the only thing they all had in common.

"Maybe we should take them up on it," Jessica said. "Their house is gorgeous, and Marty always serves incredible food." Her oozing tone annoyed him. "Besides, it would be a nice change of scenery for the boys. For all of us."

"I'd like to stick around for the holidays, Jess, be with our families."

"They'll understand that we need to get away." She put the card aside and picked up the mail again. "We don't have to decide now. I think I'll give Marty a call though." She flipped through a few more envelopes. "Funny how we never heard back from the insurance company on the claim. Did you finally get in touch with someone there?"

Sam felt his stomach curl in a knot. He knew what he had to do, but it was hard to step up to the plate and swing away.

"I did hear something," he started off slowly. "There was a letter. And a check."

"A check? You didn't tell me that." She turned to him, her expression expectant.

"Well, I didn't deposit it yet."

"Why not?" Something in his eyes told her. "Oh," she said. "How much is it for?"

He named the figure and took a breath, watching her face.

She looked confused. "That's the whole claim? Not just part, like for the house or our belongings?"

He nodded, pursing his lips. "Yes, that's it, the whole thing. It wasn't nearly as much as I expected."

"No . . . it wasn't, was it? It's not even close to the figure we talked about." She stood staring at him. He could tell she was in shock. "Can I see the letter? What did they say?"

"The letter is in the shop." He hadn't purposely left the letter there, but maybe he had done it subconsciously. When she saw the date, she would know how long he had kept if from her.

"Can't we protest it? Get a second opinion or something?"

"I've already started working on that, Jess. I've filled out all the papers and sent them in."

Her gaze narrowed. "I thought you said you just heard about this today, Sam."

"I didn't say that. I just said I didn't deposit the check yet. A lawyer told me it was better not to if we're going to argue with them."

"You spoke to a lawyer about this . . . and you're just telling me?"

"I got the letter a few days ago. I wanted to tell you, Jess. It never seemed like a good time, especially with you starting work again. I knew you would be upset."

"I am upset—about the insurance, and now, about you keeping this from me."

"I'm sorry," he said quietly. "It was hard for me to talk about it."

She swallowed hard, and he saw tears well up in her eyes. He wanted to go to her and put his arms around her. That's what he would normally do. But something stopped him. Something in the way she was holding herself so straight and still warned him off.

"That's not nearly enough to rebuild the house, is it?" she asked.

"No. It's not."

"What are we going to do? Where can we live?"

"Well, we have a few options. We could knock down the old house—they'll pay for that—and we can rebuild something different, smaller. Maybe a prefab. Those are very cost-effective, and they have some terrific styles now. Or we can just sell the land and find another house."

Jessica stared at him for a moment. Then she put her hands over her eyes and started to cry. "This can't be happening. . . . Why did all this have to happen to us, Sam? Our whole life has fallen apart, and it's not going to get any better."

Sam stepped over to her. He put his arms around her, and she leaned against him. He gently stroked her hair.

"It's a lot to think about, Jess. I could hardly handle it myself when I heard. We don't have to figure it all out right now," he said, trying to soothe her.

"It's just a house," he added in a soft voice. "We can't make it the measure of everything. We just have to deal with this and go on, try to make the best of it. I wish it were different for us, but—"

Jessica pulled back from him, brushing away her tears. "There you go again. Just . . . just steamrolling over my feelings. Can't I feel sad over this? Can't I feel angry?"

"I didn't mean that," he said quietly.

The truth was, he hated to see her wallow in those feelings. The way he looked at it, that didn't do any good at all.

"I don't know how to make the best of this, Sam. Maybe you do, but I think it's all pretty awful. I've been hanging on for a month now, believing we'll be able to rebuild and go back to our house. Now you tell me we can't. We might just knock it down and move away or . . . put up a cheap, prefab house that—" She couldn't finish, choking on her words.

He reached out to her. "Jess, calm down. It's going to be okay."

She pulled away and shook her head. She didn't say anything. She didn't have to. He knew what she was telling him. All his reassurances meant nothing. It wasn't going to be okay. That was their argument. And there was no answer to it.

Sam felt indescribably sad and lonely. He felt as if he had failed and disappointed her. Disappointed all of them.

"I would rebuild it if I could, Jessica. I would be out there right now, hammering away. You know that."

"I know you would," she said sympathetically. "Too bad for us, wishing can't make it all right again."

Sam didn't know what to say. He felt angry and hurt but didn't want to make the argument any worse than it already was.

He glanced at his watch. "I'm going to get the boys now. They should be ready to come—back." He stopped himself just before he used the word *home*.

This place wasn't their home and never would be. He didn't know where home was for them anymore. Now, with Jessica pulling away from him, it was getting harder and harder to figure that out.

AFTER DINNER, KATE WENT UPSTAIRS TO FIND A BOOK FOR JACK to read. Since the Christmas tree had arrived, they had moved their nightly story time into the living room, which now seemed to be Kate's favorite spot in the house.

Jack lingered in the kitchen, cleaning up from dinner with Julie. The phone rang and the answering machine picked up before he could get it.

"This is a message for Julie Newton. It's her brother, Peter, calling," a man's voice said.

Julie ran to the phone and picked it up. "Hello, Peter. How are you?"

Her voice was cheerful and warm, but Jack had come to know her well these past few weeks. He also heard an anxious edge in her tone. He had heard her talk to her brother before. There were clearly some strained feelings between them.

"Oh . . . well, I'm sorry about that. I did tell Marion it was going to be about ten boxes, and she said that wouldn't be a problem. . . ." Julie paused, listening. "I'd really rather you didn't put them in storage, Peter. That costs a lot of money. . . . Okay, just put them in the room we're going to use, and I'll deal with it when I get there."

Jack felt a flash of annoyance. Ten boxes. All she had in the world, except for the stuff she had packed in her car. And this guy was giving her a hard time.

Julie was still talking as he dried the last pot and put it away. He glanced at her as he left the room.

He really didn't want her to go to Long Island. He knew it was none of his business and he did not have the right to an opinion on what she did with her life. But he just didn't get a good feeling about the situation with her brother. He hated to think that she and Kate might feel unwelcome and unwanted there.

As he entered the living room, he spotted Kate crouched by the Christmas tree. She had a picture book stuck under her arm but was also busy with an armload of little packages, wrapped in tissue paper and straggly ribbons.

Jack had noticed the messily wrapped bundles piling up over the past few days. Teasing, he'd asked if she had left them, and she denied it. Now he had caught her red-handed.

He snuck up on tiptoe. She was so intent on her task, she didn't even hear him. He crept behind her, then grabbed her around the waist and lifted her high in the air. "Gotcha!"

Kate squealed, a happy sound. She squirmed but he kept a tight hold.

"Look what I caught. A real live Christmas elf, sneaking presents under the tree!"

She giggled and patted the top of his head. "Put me down, mister."

"Or else . . . what?"

She draped her arm around his shoulder. "I'm an elf. I know magic."

"Are you going to turn me into a toad or something?" He feigned a look of alarm.

"If you catch an elf, you get a wish, silly."

"A wish, huh? That's a good deal. What should I do?"

"Close your eyes and think of something you really, really, really want."

He stared at her, trying hard not to laugh and ruin it.

"Go ahead. Just do it," she ordered him.

He nodded obediently. "Okay. Here goes. I'm not that good at making wishes. But I'll try."

He closed his eyes and a vision flashed in his mind. And in his heart. An image that truly was his heart's desire. He didn't realize the soft smile that had formed on his face, until Kate spoke again.

"That's good. Keep your eyes closed, Jack," she reminded him. She counted out loud as she tapped him three times on the head. "Okay, you're done."

He opened his eyes and smiled at her. "Is that it?"

She nodded knowingly. "Your wish will come true," she promised. "Just don't tell anyone what it is, or that ruins it."

"I won't. Don't worry." He put her down and they walked over to the sofa to start the story.

He could never tell anyone what he had wished for—that Kate and Julie would stay with him forever. The image had flashed through his mind like a lightning bolt, thoroughly shocking him. Splitting his life in two parts: before and after they had arrived.

A short time later, Julie came in. She sat on the couch beside Kate and listened to the end of the story. They were taking a break from Lester tonight to read about a furry little creature named Frances. Frances wouldn't eat anything but bread and jam and was driving her parents crazy with her fussiness.

Jack wasn't sure what type of animal Frances and her family were supposed to be. Muskrats maybe? But the pictures and story were very charming, and Frances did remind him a bit of Kate.

When it was time to head for bed, Kate gave him a big hug. She had been more affectionate with him ever since she had been sick and he helped take care of her.

Julie was more affectionate with him, too, with a gentle touch from time to time. He treated her with the same casual affection, though he never managed to kiss her again.

He wanted to buy her something special for Christmas and give it to her before she left for Long Island. He had already wrapped the stuffed Lester toy and some books for Kate and had put them beneath the tree. He had a lot more shopping to do though, he realized. He could remember practically all the items on Kate's wish list and was going to make sure she had every one.

He guessed they would leave on Christmas Eve day, though Julie had not yet said precisely when. That was one week away. Too soon, he thought. He didn't want to let them go.

When Julie came back downstairs, she walked around the living room, picking up after Kate—the picture book, some shoes, and a sock.

"Kate is so excited for Christmas. She can hardly fall asleep." She sat on the other end of the sofa, near him, her arms full.

"It's fun when kids still believe in Santa Claus."

"I don't know how long this will last. But I'm trying to enjoy it. My brother's children are older than Katie. I hope they don't spoil it for her."

"That would be too bad, wouldn't it?" He caught her gaze and held it. "Do you really have to go there for Christmas? I mean, you could stay here for the holiday if you want to. I'm officially on Santa's route again. So that won't be a problem," he added, trying to keep the invitation lighthearted.

She looked surprised. She hadn't expected this. He wondered if he had waited too long to ask and now she had to keep the family commitment.

"That would be really nice, Jack," she said. "If it's not any trouble for you."

"Trouble for me? I'd just be alone all day. I don't want to put you in an awkward spot with your family, though." *No more awkward than it already is,* he added silently.

"My brother and sister-in-law won't mind at all if we come after Christmas," Julie told him. "They'll probably be relieved. The two of us moving in means they're going to have to rearrange their lives. I don't think they were too keen on rearranging their holidays, too."

"Then it's settled," Jack said. He had a feeling that he was smiling like a fool but he didn't care. "It will be fun to watch Kate open her gifts Christmas morning."

And I'd love to be with you, he wanted to say.

She already seemed to understand that, he thought, noticing the blush that rose in her cheeks. She caught his gaze and looked away again.

"Kate will be happy to stay. She wanted to make sure Santa stopped here," Julie reminded him.

"Don't worry. There will be so many gifts for her to open, she'll never doubt it."

"Jack, please. You don't have to buy out a toy store. I noticed you already left something for her. That's plenty."

Jack tried not to smile and give his plan away. "We'll see," was all he would say.

Julie picked up Kate's sweater and folded it on her lap. He knew she wasn't looking forward to leaving, but he just wasn't sure what to do about it.

He wasn't even sure what he felt for her; his tumbling emotions were so unexpected and overwhelming. He did know that here was one person, sitting beside him now, who accepted him for who he was. Who made no demands beyond what he was able to give, which at first was nothing.

Day by day, she and her daughter had pulled him up by his collar, out of his rut, and made him feel human again. Superhuman, sometimes. Julie was so impressed and appreciative when he made the slightest effort to help her. She and Kate made him look forward to waking up in the morning, to being connected to the world again. Julie had opened his heart after he had decided it was a locked door with a missing key.

She leaned over to pick up a doll from the floor, and he touched her shoulder. She turned and looked at him, a questioning look that he answered by brushing her hair back from her face.

He leaned closer and kissed her, softly on the cheek at first, then moved his mouth to her lips. She closed her eyes as he put his arms around her and held her closer.

He wasn't sure how long they stayed like that, kissing and holding each other in the magical glow of the Christmas tree.

Finally, Julie slowly pulled away. She rested her hand on his cheek and looked into his eyes a long moment.

"I'm glad about spending Christmas with you, Jack," she said quietly.

"Me, too." He smiled at her.

She seemed about to say something more but then just sighed. "I'd better go upstairs now," she said.

He nodded. "Sure . . . good night."

She kissed him quickly then moved out of the circle of his

embrace. His gaze followed her as she disappeared up the stairway, then he sat back and stared at the Christmas tree again.

He felt happy inside. As if a fireworks display were going off in his heart. It was still hard to accept that he might actually be in love with her. But if he wasn't, Jack didn't know what else he could call it.

Could he ever win her? In some rare, optimistic moments, he thought he could. She seemed to have feelings for him. Maybe not what he felt for her, but she seemed to like him, to feel some attraction.

He wasn't really that much older than her, he reflected. Five years. Was that so much?

But maybe Julie was just one of those people who aren't meant to stay. They drift into your life for a moment, do what they're meant to do, then go.

Like the Christmas tree, he thought, turning to look at it again. Its beauty and sparkling presence cheered up the house. But after the holiday, he would take it down and save the memory of its special glow in his heart.

CHAPTER TWELVE

～

*J*ESSICA HATED LEAVING HER CHRISTMAS SHOPPING TO the last minute. The stores were insanely crowded, and the items she found to fill requests were either the wrong size, the wrong color, or the wrong price.

This year, there was no way around it. On Saturday, just three days before Christmas, she and Sam headed to the mall with a list a mile long.

As they drove through the heavy traffic, she wished she had found time during the week to have made a start. But now that she was working full time, every spare minute was taken just keeping up with the basic household chores—keeping clean clothes in everyone's drawers and closets, and making quick dinners. Contrary to Sam's prediction that it would be easier to clean the small cabin, it was, in fact, harder to keep the place in order. There just wasn't enough space for everyone's belongings, and she was constantly struggling to reduce the messy piles.

It had also been hard to join this year's annual spending frenzy now that she knew the check from the insurance company would be so much smaller than they had expected. Sam had filed a protest to the claim, but it would take many more weeks until their forms were reviewed. She didn't hold out any great hopes that the situation would change. It was very hard to spend a lot of money on Christmas gifts when they didn't have much to spare.

They found their way inside the mall, and Jessica took out the list. "Where do you want to start?" she asked Sam.

"I don't know. Wherever you want. You have the list."

He usually had a list of his own and was much more excited about gift buying. She knew he felt the same concerns as she did about spending, but things had been strained between them ever since their argument on Monday night when he told her about the insurance claim.

She had tried to say she was sorry for possibly overreacting, but Sam had brushed off her apology. Her gesture hadn't changed his distant mood.

They hadn't talked again about all the decisions they now faced about the house. Or where they would live after the cabin. Perhaps it was best to wait until the holidays were over to sort all that out, she thought. It was difficult to think straight about these serious matters while they were surrounded by all the holiday cheer—so much of it seeming false and enforced.

But it would have helped some if she and Sam had just decided mutually to table all their troubles until the New Year. Instead, it felt as if they were locked in a stalemate, a frozen breakdown in communication. Though neither of them had ever mentioned the word *separation*, it was an estrangement. And, she was discovering, it felt awful being estranged from Sam.

Jessica stared around, trying to orient herself with the mall map and her list. "Um . . . let's go into the sports store, I guess. The boys both want football jerseys."

They quickly found the department that sold the jerseys, but she and Sam debated over whether to get the "official" team jerseys, which were overpriced Jessica thought, or the cheaper store brand. "These are fine," she insisted. "I don't think they'll notice the difference."

"Of course they will," Sam insisted, comparing the two shirts. "The cheap ones aren't even the right color."

"Yes, they are. The color looks the same to me." Why did he have to make this so difficult? "I think we should put money toward something more important, Sam."

"Let's skip the jerseys, then," he said. He was angry at her; she could tell by the deliberately blank look he always got whenever his temper frayed. "They won't like these, Jess. Just take my word, okay?"

"Why don't we get them hats?" she suggested. "Look, there are some Red Sox hats with the World Series patch. Don't you think they would like that?"

Sam picked up a hat and looked it over. "Nah, let's skip that. They didn't even ask for baseball hats. It's the middle of the winter."

She held her tongue and put the hat back on the display. She couldn't do anything right lately, could she.

They left the sports store without buying anything. Jessica was annoyed at the waste of time. Her head pounded with a huge headache, and she reached into her purse for some pain relievers.

"What's the matter?" Sam asked her.

"I have a headache."

"Maybe you need to eat something. It's getting late. Let's have lunch."

She looked up at him, her eyes flashing. "Lunch? We just got here. We have a zillion things to buy. I don't want to waste time eating lunch."

Sam's head snapped back, his eyes narrowed. "I get the point, Jessica. You don't have to bite my head off. The stores aren't going to run away, you know. Everything will still be here if we stop for a few minutes."

She let out a long breath, trying to get a grip on her patience. "I don't need to stop now. If you want some lunch, go ahead. We'll meet up later."

Sam frowned and dug his hands in his pockets. "I'll wait. What's next?"

"Janie. We're going to get her pajamas."

Sam gave her a look. "Kids hate to open pajamas. How about a toy or something?"

"Emily said she needs pajamas. We can get a stuffed animal to go with them, I guess."

Not that I wanted to buy two gifts for everyone, Jessica silently added.

They walked into a children's store and eventually compromised with a pair of slippers that had stuffed animal heads on the feet. More expensive than Jessica would have liked, but cheaper than buying two gifts.

"Okay, one down, one hundred to go," she mumbled to herself, crossing a single name off her list.

She had stopped in front of a jewelry store. The store was open to the mall and she stood right in front of a large glass case of glittering jewels.

A pair of earrings caught her eye, lustrous pearls set on gold wires with a small diamond at the top of each setting. She had lost so much jewelry in the fire, she didn't even want to think about it—heirloom pieces that had been passed down to her and lovely pieces of jewelry Sam had given her throughout their marriage.

Sam stood beside her and peered into the case. "Something caught your eye?"

"The pearl earrings," she murmured. "The ones on the left, toward the bottom. Aren't they beautiful?"

"They are," Sam agreed. "I can see you in those, Jess. They're perfect for you."

Jessica sighed. The price of the pearl earrings was so high, it seemed unthinkable.

She tugged Sam's sleeve. "Let's go," she said curtly.

He looked up at her but didn't budge. "I want to get them for you. You deserve something nice after all we've been through."

"That's good of you, Sam, really. But I thought we weren't buying each other gifts this year. Remember?"

After going over their shopping list, particularly the items they wanted to buy for the boys, they had agreed to forgo big gifts for each other this year. It was more important to give the boys a good Christmas. Jessica wanted to stick to their plan. It didn't take much to throw her husband off course, she noticed.

"You don't have to get me anything," he said quickly. "But let me get this for you."

"I don't want the earrings, Sam. Honestly. They're too expensive."

Sam lingered in front of the jeweler's window. She tugged his sleeve. "Sam? Let's go into the bookstore. I need to find a book my mother asked for."

"If Lillian asked for it, you'd better try a rare book dealer," he quipped.

"Very funny. At least she gave me a specific suggestion."

"Come on, Jess. I know you like them. Let's just go in and you can try them on."

She knew he meant well. But he was so . . . immature sometimes. So impractical. Why did she always have to be the level-headed one?

"I don't need such an expensive gift this year, Sam. I don't want to try them on. You know we can't afford it. Why even tempt me?"

He looked hurt, his excited expression curdling before her eyes. "I just want to make you happy, Jess. Is there something wrong with that, too?" He shook his head, looking away from her. "I can't do anything right anymore, can I?"

"Sam, I didn't mean it that way. You know I didn't. . . ." She reached out for his hand.

He pulled away, dug his hand into his jacket pocket, and pulled out the keys to the SUV. "Here. Take these. I'm leaving."

When Jessica wouldn't take them, he dropped them in the shopping bag with Janie's slippers.

Then he quickly started walking away from her.

Jessica followed, walking fast to keep up. "Sam, where are you going?" she called after him.

She felt people looking at her. She hated that.

Why did he have to do this to her—today of all days?

"Sam . . . wait. Please wait. I need to talk to you!"

He glanced at her over his shoulder, then turned and kept walking.

She stopped and watched him disappear in the crowd. She let out a long frustrated sigh, suddenly furious with him.

Fine, act out like a big baby. Take the bus. I don't care.

Jessica stalked off in the opposite direction. She was so mad, she could barely see straight, and her head pounded.

Now she was stuck with doing all the Christmas shopping, too. *Thanks a lot, pal,* she huffed to herself.

She stared around at the overdone decorations and garish displays. The herd of shoppers, jostling each other as they rushed from store to store. The irritating sights and annoying music made her feel all the more miserable.

How had she and Sam wandered into this ugly place? Jessica couldn't understand it. Even worse, she had no idea how to find her way back again.

On Sunday morning Jessica told Sam she wasn't going to church. She had too much housework to catch up on and all the gifts to wrap. Sam was about to offer to help with both chores, but he was still mad at her from their argument about the earrings. She hadn't offered an apology or even tried to talk about it. Then again, he hadn't brought it up; he didn't think he could without starting another fight.

"I can't take the kids to church either," he told her. "I have to work."

"On Sunday? You never go to your shop on Sunday."

"I've got a lot of furniture projects that people want finished for the holiday. Christmas Eve is tomorrow, Jess," he reminded her.

"Believe me, I know all about it," she said glumly. "I promised your sister I would bring pecan pies. But there's something wrong with this oven. The temperature isn't right."

"We'll just get a cake at the bakery. Why fuss?"

Jessica sighed. "That's a solution, I suppose. It just feels like I'm in a bad place when I can't even bake one pie for Christmas."

She and Sam were usually the ones who gave the annual family Christmas Eve party. It was a huge event, but Jessica had always loved preparing for it. She was a wonderful cook and a terrific hostess who knew how to decorate the house beautifully and add all the right touches.

Sam guessed that she was thinking about those parties and missed entertaining this year, despite all the work and bother. They had been invited to his sister Molly's for Christmas Eve, and to Jessica's mother's house for Christmas Day. Molly's party would be totally over the top, he knew, and at Lillian's, it would be hard to tell the day was different from any other.

Sam was not looking forward to either get-together, but he knew the boys would enjoy themselves, and it was important for them, most of all, to be with their family on the holidays.

This year, Christmas was something he just wanted to get over with. He knew that was the wrong attitude—not the Christian attitude, for sure. But that was just the way he felt.

He took one last sip of his coffee and put the mug in the kitchen sink. "Okay, I'm leaving, Jess. I'll see you later."

"Sam, aren't you forgetting something?"

Jessica looked up at him from where she now stood, folding a basket of laundry. He thought, for a moment, that she meant that he hadn't kissed her good-bye.

He felt bad. He always kissed her hello and good-bye, no matter how angry they got with each other. He walked toward her. Was she ready to talk things over and make up?

She pointed at the dog's crate. "You'd better take Sunny. The boys are going to be out all day at a basketball game, and I have to do some more shopping."

Oh, so she just meant the dog. It wasn't what he thought at all. He let out a frustrated sigh, picked up the big dog crate with one hand, and lugged it out of the cabin.

In his shop, he felt a bit calmer. He liked the quiet space and the solitude. He put on his apron and got back to work on the set of antique chairs. They had to be ready by tomorrow. It wasn't a big project and he couldn't charge for his real time, but the client was important. Mrs. Madeleine Norris was on the board of the Cape Light Historical Society. Her own Victorian house on Mariner's Way was a jewel of the historical register and a favorite stop on the annual walking tour.

The gracious old house was also perennially in need of repair. Mrs. Norris had been dangling the possibility of a substantial job—rebuilding the porch in the spring—but so far had only offered the chairs. Sam considered the smaller furniture repair both a favor and an investment.

At about noon, when he was thinking about breaking for lunch and walking the dog, he heard a knock on the shop door. He opened it to find Reverend Ben, wearing his big down jacket and earmuffs.

"Reverend Ben, come in. It's getting cold out there."

"A little colder than it should be for this time of year," Ben agreed. He tugged off his gloves and rubbed his hands together.

"Do you track down all your wayward sheep on Sunday afternoon, or am I a special case?" Sam asked, with a slightly guilty smile.

"You're always a special case for me, Sam. Very special," Ben said warmly. He sat on a stool near Sam's workbench and watched

Sam return to his project. "I was out shopping and saw the lights on. You're not usually here on Sunday."

"No, I'm not," Sam agreed.

Sam's shop took up one half of a barnlike building behind the Bramble Antique Store, which was on the first floor of an old house. The store's owner, Grace Hegmen, and her father, Digger, lived on the floors above. Half the barn was used by Grace for storage and the other half she rented out to Sam.

"I have to deliver some work tomorrow. An important client. She needs these chairs back for the holidays."

"People want their homes looking perfect this time of year." Ben gazed down at the worktable then picked up a piece of wood Sam had started carving. "This is pretty. Is it going to be an angel?"

Sam nodded, keeping his eyes on the joint of a chair leg he was gluing back together.

"When Jess and I got married, I made her a set like that for our first Christmas. She put them on the mantel every year with pine branches. I was trying to make her new ones, but I don't think they'll be finished on time."

He hadn't focused very hard on finishing the project, he realized. He had been distracted by the house and the insurance claims and by his arguments with Jessica, first about the insurance and yesterday about the earrings. A general tension about everything, he reflected. Sam could do all kinds of work for pay under pressure, but when it came to his own artistic projects he had to be in a calm frame of mind.

Ben looked over the angel once more and set it down. "How is Jessica? How did she take the news about the insurance settlement?"

"I couldn't tell her right away," Sam admitted. "But I did tell her on Monday. She didn't take it very well. We had sort of an argument. We're having some problems right now," he added. "We went shopping yesterday and had another big fight in the mall."

"What did you fight about?" Ben asked curiously.

Sam put a clamp on the chair leg to hold it in place while the glue set. "I wanted to buy her some earrings she saw in a jewelry store window. She lost so much jewelry in the fire, lots of pieces from her family that we can't replace. I thought she deserved a nice gift after all we've been through. But she got really mad at me," he said, still surprised at his wife's reaction. "As if I wasn't thinking at all about our problems and responsibilities. That's all I think about, Ben.

"Of course I'm worried about money and what we're going to do, where we're going to end up," he continued. "But I just wanted to make her happy. Is that so awful?"

Ben shook his head sympathetically. "I understand. You were just trying to do something nice for her and she misunderstood. It sounds as though she's so worried, it's clouding her perspective. It's coloring everything she sees."

"It makes everything I do or say come out wrong. That's how it seems to me."

"This is a tough time for both of you," Ben said. "One person has to bend, and one person has to step back and take control—before things go too far."

Sam set his jaw. He knew Reverend Ben would say something like that, counseling him to take the first step and apologize. As far as he could see, he had nothing to apologize for. Why did he always have to make that move toward her?

"I tried to talk things out with her the other night when I told her about the insurance claim. She just wouldn't listen to me."

"Maybe that wasn't a good time, Sam. She must have been very shocked by your news."

"Yes, she was," Sam admitted. Okay, so that wasn't entirely fair of him.

"Forgive her for whatever she did or said, Sam. She's in a lot of pain," Ben reminded him.

"I understand that. But she's not the only one. I thought we had a strong relationship, Reverend. I thought we had a really great marriage, and if something bad ever happened to us, I was sure we would stick together and work it out, not pull away from each other." He set the chair down and picked up another one. "I guess my marriage just isn't what I thought it was. We were happy when things were going smoothly and we had all the comforts. Anybody would be. But once that was taken away, our relationship began to fall apart. I think that says it all."

He and Jessica didn't always agree. But Sam had never doubted her love before. They were very different, yet that had been part of their attraction to each other, what kept things interesting, he thought. Now all he could see were their differences. And he didn't feel as if she loved him, or even respected him anymore. He felt as if all that had been lost in the fire. Or very soon after.

Ben stood up, holding his hat and gloves in his hand. "Make up with her, Sam. Be a peacemaker. That's your nature, you know. Your gift," Ben reminded him. "It's Christmas, a time to reconcile and put aside grievances. This is an especially important Christmas for your family. Show your children that bad things can happen, but life can get better, too. Not worse. Don't let this distance between the two of you grow any wider," he warned.

Sam guessed Reverend Ben meant that if he and Jessica didn't work things out, they were heading toward divorce.

Once Sam would have said that very idea was impossible. Now, he wasn't so sure.

He glanced at the minister, not knowing what to say. He wasn't going to make any eager promises this time.

"I know what you're trying to tell me," he said finally. "I'll think about it."

Ben nodded and pulled on his cap. "Fair enough. . . . Oh, one more thing." He picked up the wooden angel again. "You really ought to finish this and give it to her. It will help a lot. I guarantee it."

Sam took the sculpture in his hand. "I'll try."

"That's all any of us can do."

Ben left and Sam got to work on the set of chairs once more. The unfinished angel kept catching his eye. He would try with Jessica, he told himself. But she had to try, too. Or he couldn't say what their future would hold.

AFTER VISITING SAM'S WORKSHOP, BEN DECIDED HIS ERRANDS in the village were completed. Carrying two shopping bags of gifts, mainly for his wife, he walked back down Main Street to his car. He had parked in front of the Clam Box and though he was hungry, for once he didn't go inside. He knew Carolyn had a nice meal waiting for him at home.

The parsonage was not very far from the village, and he was home in a matter of minutes. He let himself in and hung his coat on the coat tree near the front door. He heard Carolyn in the kitchen, talking on the phone. When he walked in he saw that she was also in the middle of baking something, all the ingredients and the cookbook laid out on the counter.

"Yes, dear. I wrote it all down. Are you sure you don't want your father to come pick you up? Or maybe Rachel? She would drive down to meet you, I'm sure. . . . "

Ben's senses were alerted by the one-sided conversation. "Is that Mark?" he asked.

Carolyn nodded, smiling. "He finally got a flight in from Portland. He'll be in tomorrow night, very late." She turned back to the phone. "Your father just came in. Here, he wants to say hello. . . ."

Ben stepped closer and took the phone. "How did you ever manage that? I thought you said it was hopeless."

"I'm not sure. Mom just told me she's been praying on it," his son teased.

Ben had been praying on it, too, if the truth be told. But he didn't want to admit that right now. Not over the phone.

"Well, your mother has some sway. I always said that," he joked back. "Thanks for trying so hard. We're all very happy you'll be here."

"So am I," Mark admitted. "I didn't get to tell Mom but . . . Moira is coming with me. I hope that's all right?"

Ben felt like the wind had been knocked out of him for a moment and struggled for a quick recovery. Mark had mentioned that he was seeing a young woman he had met at school. But Ben didn't realize it was serious. Mark was not the type to bring his girl-friend home to meet the family unless it was very serious.

"Of course it's all right. We have plenty of room. Your mother will be thrilled." He glanced at Carolyn.

She was measuring out flour and pouring it into a big bowl, her reading glasses balanced on the edge of her nose. "I'll be thrilled about what?"

Ben shook his head. "I'll tell you in a minute," he said, covering the phone a moment. He turned his attention back to Mark. "Can't wait to meet her," he said to his son.

Carolyn put her measuring cup down and stared at him. He avoided her intensely curious look.

"Great," Mark was saying. "Listen, I've got to run, but Mom has all the information. If there are any delays, I'll call you."

"That's fine. Have a safe trip. We can't wait to see you," Ben added.

"Me too," Mark said happily before ending the call.

Ben set the receiver back in place. Carolyn stood inches away. "What were you talking about? Is Mark bringing someone home with him?"

Ben nodded. "Yes, he is. His girlfriend, Moira. Just like him to give us five minutes' notice."

Carolyn practically gasped. "Moira? She's coming here for Christmas? Do you think they're engaged?"

Ben sighed. "Well, I wouldn't jump to conclusions, dear. He seemed serious about that last girl, Erin, remember?"

"Oh, yes, Erin. She was very sweet. But I wasn't surprised when they broke up," Carolyn added, turning back to check her recipe.

Ben had to agree. Mark had spent last Christmas with Erin's family in California, and she had visited Cape Light last summer. Ben had found her charming and bright. But he also had a feeling she wasn't the one for Mark. His intuition had eventually proven right.

He wondered what Moira would be like. Was she going to be the one? Would Mark have big news for the family?

"Much as I would like to, I can't call back and ask him," Ben said with a laugh. "I guess we just have to wait and see."

"I suppose so. But it is fun to think about." Carolyn cracked an egg and added it to the batter. Ben could see she was already getting excited about a wedding.

Anything was possible with Mark. Ben knew that by now. Mark had never given them much trouble in high school, though he had always been intellectually challenging as a teenager, questioning the value of church and even the belief in God. Ben had been able to handle that. The truth was, he enjoyed those philosophical debates most of the time. But once Mark left for college, things changed. He began to challenge everything. To challenge and doubt. He lost his center, his very foundation. He dropped out of school after his first year and roamed around the country. Sometimes they didn't even know where he was living or how he was surviving.

Then, about five years ago, Carolyn fell ill after suffering a stroke and Mark finally came home. It was a difficult reunion, but the family finally worked out their issues and grievances. Mark stayed in Cape Light for a while, working at a bookstore in Newburyport, then decided to start school again. He went out to Portland, Oregon, and took up environmental studies. Coming to the end of his four-year degree, he had decided to pursue a career in environmental law.

Ben was proud of him. Proud of their family, too, for surviving those challenging times. If Mark was engaged to this girl, it would be something to celebrate. A real Christmas surprise.

Carolyn returned to her recipe, measuring out a spoonful of vanilla. "We'll just have to see when he gets here, I guess. I wish he had given me a little warning. I would have fixed up the guest room a bit."

"Oh, don't worry dear. Any girl Mark chooses won't be fussy about decorating, believe me." Mark was remarkably nonmaterialistic, and Ben couldn't imagine him choosing anyone much different.

Carolyn laughed in agreement. "You have a good point." She put down her measuring spoons and stared at him. "I'm a bit in shock. At first, he wasn't coming at all, and now he calls, and not only will he be here, but he's bringing a girl who could be his future wife."

"Yes, it's a lot to process." Ben sighed happily. "It's all good though, right?"

"Yes, all good," Carolyn repeated. "I'll have to get her some gifts to open—little things, perfume or something."

Leave it to his wife to think of buying gifts for a girl she'd never met and had not even invited. But it did seem the right thing to do, Ben realized. They wanted Mark's girlfriend to feel comfortable and welcome, whatever the status of the relationship and especially if they were about to announce their engagement.

"I bought a few odds and ends in town today," Ben said. "Some small things for my secretary and Rachel," he explained. He still liked to choose a gift or two for their daughter, though Carolyn was in charge of most of the shopping. "Maybe you can find a gift in there."

"Oh good. I'd rather not go to the stores again tomorrow." Carolyn gave her husband a curious glance. "Is that why you're back late from church?"

"Yes, I did a little shopping and I stopped to see Sam Morgan. He wasn't in church and I noticed the lights on in his shop."

"How are the Morgans doing?" Carolyn asked with concern.

"Not too well right now, I'm afraid," Ben admitted. He knew whatever he told Carolyn would be kept in strictest confidence, but he still hesitated to disclose personal information members of the congregation had entrusted to him. "They're having a hard time. There's a lot to figure out, and it will take a while before things are back to normal for them. Their relationship is definitely feeling the strain," he confided.

"Oh, that's too bad. They always seemed so happy together. So . . . in love. So crazy about those boys," she added.

"They are in love," Ben replied. "But marriages go through hard times—foggy weather when you can't see what's really there, right under your nose. We went through our difficult years," he reminded her.

"Yes, we did," she agreed. "More than some, maybe."

Carolyn didn't like to talk about her bouts with depression, which were, at this point in her life, very much under control. And Ben didn't like to remind her of the darkest time of that battle, which had certainly contributed to Mark's rebellion.

"Every marriage has challenges," he reminded her. "And here we are. Totally content, about to celebrate Christmas with our two children, two grandchildren, and possibly a future daughter-in-law."

Carolyn laughed, her mood brightening once more. "We do have a lot to be thankful for. I feel sorry for the Morgans, though. This time of the year is hard when your family is in such disarray."

"I had some serious talks with Sam. I've tried to give him some advice. I wish there was something more I could do for him—for all of them," Ben confessed.

Carolyn nodded sympathetically and touched his shoulder. "You have a difficult job, Ben. Everyone tells you their problems. It's hard not to feel responsible."

"I know I'm not responsible, but it is hard to feel helpless sometimes. To want to do more, but not know what I can or should do."

"I'm sure you've been a big support to Sam. I don't think he confides in many people. Just be there for him. You may have already helped more than you know."

Ben nodded. He patted her hand that now rested on his shoulder. "I hope so," he said quietly. "I really do hope so."

THE NEXT DAY, CHRISTMAS EVE, THE BOYS WERE OFF FROM school but Jessica had to work until three. Sam arranged to leave the kids with his mother, who was staying home all day to cook for Molly's party.

Marie Morgan's house was already fragrant with the scent of cookies and pastries when Sam dropped the boys off that morning.

"Are you working all day, Sam?" his mother asked as she hugged her grandsons. "What time will you pick up the boys?"

"I'm just in the shop for a few hours this morning. Then I need to do some shopping. Jessica will be off early, Mom. She'll get the boys around three, when the bank closes."

His mother watched from the door as he climbed back into his SUV. "We'll see you tonight, then," she called to him.

"That's right. See you at Molly's."

Alone in his shop, Sam began to put a few finishing touches on Mrs. Norris's chairs. He rubbed the wood with a finishing oil, then stepped back, waiting for it to dry before applying a second coat.

The wooden angel on his workbench stared up at him. He picked it up and looked it over. He had worked on it awhile the night before then had put it aside. It wasn't that far from being finished, he decided.

He picked up his tools and finished it off quickly, then rubbed the edges with wax and applied a whitewash stain. The resistance of the wax gave the finish an aged, weathered look, one that he knew Jessica liked.

While the angel dried he turned back to the chairs and applied the second coat of oil. By noon, everything was ready to load into his SUV, just in time to make the delivery he had promised to Mrs. Norris.

Sam arrived at the Norris residence and found the place swarming with caterers and servants. They all seemed to be frantically preparing for a huge Christmas Eve party. Sam guessed it was no easy task for them. Madeleine Norris was known all over town for her good taste and high standards. He wondered who would win in a match for being the most particular—Mrs. Norris or his mother-in-law? That contest would be too close to call, Sam decided.

He lined up the chairs in the spacious foyer, and Mrs. Norris examined each one carefully. "You did a fine job," she said at last. "I had a feeling I could trust you."

"I'm glad you're pleased," Sam said. He had jumped one hurdle today; only a half dozen more to go. After he collected his fee and wished Mrs. Norris a happy holiday, he jumped back into the SUV and headed for the mall.

Just walking down the row of stores brought back the bad feelings of arguing with Jessica. He tried hard to put them aside and focus on the giving feeling that Christmas was supposed to inspire. He bought the football jerseys his boys wanted and a few other gifts for them.

Finally, he came to the jewelry store, where the pearl earrings were still in the window. Sam stood a moment, unsure of what to do. He wanted very badly to get them for Jessica. He just didn't want to make her even angrier at him. It wasn't as if he was trying to prove a point, but he did believe she deserved a special gift this year.

A pair of earrings, even diamonds the size of ice cubes, could never make up for all they had lost. But the impulse sprang from his heart, because he loved her. Sam knew this was how he wanted to show her that. He just had to find a way to make her understand.

Following the impulse of his heart, Sam went into the store.

A short time later he headed back to the cabin. It was after three, and he expected to find Jessica and the boys there, getting ready for the party at Molly's house.

The cabin looked dark and empty, and the moment he opened

the door, he heard Sunny whining in her crate. Sam had had to make so many stops today that he'd left the dog at home.

Now he looked around the cabin, wondering if Jessica had returned after work and gone out again. A few of the gifts were gone from under the tree, he noticed. But maybe she had started packing up the car with the boxes they needed to bring to Molly's?

Sam had a bad feeling down in the pit of his stomach. He couldn't say why.

Then he saw a note on the counter. Had they gone ice skating again? It would be odd of Jess to do that right before a big party. But she had been acting oddly lately, that was for sure.

He picked up the note and read it quickly.

Sam—
I've taken the boys to the Cape for the night. We'll be back tomorrow morning. I need to get away for a while. I just can't face the family tonight at Molly's house. I know you wanted to stay and be with all of them, and I didn't want to argue with you. I'm tired of us fighting so much lately. I just need a break and hope you understand.
Love, Jessica

To the Cape? What in the world did that mean? Cape Cod was a big place. She could be anywhere. On Christmas Eve, no less. He stood there, stunned, unable to believe she had just packed up the kids and run off, leaving him alone.

He grabbed the phone and punched in her cell number. The phone rang and rang, but Jessica didn't pick up. Her voice mail picked up but Sam was so angry, he couldn't say anything.

Sam paced the small cabin, feeling as if he were about to

explode. He just wanted to smash something. He considered punching his fist into the kitchen counter, but decided not to bust up the place, since it belonged to his pal Luke. And it probably wasn't a good idea to risk breaking his hand.

The dog was barking now, desperate yips.

He walked over to the crate to let her out and spotted a Christmas card on the floor. He picked it up and stared at it. It was the card from Jessica's college friend, Marty Graham. Sam knew in a flash—that was where she had gone. Jessica had taken Marty up on her invitation and brought the kids to the Grahams' house on Cape Cod.

Marty had written her phone number on the bottom of the note. Sam was positive that if he called, he would learn she was expecting Jessica and the boys.

He hooked the dog to her leash and grabbed his cell phone on the way out the door. While he walked the dog around under the trees, he dialed the Grahams' number. A woman picked up and said hello.

"Hi, is this Marty? It's Sam Morgan. Jessica's husband."

"Oh, Sam. How are you?"

"I'm good, Marty," he replied, though he felt anything but. "I was just wondering if Jessica got there yet."

He waited. This woman was either going to give him the answer he expected or act as if he had lost his mind.

"Jess isn't here yet, Sam. But she just called from the Bourne Bridge. She's making good time."

"Oh, that's good." Sam felt pleased with himself for figuring out the mystery.

"Shall I tell her you called?"

"Um . . . sure. I just wanted to know she got there safely," he added.

"We were sorry to hear you couldn't come, too, Sam. Jess said someone in your family is sick and you can't leave town?"

Sam didn't know what to say to that. His impulse was to tell Marty the truth. No one was ailing—just their marriage.

But he didn't want to embarrass Jessica.

"Things looked grim for a while, but they're better now. You can tell her that when she gets there," he added.

"Oh, I will," Marty said. "Well, I hope you have a good holiday, Sam, and a very happy new year!"

"Same to you, Marty," Sam said, thinking he would soon be able to wish Jessica's friend a happy holiday face-to-face.

After they hung up, Sam put Sunny in the cabin and ran up to New Horizons' main building with Marty's card in hand. Luke had given him a key so that the boys could use the library and computers when the building was closed. Sam went to the library, booted up a computer, and typed Marty's Cape Cod address into a map site.

The house was in Brewster, an easy town to reach. He printed out directions from Cape Light and hurried back to the cabin.

He took a few minutes to clean himself up and change from his work clothes into a decent sweater and new jeans.

Then he fed Sunny dinner. It didn't feel right to put the poor pup back in her crate again, after she had been cooped up all day. On the other hand, Sam didn't think it was a good idea to take the dog with him to the Grahams' house.

He finally decided to give Sunny a few chew toys and leave her loose in the cabin. She would probably just jump on a bed and go to sleep.

"Be a good girl, Sunny," he told the dog as he left the cabin. "Santa will bring you a surprise."

Then Sam climbed into the SUV and headed for the highway.

* * *

THERE HAD BEEN A RUSH OF CUSTOMERS AT THE TREE FARM DURING the day, the typical last-minute herd that always showed up on Christmas Eve. But by late afternoon, Jack found he simply didn't care anymore. His mind was not focused on selling out his stock. His thoughts were up in the house, where Julie was already working on their Christmas Day dinner and baking cookies with Kate.

He took out a piece of plywood and painted a sign:

Free Trees & All The Trimmings.
Take what you want. Merry Christmas!

Julie came outside just as he was nailing the sign to the shed. "Jack, I can't believe you," she said with a laugh.

"I told you I was going to give the trees away."

"Yes, you did say that, I remember."

But that declaration had been made under very different circumstances. Back then he had said it in anger and defeat. This time, his heart was open and grateful. He was happy to give away whatever he had, because he had found so much more.

As they walked back to the house, Jack slung his arm over Julie's shoulder, and she slipped her arm around his waist. Their steps fell into the same rhythm.

Darkness had fallen and white stars dotted the clear, inky blue sky. A sliver of silver moon hung on the horizon.

"A perfect night for sleigh riding. Up in the sky," Jack said.

"Tell that to someone inside. She's been glued to the weather channel since noon."

Jack smiled. It had been a long day for Julie. There was no

preschool, and Kate had been bouncing off the walls all day. Julie could hardly wait to eat dinner and put Kate to bed, she privately told him. Jack could hardly wait either. He was looking forward to some time alone with Julie.

Julie had prepared a light meal for dinner, soup and sandwiches, and they ate by the fire in the living room. As she served the food, she seemed worried that Jack wouldn't like the idea. But he thought it was fun, like an indoor picnic.

After dinner, Kate led the adults in Christmas carols she had learned at school. She made her voice very deep for the "ho-ho-ho" verse of "Old St. Nick," and Jack nearly laughed out loud the first time he heard her.

The song reminded Jack of a tradition he had had with David when his son was young and still believed in Santa. Now he took out an atlas stored in his office and turned on the radio. Sure enough, a local station was tracking Santa's travels, and Jack showed Kate just where the sleigh was on the world map. Flying somewhere over Norway just then, the radio announcer reported.

"It takes a long time to fly around the entire world. Even on a magic sleigh," Kate told Jack.

"Yes, it does. But Santa will be here tonight while you're sleeping, don't worry."

"That reminds me, it's time for bed. Santa can't come if you're still awake," Julie said.

"Okay, but we need to leave a plate of cookies and some milk for him," Kate reminded her mother.

"I almost forgot. Let's go get some."

Julie and Kate returned quickly. Kate carefully carried a plate of cookies, and Julie held a cup of milk. Kate put everything on the brick skirt of the fireplace. "Right where he can see it when he comes in," she said.

"Good idea," Jack agreed. Chocolate chips again, his favorite. He might have to support the cause by eating them.

"Do you want a story tonight?" Jack asked. His heart ached a little, realizing this could be the last time he shared the adventures of Lester and made the "rabbit voice."

Surprising both the adults, Kate shook her head. "I don't think so. . . . Can Jack come upstairs and tuck me into bed, too, Mommy?"

Julie glanced over at him. "If he wants to."

"I would be honored," he answered quietly.

When Kate was washed and dressed in her nightgown, Julie called to Jack, and he came in and sat on the edge of the girl's bed. Kate was already snuggled under the covers, with the blanket pulled up to her chin.

"I know it might be hard for you to fall asleep tonight," Jack told her. "But just close your eyes and think of something happy. And morning will be here before you know it."

Kate nodded. She did look sleepy. Julie kissed her cheek and then Jack bent down and did the same. Kate closed her eyes, her breathing already slow and even.

Julie turned off the light, but Jack stood there a moment, watching Kate in the dark.

Julie tugged his sleeve and tilted her head to the door. He followed her out of the room, holding the precious image in his mind.

Julie quietly shut Kate's door, something she almost never did. "I don't want her to hear me setting up her presents," she explained on the stairway.

"Right, good idea. I have a few for her, too," Jack whispered.

They spent the next hour retrieving gifts from various hiding spots around the house. When Jack finally carried up a pink bike from the basement, Julie stood with her hands pressed to her face, her expression one of complete disbelief.

"Jack! What did you do? You were much too extravagant. You can't give her all these things. You have to take some of it back."

He was secretly pleased at her outrage. It just went to show that he'd done well, he thought.

She couldn't scold him too loudly, either, at the risk of waking Kate. That was in his favor, too.

He walked over to Julie and put his hands on her waist, pulling her closer. "There are a few for you under there, too. They're not all for Kate."

She tried to keep a stern expression, but he saw he was wearing her down. "Jack, you're too generous. You're too good to us. You're making it very hard for me to—"

She stopped mid-sentence. "I didn't get you that much," she said sadly.

Then he felt bad, too. He hadn't meant to outdo or embarrass her. "You didn't have to get me anything," he insisted. "You've already given me so much. You and Kate . . ."

He wanted to say more, but he didn't dare. His heart was so full, he could hardly speak. He didn't know what else to do but kiss her. She moved, willingly, into his arms and he felt her return his kiss with a wave of emotion that nearly swept him off his feet.

Then she pulled away and pressed her face to his chest. "I can hear your heart beat," she said quietly.

It was beating out of control. He was sure people could hear it all the way in town.

He stroked her back and touched her hair. He inhaled the sweet scent of her.

"No . . . I was mistaken," she said quietly. She looked up at him a moment. "That wasn't your heart. It was Santa's reindeer, on the roof. I think he's here at last. We'd better leave or he won't come in."

Jack nodded, feeling a wistful, sweet yearning for her. She was so wonderful. He had never thought he could feel this way about another woman, after Claire. But he did now.

Why did he have to feel it for a woman who was about to leave him to start a new life? He couldn't ask her to take things further. That wouldn't be fair to either of them.

Finally, he sighed and released her. "We've done everything right. We can't mess up now," he said.

Julie just nodded and they parted quickly.

Julie went upstairs and Jack unplugged the tree lights and cleared up the incriminating evidence from the living room. Then he ate most of the cookies and sipped some milk, leaving just enough crumbs on the plate for a convincing display.

The stage was set. Santa had come and gone, unloading most of his sleigh in Jack's living room.

CHAPTER THIRTEEN

‿✦

𝒥ESSICA FOUND MARTY GRAHAM'S HOUSE IN BREWSTER
easily. There wasn't much traffic once she turned off the
main highway and crossed onto the Cape.

She reached the town of Brewster at about six. She knew Molly's party was just about starting back in Cape Light. She felt no
regrets about missing it. All she was really missing out on was being
the object of everyone's attention—and pity. She wondered if Sam
was there alone. That thought made her feel a pang of regret, but
not enough to turn around and go home.

Marty greeted her happily and showed the boys to a spacious
family room, where her own children were watching a huge, flat
screen TV.

Jessica followed Marty to the great room, which was indeed
enormous. A Christmas tree stood in front of a tall cathedral window, and a side table held hors d'oeuvres and cocktails. Everything

was perfectly arranged and displayed. Jessica helped herself to an hors d'oeuvre then took a seat on the large sectional sofa that faced the fireplace. She couldn't help feeling that at any minute *Architectural Digest* might swoop in for a photo shoot.

"Dinner's being catered by the Blue Door," Marty told her. "It's one of the best restaurants in town. And dessert is coming from La Patisserie, that incredible bakery I took you to last time you were here. I special-ordered a Bouche de Noel for us."

"That sounds great," Jessica said, wondering why she couldn't feel more enthusiastic. The Bouche de Noel was a fantastic chocolate cake that looked like a tree log and was a holiday tradition in France. Jessica knew all about them because Molly made one every year for the family.

Beyond those special touches, though, there wasn't much to indicate the holiday. Marty had no other guests coming besides Jessica and the boys. It promised to be a quiet evening.

Driving there, Jessica had thought that was exactly what she wanted. But now that she was here, she wasn't so sure. What had she done? What was Sam thinking right now? He had called on her cell phone, she knew, but hadn't left a message.

"Sam called," Marty said suddenly, as if reading her mind. "He said to tell you to call when you arrived and let him know you got here safely. His relative in the hospital? He said things looked grim, but they're much better. Isn't that great?"

Jessica nodded, not knowing how to respond.

So Sam had figured it out. He was probably furious. But what was that bit about his relative—sarcasm or some kind of coded message?

Jessica considered calling Sam's cell, to let him know they were all right, then got distracted by Marty's flow of conversation.

". . . the bathrooms and kitchen were a disaster, but the property was exactly what we wanted, and there was plenty of room to expand. . . ."

"It's really very lovely," Jessica said.

Classical music played softly on a sound system. The decor was sleek and modern, the couches and rugs in tones of gray and pale blue. The fireplace, edged by a gray marble mantel, was lit but seemed to provide little warmth. Jessica's eye was drawn to the tree. All the decorations were white and gold—long gold ribbons and white and gold ornaments, with a golden star on top and small white lights tucked in the branches. It was all incredibly tasteful, but it made Jessica miss her own family's tree, the one they put up before the fire, with its colorful mix of ornaments, each one unique and with a story to tell. Even the tree in the cabin with Tyler's paper snowflakes seemed more personal—and somehow more genuinely festive—than this one.

Marty's husband, Kevin, walked in with a tray of drinks and another dish of hors d'oeuvres. "Here you go, ladies. Teresa said dinner will be ready in about twenty minutes."

Teresa was their housekeeper, Jessica had already learned. She wondered if the woman would stay the whole night or be allowed to go home to her own family.

Marty and Kevin launched into an animated conversation. Jessica was content to listen as they reported on the progress of their two children, various trips to New York and Boston, and interesting vacations. She had very little news of her own to report—little that was good and even less that she wanted to share.

"We'll probably do some skiing in Vermont this week," Marty told her. "Kevin wanted to go to Utah, but we didn't plan in time. As usual." She made a face.

"Still working at the bank, Jess?" Kevin asked. He was a financial advisor; at least they had that subject in common.

Jessica nodded and sipped her wine. "I took some time off, but just went back again."

"Full time? I don't know how you do it," Marty said enviously. "I can hardly do my volunteer work once a week. I'm just not that organized. I think of going back to work somewhere, but I can't figure out what I'd like to do."

Kevin wore an amused expression and shook his head.

Jessica did her best to smile, too, but she was keenly aware of the differences between them. She couldn't imagine that Marty was considering returning to work because her family needed a second income. She couldn't imagine Marty going back to work at all.

While it was pleasant to catch up with Marty and Kevin, and their house was the complete opposite of the dank little cabin, Jessica knew in her heart it just didn't feel like Christmas here. It had been nice of Marty to invite her, but the truth was, they weren't that close and Jessica didn't feel as if she belonged here. Not without Sam. Not tonight, of all nights.

The doorbell rang. She wondered if other guests were expected after all. Maybe it was just a neighbor, stopping by to wish the Grahams a good holiday?

"I'd better get it," Kevin said. "I think Teresa has her hands full in the kitchen right now."

"It's a shame you can't stay a few days, Jess," Marty said as her husband left the room. "The beach is beautiful this time of year. No tourists and some great bargains in the shops."

"I love the beach in winter," Jessica said honestly. "But we really can't stay."

She didn't bother to add they had a beautiful beach right in

Cape Light or that she probably shouldn't have come here in the first place. She wished desperately that she and the boys were home with Sam, even if home was the shabby little cabin.

Then Jessica heard voices coming from the foyer. A man's voice, deep and unmistakable. It was Sam. He had followed her here.

Her hand trembled as she put her glass down on the coffee table. She wanted nothing more than to run into Sam's arms. The question was, what did Sam want? He couldn't be happy about her taking off with the boys on Christmas Eve. She would have to get him outside quickly so that they didn't end up arguing in front of the Grahams.

"Look who's here," she heard Kevin announce in a jolly voice. He stood aside as Sam walked into the living room.

Marty's eyebrows arched. "Sam! What a nice surprise."

"Yes . . . it is a surprise." Jessica quickly rose. She felt a lump in her throat the size of a golf ball.

"Hello, Jess." Sam met her gaze and held it. "I'm glad you got here safely."

"There wasn't much traffic."

"I noticed that, too."

He must have broken every speed limit to get here so quickly, she thought, traffic or not. She couldn't tell what he was thinking at all. All she knew was that he looked very handsome, dressed in a black sweater that had a half zipper with a blue shirt underneath.

"Where are the boys?" he asked.

"They're in the media room with our kids." Marty smiled and stuck out her hand. "Nice to see you, Sam. Merry Christmas. So glad you came."

"Merry Christmas, Marty. Thanks for inviting us." Sam smiled politely, then gazed around the room. "This is a beautiful house. Really . . . spectacular."

Jessica knew the architecture wasn't at all to his taste, but Sam, as usual, was being kind. The Grahams were obviously so proud of their home.

"Have a seat," Kevin said. "Let me get you a glass of wine."

Sam didn't much like wine. He preferred beer, Jessica knew.

"I'm okay for now, thank you. I'd like to talk to you for a minute, Jess. Outside?" He glanced at Marty. "I have a surprise for the boys in the car. I just want to show Jessica."

Her friends nodded in agreement.

Oh dear, here it was. Jessica met his gaze again. At least he had the decency to avoid embarrassing her.

She managed to smile at the Grahams. "We'll be right back."

She followed Sam back to the foyer, grabbed her jacket from the front hall closet, and slipped it on. Sam held the door for her and let her go out first.

She set off quickly down the long path to the driveway, trying to get a good distance from the house. She didn't want Marty and her husband to hear the shouting match that was sure to follow.

"Where you going, Jess? Trying to walk back to Cape Light?"

She turned and crossed her arms over her chest. "Go ahead. I know you're angry at me, Sam. Let's get this over with."

"I was angry with you," Sam admitted. "But I had three hours in the car to think about it."

"More like two. You must have been driving like a maniac."

Sam shrugged and she saw a glint of amusement in his eyes. "Well, I am crazy for you, but you already know that. That's not what I came here to tell you."

"Why did you come?" she asked, allowing herself a glimmer of hope. Maybe things between them weren't quite as terrible as she had thought.

"I don't want us to fight, Jess." Sam held up his hands, as if surrendering. "I know it's been tough, losing the house, losing all our things and not knowing where we're going to end up. But please, let's not fight and pull apart like this."

Jessica saw the pain in his eyes. She wanted to hold him and tell him their problems were over, that everything was fine. Except that everything wasn't fine. She had to be honest. Things would never be good between them if she hid her feelings now.

"I don't want to fight with you either, Sam. . . . It's just that I don't think you really understand how I feel about things. I mean, you wanted to be at Molly's tonight, and I understand that. But I couldn't bear the idea—I felt as if everyone would be pitying us. I can't feel the same way you do, Sam. I just don't."

"I know," he said simply. He ran a hand through his dark hair. "You've got a right to your feelings, and I need to stop assuming you'll see things my way. But I wasn't trying to—what did you call it?—*steamroll* you. I just wanted things to be better. Instead, I feel as if I've failed you, Jessica, like you've lost your respect for me."

She stared at him, shocked. "Why would you think that? I don't feel that way at all. But I have felt like some sort of bitter, bossy wife who's always reprimanding you and trying to be the practical one," she admitted. "I don't want it to be that way, Sam. I'm just worried. I'm scared."

He nodded. "I am, too. But I would feel a lot better if we could be together in this. You can't just run up to Cape Cod and forget that we're a family—first, last, and always. We have to be together on Christmas. It's even more important for us this year," he said, echoing Reverend Ben's sentiment. "What are we teaching our kids by running away, falling apart? What does that say to them? Bad things are always going to happen, honey. That's part of life. We have to handle this and show the kids things can get better. I know they can if we stick together and work on it."

He took hold of her shoulders and gazed down into her eyes. She didn't say anything for a long time. Her thoughts were whirling, and she wanted to choose the right words. She needed to be honest, and she wanted to find a way for them to stop hurting each other.

"I'm sorry, Sam," she said at last. "I could have handled some of this better, I guess. Maybe I was trying to hurt you by running up here," she admitted. "Because I was so disappointed by everything. But I shouldn't have run out. You've been hurt by all this, too, and it's not your fault if things haven't worked out as we both hoped. I know you only meant well, saying you could fix the house again."

Her words gave him hope. He felt his heart opening up to her again. "We'll get a new house, and it will be just as beautiful as the old one," he said. "It doesn't matter where or how. You have to have faith in me, Jess. You have to trust me again. We have to trust each other and stick together, not snipe at each other." He paused and took a ragged breath. "We can't let the fire destroy our marriage, too. We have so much, Jessica, so much the fire could never touch. Do you see that now? I do," he promised her.

Jessica nodded, her eyes glassy with tears. "I do," she said, and it almost felt like a new marriage vow. Still, she had to explain, to make him understand. "I—I wanted things to stay the same, to go back to just the way they were before the fire. But I see now that they'll never be the same. Even if we could rebuild the house exactly, we're changed inside now, forever. So we'll have something new—just as good, but different. I know I've been hard to be around. But I don't want to lose you, Sam."

"Oh, honey." He hugged her close. "You couldn't lose me if you

THOMAS KINKADE AND KATHERINE SPENCER

tried." He grinned at her. "Actually, you tried tonight. You didn't get very far, did you?"

Jessica finally smiled again. He kissed her and hugged her close. When they parted, he knew they had finally made it out alive, and he sent up a silent prayer of thanks.

"Let's get the boys. We could be home by nine thirty."

She glanced at him, and he was sure she was going to insist that they do the polite thing and stay and have dinner with the Grahams.

"Okay. I'll make some excuse to Marty," she said instead.

"My sick relative again?"

"No, I need something better."

"The dog is home alone. I decided not to put her in the crate."

Jessica grinned. "That will do it. She might chew up all the Christmas gifts, you know."

"Let's hope not," Sam said. Sunny had better not eat those earrings, he thought. He didn't feel like visiting the twenty-four-hour vet clinic again.

The Grahams were puzzled when Jessica and Sam announced their need to depart. Jessica hugged Marty and thanked her again. "I'll call you soon and we'll have a good talk," she promised.

She hoped that sometime in the future she could explain to Marty what had happened, but she wasn't quite sure when that would be. Perhaps when it didn't seem so embarrassing.

Since they had two cars, Darrell rode with Jessica, and Tyler rode with Sam. The boys also seemed puzzled about the change in plans but happy to be going back to the cabin, Jessica noticed. Despite the flat screen TV, they hadn't really been happy to be at Marty's house, away from their dad on the holiday. Fortunately, things had been set right again, just in the nick of time, she realized. They really had to be together for Christmas. What in the world had she been thinking?

A few hours later, they all arrived at the cabin. Jessica made hot cocoa and sandwiches for everyone while Sam built a fire in the wood-burning stove. They all sat together by the Christmas tree, with the boys trying to guess what was in the wrapped boxes, and Sunny contentedly curled up between them.

Jessica found that she, too, was content. More than that, she was genuinely happy to be back in the cabin. Though she had always thought it small and dreary, tonight it didn't seem that way at all.

At least her impulsive trek to the Cape had caused her and Sam to clear the air and come closer again. That was a surprise and true gift from the universe, she realized.

Jessica had brought a few of the boys' packages to the Cape, to give them something to open. After they went to bed, she retrieved the boxes and added them to the others under the tree. Sam sat nearby, watching her.

"Sunny was a good dog," he said. "She didn't eat any of the presents, I don't think."

Jessica checked the boxes. "You're right. They're fine."

She turned to Sam, and he held out a small gift bag to her. "How about this one? I think the ribbon's been gnawed a little. Want to check it?"

She took the bag from him. "Sam . . . what did you do?"

"Open it and see," he suggested.

She sat next to him on the couch and opened the bag, then took out the small velvet box that sat atop a nest of tissue paper. She clicked open the box to see the beautiful pearl and diamond earrings she had admired at the jewelry store.

She looked up at her husband. "You didn't have to do this," she said quietly. "But they are beautiful."

"Does that mean you're not mad at me for buying them?" he asked cautiously.

She felt her eyes fill with tears. "I love you so much, Sam. You're so sweet to me, and I've been so awful. . . . How can you give me this beautiful gift? How can you still want to be married to me?"

Sam practically laughed out loud at her question. He took her in his arms and held her close. "I love you and the boys more than anything in the world. Don't you know that by now? I've made mistakes; I've been difficult, too. But I love you, Jess. Maybe that makes most of it all right?"

"It makes everything all right," she agreed.

Sam gazed down at her, looking deeply satisfied by her answer. "There's something else in that bag. Under the tissue paper," he said.

Jessica realized the bag did still feel heavy. She reached down and pulled out a small tissue-wrapped bundle.

"Oh," she breathed as she unwrapped it. She couldn't quite believe her eyes. "One of the angels . . ." She picked up the carved wooden figure and turned it around in her hands. "Did you find this in the house? I thought for sure they were all burned to ashes."

"This one is new, Jess. I finished it just in time. I'm going to make you a whole new set just like the ones you lost. Well, not exactly like the old ones, but they'll be just as nice," he promised.

"They'll be beautiful." She set down the single angel on the little table by the couch, where they both could see it. "They'll be even better."

She turned to him and pulled him close. When he put his arms around her and they kissed, she felt their life was finally starting to get back on track. Finally starting over, in a new direction. Different, but maybe even better.

"JACK! JACK . . . WAKE UP! QUICK! COME AND SEE!"

Jack opened his eyes with a start. He thought there was an emergency, a fire maybe. The room was practically dark, though he could see the first glow of light under the edge of the shades in his bedroom window.

Kate jumped up and down at the side of his bed, doing an excited little dance. Before he could ask what all the shouting was about, she darted right out again.

Then he remembered. It was Christmas.

She had seen the gifts under the tree and knew Santa had come.

He jumped out of bed and pulled a thermal Henley shirt over the T-shirt and sweatpants he had worn to bed. Then he walked out to the living room, hoping he hadn't missed anything.

Julie sat on the couch in her blue bathrobe. Her long hair was mussed from sleep, and she looked tired but extremely pretty, he thought. She gave him a sleepy smile. "Merry Christmas, Jack."

"Merry Christmas," he said with a yawn. "What time is it?"

"You don't want to know," she assured him.

A few boxes were already open, but Kate was pulling more packages and boxes from under the tree and handing them out to Julie and Jack. Most of the gifts, though, were for her, from Santa.

"Look at what I got, Jack!" she said as she tore open a box containing a fluffy pink sweater. She put it on at once. "It's pretty, isn't it?" she asked, holding out one arm and admiring it.

"That it is," Jack agreed, though he was trying hard not to

laugh. She was already wearing a bike helmet, a charm bracelet, and a ballerina tutu over her pajamas. Kate, apparently, believed in wearing all her gifts immediately. And simultaneously.

"You look like a pink bunny rabbit," her mother told her. "Lester would probably think you were one of his cousins."

Kate looked pleased at this idea, but she was already into the next box. Jack *ooh*ed and *aaah*ed with surprise at all her gifts from Santa, the ones he had bought and wrapped. He was content to give the big red guy the credit and simply bask in her happiness.

The very last package she found was Lester; Jack recognized the shape and wrapping. This gift tag he had signed with his own name. He watched intently as Kate tore off the paper. The expression on her face was priceless.

"Lester!" she said breathlessly. "He's beautiful." Kate hugged Lester to her chest. "I love him," she told Jack.

Jack leaned over and hugged her. "I love you," he said.

Kate slipped her arm around his neck and kissed his cheek. "I love you, too, Jack."

He felt shocked by his admission and by Kate's. He hadn't meant at all for that to come out. He looked over at Julie. Her expression was unreadable, and she didn't say a word.

Finally, it was time for the adults to open their gifts. "Open that one first," he told Julie, pointing to a large box.

He felt nervous as he watched her begin to open the layers of tissue paper. "Now if this isn't right for some reason, you can exchange it and get something you like," he said.

"Oh my goodness . . . what a beautiful jacket." She lifted out a dark red down jacket with fur trim on the hood. Her own jacket was old, Jack had noticed, and working with the trees and pine sap had ruined it.

"You think I'd exchange this?" She looked at him as if he had lost his mind. She got up and tried it on over her bathrobe, giving a little turn, like a runway model. "What do you think, guys?"

"You look pretty, Mommy," Kate said.

"I'd never argue with that," Jack agreed, meeting Julie's gaze.

Julie just blushed, making her look even lovelier.

The rest of her gifts were less extravagant but chosen with care. A hat and glove set to match the jacket, a bottle of perfume that he knew she wore, and a box of art supplies. In the evenings, when Kate was asleep, Jack had often seen her sketching with charcoals. So he had gotten her a set of charcoal pencils but also rich, creamy pastels and a little metal traveling case of watercolor paints.

Julie looked at him in astonishment. "These watercolors and the pastels . . . Did you somehow read the wish list I never got around to writing?"

Jack shrugged awkwardly. "I just picked out what I thought you might like."

She shook her head, laughing. "I'm beginning to think you really do have a direct line to Santa."

She got up from her chair then walked over to where he sat. She leaned down and hugged him. "Thank you, Jack. I love my presents."

Her cheek rested next to his for a moment and her soft hair trailed along his shoulder, enveloping him in her warmth and softness. Why couldn't moments like this last, he wondered.

Julie straightened up, her eyes alight with anticipation. "Now it's your turn to open presents," she said.

Jack scratched his head as he stared at the pile of wrapped boxes at his feet. "I don't even know where to start."

Kate jumped up to advise him. "This one is from me. Open that," she said.

He tore off the tissue paper and found a round cylinder-shaped object made of clay and painted in a colorful, messy design. "Wow! You made this? For me?"

Kate nodded, looking very proud. "You can put pencils in there. And pens."

"I can see that," Jack said quickly, though he had not guessed the object's purpose. "I will put my pencils and pens in there. I'm going to keep it right in the kitchen, by the phone. Where everyone can see it," he added. "That is really, really special. Thank you, Katie."

Kate shrugged. She still wore her eclectic outfit, with the addition of puffy snow boots. "You're welcome," she said.

Jack opened a few more gifts from Kate, the little ones she had snuck under the tree—a small stuffed animal, a tiny baby doll, and a little book. Jack was very touched that she had chosen from her own possessions.

"Wow, Katie . . . I love all these toys you gave me." He picked up a little stuffed tiger and patted its head. "Are you sure you want me to keep them all? You won't miss anything?"

Kate stared at the toys a minute. He thought she was going to change her mind, but she shook her head. "I won't miss them. They're all for you. You don't have any toys and I have a lot now, from Santa."

Jack glanced at Julie. He couldn't help smiling. He tilted his head. "Well . . . that's true. But thanks anyway."

The next gift he opened was from Julie, a pair of new work gloves, the expensive, heavy leather kind. "Julie, these are great." He slipped them on and admired his big hands. "They're exactly the right size. Do you really think I need them?" he teased her.

"Your old pair is held together with duct tape," she reminded him. "Maybe they can be retired—to the Work Glove Hall of Fame or something?"

"Maybe," he agreed, trying to keep a straight face. He reached for his next package, a medium-sized box. First, he was sure it was clothing. But as he opened it he realized he couldn't quite guess what was inside. He pushed back the tissue paper to find a picture in a frame. It was a sketch of him and Kate, sitting together on the couch, reading a Lester book. The drawing was so finely detailed that he could even make out Lester's whiskers on the book's cover. And Kate . . . Kate somehow looked even more real than she would in a photograph. Julie had caught the shine in her hair, the softness of her skin.

Jack's throat felt thick. He couldn't speak. He took the picture out for Kate to see, too. "Look at that," he said quietly. "Your mom's a real artist. That looks just like you, Katie."

"That looks like you, too, Jack," Kate said.

"So it does." His eyes met Julie's. "This is amazing."

She scooped up a few of the discarded ribbons and began to untangle them. "It's just a sketch, Jack. But I'm glad you like it."

"I love it. It's really . . . beautiful." It was beautiful, preserving a perfect moment in his life. He wondered though if he would be able to keep it out once they went away. Looking at it might simply be too painful.

He sighed. "Well, I don't know how you did that. But thank you. That's about the nicest gift you could have given me."

"You're very welcome," Julie said softly. Her dark eyes seemed serious for a moment, as if there were something she was trying to tell him. Then her expression brightened as she handed him another box. "But you're not done yet. You have a few more boxes to open."

Jack winked at Kate. "I can't believe all the great stuff I was missing when Santa didn't stop here. It's a good thing he finally found me."

He opened the box, which held a sweater, and another box, which contained a matching shirt. The sweater was finely knit, the dark blue color she said looked good on him. The shirt was stylish, a blue-gray he never would have chosen for himself. Then again, if Julie told him he looked good in leopard print, he would probably wear that to please her.

She looked apprehensive, watching him examine the clothes. "Are they all right?" she asked doubtfully.

"This all looks great," he told her. "You have terrific taste, Julie. Maybe you should pick out a whole new wardrobe for me."

She smiled again. "Oh, I think you have your own style. I wouldn't want to change that."

He grinned at her. "I do like the shirt and sweater. Maybe I'll wear them today."

Julie rose and began picking up the scraps of wrapping paper. "We have some special things for breakfast that Kate and I baked. Date-nut loaf and cinnamon bread."

"How about some of those chocolate chip cookies?" Jack asked brightly. He got up and began to pick up paper and boxes, too. "They were good. I mean they *looked* really good. Santa got to eat a whole plate last night."

"Mom doesn't let me have cookies for breakfast," Kate said wistfully.

"Well, it is Christmas." Jack glanced down at her and winked. "I don't think once a year would hurt you."

"I suppose not," Julie agreed. "Which reminds me, Kate and I are going to church this morning. . . . It's going to be a very nice service with lots of music. Would you like to come with us?"

Julie kept picking up the wrapping paper. She didn't even glance at him. Perhaps she was being considerate, not wanting him to feel put on the spot. Inviting someone to church could be a touchy question.

Jack put the lid back on his sweater box and took a breath. "Sure. I'll come. Why not?"

"Once a year won't hurt you, Jack," Kate said, echoing his own words.

Jack stared at her then laughed. He could not remember having had a Christmas morning like this in a very, very long time.

JACK PULLED UP TO THE CHURCH ON THE GREEN, SHOCKED TO find the parking lot full and all the spaces nearby lined with cars. Did this many people really go out on a cold Christmas morning to attend church?

Of course it *was* Christmas. *Everyone goes to church today,* he reminded himself. *Even me.*

Once inside the church, they made their way through the crowded foyer. They were a few minutes early and many people were still milling around, exchanging holiday greetings and catching up on news.

"Hello, Jack. Merry Christmas." Lucy Bates and her family were just behind them. Lucy smiled at Julie. "Hello, Julie," she added. "Is this your little girl?"

"Yes, this is Kate. This is Lucy, Katie. Say hello."

Kate politely said hello but suddenly seemed shy. Jack was not used to seeing her like that anymore and gently smiled. With her mother's permission, she had brought along Lester and now hugged the toy rabbit close, as if it would protect her from strangers.

"Oh, she's so cute," Lucy said. "You have a great Christmas," she added, moving along with her family again.

Jack touched Julie's arm, trying to steer her toward the entrance to the sanctuary. He noticed the Morgan family coming in with their two boys. Jessica Morgan suddenly stood right near him as she helped her younger son take off his jacket. "Oh, Jack . . . how are you?" He could tell by the way she stared that she hadn't recognized him for a moment without his beard and long hair.

"I'm fine. Couldn't be better," he said honestly. "It was awful about your house. I was so sorry to hear that."

"Yes, it was an awful situation for us," Jessica admitted. "But we're doing better now. Things are coming along," she said with a hopeful note. "Thanks for the Christmas tree. That was very nice of you."

"Oh, that was nothing. When you get set up in a new place, you let me know. I'll help you with the landscaping, okay?" he offered.

He wasn't sure where that generous offer had come from. It had just popped out. But once he said it, he was glad. Jessica looked so pleased.

"Thank you, Jack. I'll remember that."

Julie had been helping Kate get her coat off, and now returned. "Merry Christmas, Jessica," Julie greeted her.

"Merry Christmas, Julie." She gave Julie a quick hug then left to join her family.

Jack stood aside, suddenly realizing Julie had been coming to church these past few weeks and already knew people here. Perhaps as many, or more, than he did.

They followed the crowd slowly moving into the sanctuary. Jack looked around at all the decorations, garlands of pine and

long white looping scarves of sheer fabric, red and white poin-
settias around the altar, and many white candles.

Tucker Tulley, whom Jack knew better as a police officer than as
a church deacon, handed them programs. "Good to see you, Jack,"
Tucker said. "Merry Christmas, Julie," he added. "Merry Christmas, Kate."

So, she knew Tucker, too. Jack smiled at Julie and let her walk
ahead. So many people here seemed to know her, and like her. She
was just that type, the kind who made friends quickly. She had
that same gift of being easy with people that Claire had.

He spotted three seats on the left side of the center aisle, a few
rows from the back, and gently steered her in that direction.

"Julie! Merry Christmas, dear . . ." Sophie Potter sprang up
from her seat on the aisle and greeted Julie warmly. "I have a little
something for Katie," she said, pulling a small package out of her
big handbag.

"Sophie, you didn't have to do that."

"Oh, it's just a little something. Some mittens I made for her
and a chocolate Santa Claus. Here you go, sweetheart. Now don't
eat that in church. Save it for later, okay?"

Katie nodded. "Thank you," she said politely.

"Did you ever meet my granddaughter, Miranda?" Sophie
turned to a young woman who sat next to her in the pew. "And this
is her husband, Jeff. They just got married this summer. They're
living in Boston now, but they came back to visit for the holiday."

The Potters were a large family, Jack remembered, though it
was only Sophie and her oldest daughter left in the area now. Jack
had heard that last winter a young man who had lost his memory
had been found on the Potter orchard, and that Sophie and her
granddaughter Miranda had taken him in. The story had been in

the local newspapers, but it had taken weeks before someone who knew him appeared. Jack had seen that part on the TV news—an ex-fiancée or someone had shown up to claim him.

After that, though, Jeff had obviously come back for Miranda. Jack, who had been out of the town gossip loop, didn't know that part of the story. But now they were married. There was a happy ending for you. Was that pure luck? Jack wondered. Or was there some way you could make the impossible happen?

Music started. The introit. The service would soon begin.

"Well, I won't keep you. You'd better get your seats," Sophie said.

They moved along, but the space Jack had spotted was now gone. He looked around for another opening. Practically all the seats were filled.

Tucker came by, aware of their dilemma. "There are some seats up front, folks. Follow me." He led them to a front row and stood by as they made their way in.

Jack suddenly felt self-conscious, following Julie and Kate to the empty seats. The Warwick family sat nearby. Everyone knew Emily Warwick and her husband, Dan Forbes, their daughter Jane sitting between them. Emily's grown daughter, Sara, and her husband, Luke, sat alongside Emily, and the Morgan family sat just behind them. Presiding over the entire clan, in a huge fur coat and pearls, sat Lillian Warwick. The old woman turned her head slowly and stared at him, unsmiling. Then she looked at Julie and Kate and turned away again, her expression tight and disapproving.

Jack's good mood vanished. He didn't know why Lillian Warwick's look had gotten under his skin. It was silly, but he suddenly felt as if everyone was looking at him and not in a welcoming way. He felt as if the entire congregation, who had known his wife,

Claire, so well, worked with her on committees, known her as a friend and active member of this church, was noticing that he was here with another woman.

He felt . . . guilty. He tried to brush the feeling aside. The day had started on such a bright note, and it would be his last day with Julie and Kate. He didn't want to ruin it. Perhaps coming to church wasn't such a good idea after all.

The choir walked in down the center aisle, singing "Joy to the World!" Reverend Ben Lewis followed in his flowing robes, his head bowed. The congregation rose. Jack felt a strange stirring in his heart. The bright voices and music moved him, though he wasn't sure why.

"Welcome, everyone. Merry Christmas. And a special welcome to all our visitors today," Reverend Ben began. He quickly reviewed some church announcements then looked up again.

"Now let us clear our minds and open our hearts to receive God's word. Today is a very special day, a celebration of the birth of our Lord, Jesus Christ. A blessed miracle. Let us lift up our hearts and rejoice. . . ."

The choir began another hymn, "Come All Ye Faithful."

Everyone stood, so Jack did as well. Unprepared, he grabbed a hymnal and fumbled to find the page. Julie, standing next to him, gently touched his arm and held out her book. He leaned his head close to hers and started to sing, catching up with the lyrics where her finger marked the place. Her nearness was distracting, but he forced himself to concentrate.

She turned a bit and smiled up at him. He felt himself glowing inside. He could sing all morning standing next to her like this.

After the hymn Reverend Ben led the congregation in an opening prayer. When it was time for the Gospel reading, an older woman rose and walked up to the pulpit. She wore what Jack thought of as a thrift-shop outfit—a long blue cardigan sweater with a white blouse underneath and a Christmas brooch on the shoulder. Her loose gray skirt came down just below her knees, revealing black tights and thermal snow boots. Her straight brown hair was streaked with gray and held back at the sides with bobby pins.

She walked to the front of the sanctuary quickly, slipped on reading glasses, and stared down at the big Bible on the pulpit.

Jack vaguely recognized her. Grace Hegmen, who owned the Bramble Antique Store in town. He glanced around the sanctuary and looked for her father, Digger, wondering if the old man was still alive. Jack finally did spot him, sitting near Sam Morgan.

It was hard to guess Digger's age, Jack reflected. Digger always looked the same, with a wool seaman's cap on his head—even in church—a long white beard, and a navy peacoat.

From his vague expression and wandering gaze, Jack wondered if the old man was entirely with it these days. He was lucky his daughter Grace was so devoted to his care. But she didn't seem to have much more in her life except her shop. Jack knew that she had once been married and had a little girl. The child had died in a car accident, and her husband had left her. Grace had isolated herself, more or less giving up on life.

Jack sure knew what that was like. Looking up at her now, as she read a passage from Luke, he felt a pang of sympathy. He could have ended up like Grace, he realized, if not for Julie. He still could, in fact, if he gave up again after she left.

" '. . . And there were in the same country shepherds abiding in the fields, keeping watch over their flocks by night,' " Grace read. " 'And, lo, the angel of the Lord came upon them, and the glory of the Lord shone round about them; and they were sore afraid. And the angel said unto them, Fear not: for, behold, I bring you good tidings of great joy, which shall be to all people. For unto you is born this day in the city of David a Savior, which is Christ the Lord. And this *shall be* a sign unto you; ye shall find the babe wrapped in swaddling clothes, lying in a manger. . . . ' "

Grace read on, concluding the passage that told the familiar story of the first Christmas Day. Once finished, she returned to her place and Reverend Ben took the pulpit.

Jack shifted in his seat. It had been a while since he had listened to a minister's sermon. He couldn't remember now if Reverend Ben was the long-winded kind or kept it short and to the point. He crossed his arms over his chest, preparing himself to be bored.

Reverend Ben looked out at the congregation and pushed his glasses a bit higher on his nose. "No matter how many times I read the Scripture passages that tell the story of Christ's humble birth, there's always something new to see. Something new to learn and think about," he began.

"As if the story is a favorite decoration, hanging on a Christmas tree. An ornament with an amazing, unique design. Every year we turn it in our hands, or hold it up to the light and see it differently, from a new perspective. We see it in a way we never have before." He paused, smiling slightly. "That's fortunate for me, since I'm obliged to give a new sermon on the subject every year."

A few laughed quietly, Jack among them. He had always liked this minister's honesty. He remembered that now.

"What struck me most this year was the isolation, and even alienation, this young couple must have felt on their journey and during their stay in Bethlehem. Forced by a government decree to up and leave their home and all that is familiar and comfortable to them and travel a great distance. And all this just as Mary is about to give birth. It must have been hard enough in those days to give birth to a healthy child. Just think of it," he encouraged his listeners. "At that time and in that culture, a young woman expecting her first child was most likely surrounded by her female relatives, counseled and coached by her mother, a midwife perhaps, and other women in her community. Even these days, so much excitement and preparation surround the birth of a new child. Relatives, especially grandparents, rallying around the new parents, eager to give advice and support.

"But Mary and Joseph were utterly alone, arriving in a foreign place where they had no relatives or even an acquaintance to turn to for their most basic needs—food and shelter for the night. Imagine their feelings, their exhaustion and discomfort. No sense of relief and safety when they arrive in the town. Instead, they go from inn to inn, trying to find a place to stay. They must have felt frightened and perhaps even a bit desperate as Mary's time approached.

"Think of the shepherds in vast empty fields, staring up at the dark sky and stars as they fell asleep that night, perhaps feeling very distant from any kindred soul. And the three wise men, traveling down long dusty roads, through foreign lands and empty stretches to reach the town of Bethlehem.

"And as the Scripture says, an angel appears to the shepherds and wakes them. The angel tells them not to be afraid but to follow the brightest star in the sky and find the child born in the manger. They choose to believe their vision and set off on the quest. And the three wise men have also been advised by a vision, and they, too, are inspired to find the child.

"And finally, all the players in this ageless tale come together in the stable with the new family. What could Mary and Joseph have been thinking as these strange visitors arrived, asking to see their baby? They didn't know anyone for miles. They didn't think anyone had given them a thought, a poor couple bedding down with the animals, struggling to bring their son into the world. Yet the shepherds show up, probably bearing some type of humble gift, perhaps even a new lamb, and they ask to see the new baby.

"Can you imagine Mary and Joseph's surprise? Quite possibly, their pleasure, too, at having someone—anyone—to share in their great joy and this huge milestone in their lives.

"Then the three wise men, aristocrats, possibly even kings, approach the manger. Men who are dressed in rich clothing, doubtless of a high social rank. The new mother and father must have been frightened at first by these visitors. But the kings are humbled by the sight of the baby and eagerly present their costly gifts. Just imagine how these presents must have awed Mary and Joseph—incense, frankincense, and myrrh. Those are the gifts of the wise men. Yet, they bring another gift that is not part of the list. The gift of unconditional, unquestioning love for the tiny child. A gift that surprises the young parents as much, if not more, than their tribute of treasures."

Pastor Ben smiled gently and glanced down at the pulpit to turn a page of his notes. Jack realized he was enjoying this version of the familiar story, the minister's retelling bringing it to life in a new way.

"So the night is filled with unexpected visitors and gifts. The young couple's abject isolation, even fear, miraculously transformed to connection, goodwill, and joy. The dark, lonely scene in the stable turns into one of celebration, with lowly shepherds and kings brought together by the same mission and message. A kind of surprise party, if you will," he added with another smile.

"Certainly, a scene of reunion and even reconciliation. For these visitors have come from far and wide to honor the child who, the Scripture has foretold, would reconcile God and mankind.

"Connection. Reunion. Reconciliation. Unconditional love. Those are a few of the deep threads that run through this story's rich tapestry. Those are lessons we can all take to heart."

Reverend Ben paused. His gaze scanned the rows of church members, listening intently. For a moment, Jack felt as if the minister was looking straight at him. No, he told himself, that must just be a trick of the light.

"How many of us experience the sense of being set apart, isolated, even in the midst of a roomful of people?" Reverend Ben continued. "I suspect we have all experienced that feeling at one time or another, even in a room filled with those nearest to us. In this story, we learn that this day is a time for connection. A time to put aside fear and open up our hearts. To strangers, surely. And also to family and friends, which is sometimes even harder.

"It's difficult to put aside differences and grievances. It's hard to offer the gifts of forgiveness, trust, and love. But that example, that challenge, is one beautiful idea we can take away from this story and live out in our lives today and every day of the year ahead.

"Do I make it sound too easy? If I do, I apologize for that. Many times, it's not easy at all. As the story suggests, it can be a frightening journey through a dark, foreign place. But the reward is great for those who persevere, who hold fast to their faith and try to live in this isolating, alienating world. Those who try to express the best part of themselves. The inspired part that strives for connection and forgiveness and unity, refusing to be guided by a fearful, alienated instinct. But instead by our spiritual and loving selves—which is the divine image in each of us."

He paused again and looked down briefly. Then raised his head and smiled. "'Fear not; for . . . I bring you good tidings,'" he said, quoting the Scripture Grace had read. "Peace on Earth. Goodwill toward men . . . Merry Christmas, everyone."

Jack watched the minister gather his notes and take his seat again in the first pew near the pulpit. The choir rose and began to sing "Silent Night."

He turned to Julie and met her glance then reached over and took her hand. It just felt . . . right.

AFTER THE CHURCH SERVICE, JACK, JULIE, AND KATE RETURNED to the tree farm. They all changed into comfortable clothes, then Jack took Kate outside to try her new saucer snow dish while Julie finished fixing dinner. Fresh snow had fallen during the week, and the little girl couldn't get enough of spinning down the hill that sloped from the house to the bottom of his property. The ride she had once taken on her waterproof bottom, he recalled.

By the time Jack and Kate came back into the house, everyone was ready for dinner. Jack almost felt dizzy, inhaling the tantalizing smells that wafted out of the kitchen.

The table looked like something from a magazine, and Julie's dinner was amazing. Jack had never tasted roast goose before. He found it delicious, the rich flavor perfect for Christmas. And that was only the main dish. Julie had prepared a true feast with potatoes and chanterelles baked in cream, green beans and almonds, honeyed yams, and an assortment of desserts that he barely had room for.

After dinner, they sat by the fire and played games with Kate. It was one of those rare, perfect days, Jack knew; one of the best of his life. He didn't want to be greedy, but he wished this sweet time would never end.

CHRISTMAS DAY AT HER MOTHER'S HOUSE WAS MORE OR LESS AS Jessica had expected. Tyler and Jane were occupied with new Christmas toys, and Darrell had brought his iPod, which kept her mother's complaints about their behavior to the minimum.

Sara and Luke had cooked the meal, serving a rib roast with all the trimmings, so the dinner was tastier than the usual bland fare her mother had brought in, or even Emily's well-meaning, but questionable, cooking.

"A very rich cut of meat," her mother remarked as she was served her entree. "Difficult to digest," she warned.

"A little red meat builds the blood, Lillian," Dr. Elliott countered. "What would Christmas be without a challenge to the digestive system? Personally, I think you're up to it."

Jessica struggled not to laugh out loud. Ezra glanced at her across the table and winked. He was still the only one who could get the last word on her mother.

Lillian waited until they were almost done with the main course before saying, "Jessica, I noticed you and your family weren't at Molly's party last night."

Jessica and Sam exchanged a glance, then Jessica said, "We wanted to have a smaller celebration this year, just us and the boys."

Emily, of course, didn't press the point. Jessica could tell from her sister's sympathetic expression that she knew it was hard for them to socialize right now.

"You didn't miss much," Lillian said, patting her mouth with the corner of her napkin. "It was sheer mayhem. All those children running around. All that food. And when they opened the gifts at midnight . . . well, I've seen better manners during feeding time at the zoo."

Jessica stiffened at her mother's critique of Molly's party. She seemed to forget that Molly was Sam's sister. On second thought, she probably had not forgotten at all and was intentionally trying to get under Sam's skin.

Jessica usually loved Molly's parties. She used to give the same type of party at her own home—a loud, lively gathering, with lots of good food and conversation and overstimulated children. There was always a crescendo of excitement when the gifts were handed around. It was impossible to avoid that, and who would want to?

Emily shook her head. "We all had a wonderful time. I think you did, too, Mother. You just don't want to admit it. After all, you always show up when Molly invites you."

Lillian sniffed and pushed her food around her plate with her fork, trying to select the next acceptable bite. "I only agree to attend because if I don't, you all nag me to death about staying home alone. We come into this world alone and we leave it alone. I have no respect for a person who cannot entertain themselves and abide their own company, believe me."

"Well, no one likes to be alone on Christmas," Dan offered. "Even you, Lillian."

Jessica noticed that her mother didn't answer. She took a sip of water and peered at her son-in-law over the edge of her glass.

Jessica realized that she had thought she wanted to be alone last night. Not totally alone, but away from Cape Light and practically everything familiar to her. But that had been a mistake. She was thankful that Sam had cared enough to come after her. Now he sat beside her at the table, and she reached for his hand and squeezed it.

He glanced at her and smiled back, and she knew he wasn't bothered by what her mother had said. Sam, too, was just glad that they were all together again. He turned to the others. "Sara, Luke, that was a great meal," he said. "Everything was delicious."

"I suppose you aren't able to cook much in that little shack in the woods," Lillian said to Jessica. "The facilities must be very . . . basic."

"The kitchen is basic," Jessica had to agree. "But we're managing all right so far."

"The boys love their bunk beds. It's very cozy," Sam said.

"*Shabby* would be a better word for it," Lillian replied.

Leave it to her mother. Just as Jessica was starting to get past her negative feelings about the cabin, her mother insisted on reminding her of all the reasons to dislike living there.

"How much longer do you think you'll remain in that situation? Not indefinitely, I hope."

Jessica couldn't see why that mattered to her mother. She hadn't wanted them to live in her house. Why did she care how long they stayed in the cabin?

"Not indefinitely, by any means," Sam cut in. "But we're still trying to figure out what to do about the house. We're not sure now we can rebuild it," he admitted. "There's a lot to think about."

"Oh, that's too bad." Emily glanced at Jessica. "Are you positive?"

"Yes, I think so," Jessica said. "We need to figure out an alternative." She made herself smile. "Let's not talk about this now. It's Christmas. Why don't we clean up and have some dessert. Then we can open the gifts."

"Not so fast," her mother said. She leaned back and reached into the pocket of her sweater, a pale blue cashmere cardigan.

She pulled out an envelope and gave a long, exasperated sigh. "I was going to give this to you later, Jessica. But the conversation is irritating me. I'm having enough trouble digesting that roast."

Emily passed Jessica the envelope, Lillian's trademark vellum stationery with her LMW monogram on back.

Jessica stared at the envelope for a minute, then glanced at Sam.

"Well, open it. It won't explode," her mother promised.

Ezra laughed. "Maybe not. But knowing you, she has a good reason to suspect it could."

Lillian glared at him. "Oh . . . you. Be quiet now. Silly man."

Jessica slipped her finger under the flap and pulled out a note card. She opened it up to find a check inside. She unfolded the check and saw it was made out to her and Sam. She gasped at the amount. Enough to rebuild their house in grand style.

Jessica opened the card and quickly read the note.

Dear Jessica and Sam,
Here is your Christmas gift. A little more extravagant this year than usual, but your family appears to need more than the usual.

Her mother's gifts were usually along the lines of a useful book, like an atlas or dictionary, or a pair of quality leather gloves. Jessica kept reading.

Quite frankly, your family looks like a band of gypsies roaming about. People are starting to talk. I hope this gift helps you to return quickly to a respectable new home.
Your loving mother

"Lillian." Sam's voice was uncharacteristically hoarse. "Thank you. From the bottom of my heart."

"Nonsense. I had to do something," Lillian said curtly.

Jessica could see her mother was uncomfortable being thanked. She was always uncomfortable with displays of emotion, even a kiss hello or good-bye. This moment was off the charts.

But Jessica rose from her chair, walked to where her mother sat at the head of the table, and put her arms around Lillian's bony shoulders. "Thank you, Mother. Thank you so much. I'll never forget this generosity."

Lillian tolerated the hug for a moment, awkwardly patting Jessica's arm. Then she returned to her usual tart mode. "What's the difference to me? You'll all get my money once I'm gone anyway."

"You're not going any time soon, Lillian," Ezra promised. "It was a good idea to give some of it away now when it can be put to good use. I'm very proud of you," he added, knowing the compliment would goad her.

She glared at him. "Thank you very much, Ezra. I'm tickled pink at your approval."

The rest of the guests laughed out loud. Sam leaned over and whispered in Jessica's ear, "I promise I'll never say another bad word about your mother."

"Yes, you will," Jessica whispered back. "But that's okay. She's sort of a puzzle, isn't she?"

Sam nodded, still looking dumbfounded as they stared at the check again. Jessica would never understand her mother in a million years. She would never understand life. How she could be so downhearted and hopeless one minute, and so buoyed up and renewed the next.

Bad things happened sometimes; that was inevitable. But good things happened, too. Sometimes it was hard to remember that. She decided one resolution for the New Year would be to try to take a more philosophical view and to hold on to a more thankful perspective.

IT HAD BEEN A LONG DAY FOR EVERYONE, JACK THOUGHT, especially little Kate, who had woken up at daybreak. Now, it was only early evening, and Kate was already rubbing her eyes and asking for her story.

"Sure," Jack said. "Go get your book."

They sat together by the fireside, and Jack read one of the new Lester books aloud while Kate sat in his lap and the stuffed Lester sat in Kate's lap. She had hardly let the toy rabbit out of her sight all day, and Jack felt gratified that his gift had been such a big success.

This story was about Lester's family looking for a new rabbit hole. They faced some difficulties—mud sliding in and interference from other animals—but in the end, they found the perfect, cozy underground nest.

Lester helped, of course.

"That was a good one," Kate said, yawning. "Now Lester has a home with me. I'll take him everywhere."

Kate's promise made Jack sad. This was their last story time together. Tomorrow Kate and Julie would be off to Long Island. Along with Lester.

It had been such a joyful day that he had kept pushing those thoughts away, denying it would really happen. It didn't seem real.

Even as he helped Julie tuck Kate in for the night, he still couldn't face it.

"Go to sleep, sweetie," Julie said as she shut out the light. "We have a big day tomorrow."

He followed Julie downstairs. She started to pick up in the living room, but he took her hand and drew her to the couch. "Come here, that can wait. Sit down with me a minute."

She looked at him shyly and let him lead her to the sofa, where they sat side by side. Jack put his arms around her. He kissed her forehead but purposely avoided her tempting mouth.

"I'm not a big talker," he began.

"Yes, you've told me that," she said with an amused smile.

"Not about . . . personal stuff, I mean." He struggled, trying to find the right words. This was so hard. "Julie . . . you must have figured out by now how I feel about you. It must be pretty obvious."

He looked into her eyes. Her look of amusement was gone. She looked serious—and surprised. And full of anticipation, he thought.

"How do you feel about me, Jack?"

He swallowed hard. "I think you're wonderful. You're . . . amazing. I've never met anyone like you," he said honestly. He stroked her hair away from her face. "I care for you, Julie. I really do. You and Kate, you've changed my life completely, and I don't know how I can ever thank you."

A veil dropped over her expression. A subtle thing, really. But the look of anticipation he noticed just moments before had vanished. She looked down at their hands, twined together.

"There's no reason to thank me, Jack. You're the one who's done so much for us. Not just letting us stay here these past weeks, but the way you've treated Kate. And me. I was such a mess after the divorce. I felt so bad about myself. But you've always acted as if everything I do is so special. That's meant a lot to me, Jack."

"Everything you do *is* special." She was perfect in his eyes. He loved her. He just couldn't say it out loud.

"You sure fooled me," he went on, trying to glide over the awkwardness. "You always seemed so positive and fearless, confident. As if you didn't need my help, or anyone's."

Julie gave him a rueful smile. "That was just an act for Kate, I guess—and for myself, to keep from falling apart. But you gave us the time here, and things started to shift. I feel so much better about everything now. Though it's going to be hard living with my brother in New York, I think I can do it and pull my life together. That's what you've really given me, Jack."

It took a moment for her admission to sink in. He never thought he was giving her anything. To him, it all seemed the other way around.

He let out a long breath. "I . . . I don't really want you to go," he said finally. "You know that. But I don't think you should stay here, either. I'm just not sure I can ever give you what you need, Julie. What you really deserve. You need someone different from me, someone . . . younger, who hasn't been through so much."

"Jack, you're not old. I don't know why you always say that." She rested her hand on his chest and sighed. For a moment, he thought she was about to argue with him, but all she said was, "If that's the way you feel, I understand." She gave a little shrug. "Maybe it's just bad timing for us—too soon after losing your wife."

"Maybe," he agreed.

He wanted with all his heart to ask her to stay, but he just didn't think it was right or fair of him. If he let her go now, Julie would find someone better, someone younger. Someone more like her, alive and engaged in the world.

"It's probably not the best timing for me, either," she admitted quietly. "I'm just getting over my divorce, and Katie has been through so many changes. You and I haven't really known each other very long. If things didn't work out, it would be hard—hard for us and for Katie."

Jack nodded. He had worried about that, too. "I understand. I wish you didn't have to go," he finally admitted. "But I would never want to hurt or disappoint you. You or Kate."

He stared into her beautiful brown eyes and told himself he was doing the right thing. Someday she would look back on this moment and be grateful she hadn't stayed.

He didn't know what else to say. He leaned over and kissed her. He tried hard to control his emotions, but it was no use. The way she responded didn't help. A wave of pent-up love and desire swept through him. His kiss revealed everything inside, all the feelings he didn't dare put into words. Their embrace was passionate and heartfelt but also bittersweet, both of them knowing this was really a farewell and not the start of anything.

Slowly, Jack pulled away. He risked one more look into Julie's eyes, and he saw her own disappointment and aching sadness. A sharp wave of regret sliced through him. He never meant to make her sad. He had thought he was the only one who was giving up so much.

Julie had deep feelings for him, too. He finally knew that.

And it was too late. It seemed best now to just leave things as they were. To let her go tomorrow, as she planned, to start her new life.

This time together had been just a resting place for her. And a special gift for him.

He held her in his arms a moment longer, not yet willing to let her go. The lights in the room were low and as he looked out at the fire and the Christmas tree lights, he felt his vision blur.

He didn't want to cry in front of her. *Get a grip, Jack,* he told himself.

A knock sounded on the door, shattering the silence. Jack jumped up and walked to the foyer to answer it. "I wonder who that could be," he said, wiping his eyes and nose quickly on a hanky.

He pulled the door open. A young man stood on the doorstep. He wore a military uniform. The cap shadowed his face in the porch light. He stood tall and strong, staring at Jack.

Jack blinked. His eyes were playing tricks on him, his vision still blurry from the waterworks over Julie.

"Yes? Can I help you with something?"

The young man smiled hesitantly. "Dad, don't you recognize me? It hasn't been *that* long."

Chapter Fourteen

$\mathscr{J}$ACK PRESSED HIS HAND TO HIS HEART. "DAVID? . . . IS IT really you? I don't believe it."

David took a step forward. He stood near Jack awkwardly, looking as if he wanted to embrace his father, but not knowing if Jack would allow it.

Jack threw his arms around his son and hugged him, practically lifting the young man right off the ground.

He felt himself simply fall apart, and he started sobbing, his head dropping to David's shoulder. "David, my boy. I didn't think I'd ever see you again. . . . "

David hugged his father back. "I'm sorry, Dad. I'm really sorry. I've been such a jerk."

"Come in, come in." Jack pulled his son inside and wiped his eyes with the back of his hand. "Julie, come here. You won't believe this. You won't believe who's here. . . ."

Julie walked in from the living room. She smiled with a curious expression. Jack felt suddenly awkward. He didn't know how David would react, finding his father with an attractive woman. Would he think Jack was being terribly disloyal to his mother's memory—sitting here with a strange woman on Christmas night?

But David didn't seem to think that at all. He stepped forward and smiled, politely extending his hand. A real gentleman now, Jack thought with amazement.

"How do you do? I'm David Sawyer, Jack's son," he introduced himself.

"I gather that," Julie said with a grin. "I'm Julie Newton, a friend." She glanced at Jack and he smiled back, struggling to get his emotions under control again.

"Julie's been staying here the last few weeks with her daughter. She's been working at the tree lot," Jack explained. "They're leaving for New York tomorrow," he added.

David glanced into the living room, his gaze lingering on the tree and all the gifts piled underneath. "Looks like you've had a good Christmas."

"We did," Julie said. "The best." She gave Jack another smile; she looked genuinely happy for him. "I'd better turn in now. We have to get up early tomorrow. And you two must have a lot to talk about. Nice to meet you, David."

"Same here," he said.

She touched Jack's arm as she passed by on her way to the stairs. "See you tomorrow, Jack. Good night."

Jack said good night to her and watched as she disappeared upstairs before turning back to his son.

"Come into the kitchen. Can I fix you something to eat? We

have a lot of leftovers from dinner. Julie made a roast goose. Ever try that?" he asked David eagerly.

David shook his head. "No, sir. But I am hungry."

Of course he was, Jack thought. Some things never changed.

Jack reheated the food and served David, barely able to keep his eyes off his son. He kept wondering if he was imagining the whole thing. He knew he wasn't. It was just that he had imagined David returning so many times that seeing him again now felt as if he were living a dream.

He sat across the table from David while he ate. He didn't want to overwhelm the boy with questions but couldn't help asking what he had been doing, where he'd been. David didn't seem to mind. He seemed eager to fill Jack in on the time they had been apart.

"I traveled south first, down to Florida. You know how I always fantasized about living someplace with palm trees."

"Sure, I remember that. You started to hate New England and the cold."

"I worked construction jobs mostly, pretty low on the food chain. I didn't have any real skills like carpentry or an electrician's license. It's hard to break into those unions."

Jack opened a beer and offered one to his son. David was certainly old enough now. "Did you stay in Florida?"

"No, I got tired of it. I went to Louisiana and Texas next. Then up to Colorado and west, to California and Washington."

"Wow, you put on some mileage. Did you work construction in all those places?"

David shook his head. "Those were the good jobs. I had some awful jobs, too, and I didn't find work at all some places."

Jack hated to think of his son wandering around, out of work, possibly even homeless. "Why didn't you get in touch? Why didn't you call when you needed help?" he asked. "Why didn't you at least just let me know you were alive?" He didn't mean to sound angry, but emotion took over all the same. He stopped himself and sat back. "Sorry. I didn't mean to lose it. I've just been . . . upset, worrying about you. It's been on my mind all the time, night and day. Since the day you left."

David looked at his father with amazement. "You've never apologized to me before for losing your temper. Not once. Do you know that?"

Jack sighed and shook his head. "You're probably right. I'm not going to argue about it. Maybe I've learned a thing or two, living alone these last two years. Maybe I've had some time to think things over. But you did some shouting, too, as I recall."

David nodded and pushed back from the table. He sipped his beer. "I did. I know that. I was angry about Mom dying. You seemed lost on your own planet of pain, Dad. You wanted me to act differently or something. I don't know. I couldn't handle being here anymore, with her gone. I had to go. That's all I knew. I didn't think too much about it when I left."

Jack didn't answer for a long moment. "You're right. I was on my own planet. I can see that now. But why didn't you ever get in touch? I mean, after all this time. You seem to have grown up, David. You seem like a real man to me now. You must have realized I was worried to death about you."

David sighed. "Well, I did. That's why I came back. Mostly why," he added quietly. He looked up at Jack again. "After I left, I guess I was just being stubborn or something. Trying to teach you a lesson, Dad," he admitted. "Trying to get back at you for not understanding me. I also thought you were so angry at me that if I called, you would just yell at me over the phone."

Jack blinked in surprise. Didn't David know how much his father loved him? *I guess not,* he realized. *Maybe kids never do—until they have their own kids.*

"I guess I deserve that," Jack said finally. "I haven't always been the most understanding guy. So, you signed up to be a soldier," he went on, carefully keeping his tone calm. In truth, though, he felt anything but calm about the sight of his son in uniform.

David laughed. "I didn't know what else to do. I thought at least I'd get some structure in my life and maybe an education someday."

Some structure and an education. Isn't that what his parents had been offering him his entire life? Jack had not gone to college himself but had always encouraged David to continue after high school. But David had argued about that, too, and brushed off his schoolwork, though he was certainly smart enough to get good grades.

Jack held his tongue. It wasn't the time to rehash that old story. What had happened in this house when David was a teenager was now . . . irrelevant, he realized. The sight of the uniform seemed to underscore that point.

"How do you like the army so far?" he asked instead. "Are they tough on you?"

"Basic training was tough. They made me work. They make you sweat. I had to grow up pretty quickly. And you know something?" He laughed, a sound that amazed Jack, at once both strange and familiar. "I had this sergeant during training. He was just like you, man. He looked like you, he walked like you, he even sounded like you."

Jack grinned. "Sounds like a great guy. I bet he taught you a lot."

"He was okay," David said, his smile subdued now. "I have to tell you, I felt like someone was trying to send me a message."

Jack felt himself relax. "Looks like you heard it."

They moved into the living room and talked for several hours more. Jack was careful to sidestep the old touchy subjects and also to remember that David was no longer the moody eighteen-year-old who left home. It wasn't that hard. David seemed so much easier with Jack and with himself, all the old rebellion melted in the time he had been away.

Jack couldn't get enough of his son. He didn't want to let David out of his sight, as if David were a dream that would disappear with the dawn. But finally, they both admitted to needing some sleep.

"You take your old bedroom," Jack insisted. "I'll stay out here on the couch."

"No, Dad, it's okay. It's too late to start messing around like that. Just give me a pillow and some blankets, I'm fine out here."

Jack didn't want to do that. He wanted David to be comfortable. But after arguing a few more minutes, he finally gave in.

"Okay, but just for tonight," Jack said. "Then you take the room. I'll clean it up for you tomorrow." His son had become so sensible and mature. "How long can you stay?" he asked suddenly.

David looked at him and then looked away. "A few days. I have to report on January one to Fort Bragg in North Carolina."

"Are you being reassigned there?"

"Not permanently. My unit is being sent to the Middle East, to Iraq, Dad." David paused and met his father's gaze. "That's another reason I came home to see you."

To say good-bye, Jack realized. He sat down heavily. He felt shaken to the core and wanted to grab his son again and hug him to his heart. His boy, the child he had held in his arms as an infant. The boy he had taught to walk, to ride a bike, to swing a baseball bat—going off to fight a war? It didn't seem possible.

David crouched down next to him and touched Jack's arm. "Dad? Are you okay? Do you want some brandy or something?"

Jack shook his head. He glanced at David but still couldn't speak.

"I didn't mean to shock you like that. . . . I wasn't sure when to tell you," David admitted.

Jack sighed and covered his son's hand with his own. "It's okay. There wasn't any good time to deliver that news, believe me."

David just nodded.

Jack stared straight ahead and took a long breath. "We'll talk more in the morning, son. I'll get you some blankets and stuff for the couch."

He walked back to his room to find some extra bedding. It was funny how God gave with one hand and took away with the other.

He had waited so long to see David again. Now, here he was finally, home again. But maybe for the last time.

After getting David settled and saying good night, Jack lay in bed, staring at the ceiling. He was exhausted but couldn't sleep. The night had been a roller-coaster ride of emotions.

There were no solutions. You just had to grasp and enjoy what you could, Jack realized. You had to be alert and aware. You couldn't sink into a shell. You couldn't hide on some private planet of pain.

Julie would leave tomorrow and he had to let her go. But he had been given a great gift this Christmas night: a few precious days with his son. He was determined to put aside his worry and despair for David's future and make the most of their time together.

* * *

JULIE WAS UP AND READY TO LEAVE EARLY THE NEXT MORNING, as she had planned. Jack helped her pack up her car, but they couldn't fit in all of Kate's presents, and he offered to mail the extras down to her brother's house.

When it finally came time to go, Julie strapped Kate into her car seat in the back, with Lester in her lap.

Jack leaned over and checked the seat belt, just to make sure. He quickly kissed Kate on the cheek and forced a smile.

"Good-bye, Kate. Have fun with your cousins in New York," he said, unable to think of anything to say that wouldn't be too sad.

He knew Kate did not completely understand what was happening. Neither did he, for that matter.

"Will you come and see us, Jack?" Kate asked. "Mommy said Long Island isn't very far."

"Sure, I can do that. Someday," he said vaguely.

He glanced at Julie, who watched them from the front seat.

"Okay, good-bye now." He kissed Kate again and closed the door. Then he stepped up to the driver's side window. He had already given Julie a heartfelt hug inside. All that needed to be said between them had been said last night, he thought, and yet, if it hadn't been for the distraction of David in the house now, he wouldn't have been able to handle this. He was sure he would not have been able to let her go.

"So, drive safely. If the car gives you any trouble at all, just stop somewhere and call me."

He hoped to heaven the car broke down before she even reached the highway.

"I'll be fine, Jack. Don't worry," she said quietly. She offered him a small smile.

"Call when you get there, okay? I just want to know you got there safely."

She nodded. "I can do that. No problem. Enjoy your time with your son. He seems like a great guy."

"He is a great guy. He's a real man, now," Jack said with pride and a bit of amazement.

"He's a lot like you." Her eyes sparkled. "I mean that in a good way," she added, making him laugh.

He smiled at her, then leaned over and kissed her again. He couldn't help it. He touched her hair lightly with his hand and stepped back from the car.

"Okay . . . have a good trip," he said, his voice thick.

She nodded and waved, then steered the car down the narrow drive to the main road and disappeared.

All he could see at the end was the pink bike he gave Kate, secured to the trunk on a bike rack.

He sniffed and took a long, shaky breath. Had he done the right thing by letting her go? *God only knows,* Jack thought sadly. *Life must be lived forward, but can only be understood backward,* he recalled Julie saying. That was just the problem, wasn't it?

THE NEXT FIVE DAYS WITH DAVID PASSED QUICKLY. THEY FELL into an easy routine, and in some ways it seemed as if his son had never left. On the third day of David's stay, they decided to visit the cemetery and put flowers at Claire's headstone.

"I haven't gone there since the funeral," Jack confessed.

"We'll go together then. It's okay, Dad. I understand."

David patted his father's back. It was odd for Jack to have his son offering support, being the comforter. It had always been the other way around. He was so grown-up now. Jack wished Claire could see it. But maybe she did, he reasoned. Maybe she had sent David here.

On the way home from the cemetery, they drove through town. David looked around curiously.

"Does it look very different to you?"

"Not so much," David said. "Is Emily Warwick still the mayor?"

"She sure is. She'll be the mayor for as long as she wants, I think. Charlie Bates keeps nipping at her heels, but nobody really likes him."

David laughed. "See, it hasn't changed at all."

Jack had to stop at the post office and mail the packages of gifts down to Kate. David helped him carry the boxes in.

"So, did you hear from Julie? Is she okay?"

"She's fine." Jack kept his eyes focused on an address label, carefully filling in the information.

"So . . . how did you leave it with her?" David asked.

Jack looked up at him, surprised at the blunt question. "What do you mean?"

"Are you going to see her again? Go down to New York and visit? It's not all that far, Dad. Only takes a few hours."

Jack shook his head. "I don't know. I don't think so." He took another label and started writing.

"Why not? I know you like her."

"How do you know that?"

"It's written all over your face when you look at her. When you say her name."

Jack sighed. "That obvious, huh?"

"Yeah. Sorry to break it to you." David leaned over and took a label, and started writing, too. "I know you loved Mom, Dad. I think it's okay if you've found somebody new. I don't think Mom would want you to be unhappy and all alone. I don't want you to be left here all alone, either."

Left here all alone. He meant if something happened to him in Iraq. If he didn't come back.

"Julie seems pretty special," David continued. "I don't think you should just let her go."

Jack stacked up the labels and counted them out. He was one short, then he saw the one David had filled out. "Okay, I get your point. I'll think it over, okay?"

They left the post office and headed home. At the end of Main Street, they passed the drugstore where Jack had met up with David's old girlfriend, Christine. David had not asked about her, and Jack had forgotten to tell him about the encounter.

"Listen, speaking of special girls . . . I ran into Christine a few weeks ago." David sat up straighter, Jack noticed.

"You did? How is she?"

"She's fine, doing very well. She's in college, studying to be a teacher." Jack paused. "She told me she just got engaged to be married."

He glanced at David, trying to see how his son was taking this news. "She's moved on with her life, I guess. She asked me about you," Jack added. "She asked if I ever heard from you and said, if I did, to tell you she said hello. Or something like that." Jack shook his head. He wasn't good at this stuff. Did the boy even care? He must have had a lot of girlfriends over the past two years.

"She did?" David's voice was sharp with interest.

So he did care. Jack wasn't surprised. There was something real there. He had always thought so, even though they were terribly young. But he and Claire were young when they met, and that had lasted, Jack reflected.

"Maybe you should call her," Jack suggested. "I think she'd like to hear from you."

David looked out the window as they approached the tree farm. "Sure, I'll call her. I was thinking of doing that anyway."

That night, David went off to visit Christine, looking eager and nervous as he left the house. But he also looked very handsome and mature. Jack was certain that if Christine had any feelings left for David at all, she would be bowled off her feet by the new-and-improved version.

Jack was sleeping in the living room now, having forced David to take his old room back during his stay. When David came in at midnight, Jack was still awake, reading a book about orchids.

"So, how did it go?" He put the book down and looked up at his son.

"She was angry at me. Really angry." David sat down and pulled off his wool hat. "But then we talked and sorted things out. She has two more years of school left. She's not getting married until she graduates. She told me that they decided to wait. Two years is a long time," David noted. "I should be home by then," he said hopefully.

"I sure hope so," Jack agreed.

He could have posed the same question David had posed to him about Julie—*how did you leave it with her?*—but he held back. He didn't want to pry.

"She's going to write to me. She said she would, anyway."

"I think she will if she said so," Jack assured him.

David rose. "I guess that's something. That's about as much as

I could hope for," he admitted. "I didn't treat her very well, leaving town without a word. It wasn't right."

"I think you know better now," Jack told him. "I bet she realizes that, too."

David sat with him a while longer then headed off to bed.

Jack hoped the girl kept her promise, even if nothing came of it. A soldier needed someone at home, something to look forward to. He hoped Christine wouldn't disappoint his son, at least in that way.

Jack wished that David could stay, so they could at least see in the New Year together. But David had his orders and there was no arguing with that. On the morning of New Year's Eve, Jack drove his son to a bus station in Ipswich.

Jack was getting weary of saying good-bye to people, of sending off those he loved. But he tried to do his best so that their leave-taking wasn't harder for David than it had to be.

He waited with David in the station, sitting on hard plastic chairs, making small talk until the bus pulled in.

They heard the bus announced. David stood up and grabbed his large green duffel. He was in uniform and people glanced at them. Jack felt proud, even though he didn't necessarily agree with what was going on in the world.

David turned to his father and hugged him tight. "That's my bus. I'd better get going. . . . Thank you, Dad." His voice was choked with emotion. "Thanks for everything. It's been great spending time with you and being back home again."

Jack held him fiercely, his eyes welling up with tears.

"I'm the one, David. I'm the one who should . . ." He couldn't finish. "Thank God you came home, that's all I have to say. You'll be back. I know it. I know you will," he promised his son.

David nodded and swallowed hard. "I'll call you, Dad," he said. Then he turned and boarded the bus.

Jack stepped back, waiting. When David's face appeared at a window, he forced a smile and waved. The bus door closed. The engine heaved a giant gust of exhaust and it pulled away.

"Happy New Year, David," Jack called silently after him. He had forgotten to say that, he realized. He had forgotten to say a lot of things.

Jack cried most of the way home. It was hard to drive, and at one point he just pulled over at the side of the road and wept uncontrollably.

At home, he decided to ignore the holiday. He didn't feel like seeing the New Year in on his own. He felt bleak and empty with both David and Julie gone.

He heated up some canned soup and sat at the kitchen table to eat it. Tomorrow he planned to start to clean the tree lot. The extra garlands and wreaths would be tossed in a grinding machine, the trees would be chopped for firewood. It was hard work and he wasn't looking forward to it.

Being perfectly honest with himself, Jack knew he didn't feel like doing anything. He felt as if he might be overwhelmed again by sadness, sinking into a dark place. All he could see was the dim shadow of David's face, looking at him through the bus window and then gliding away. It was hard to get that image out of his mind.

During his stay, David had taken out old photograph albums. They were all still piled on the kitchen table. Jack pulled one over and paged through. It was hard to look at the photos of happier days, days when David was a little boy and Claire was with him.

Jack reached the end of the album, noticing for the first time that it was filled with blank pages. That seemed odd to him, seeing all those pages blank and empty.

Where were the pictures, he wondered. *In the future, yet to come,* an inner voice answered. A picture of Julie and Kate came to mind, one fixed in his heart. He wished now he had a real photograph of them.

That wouldn't be too hard, he knew. Not at all impossible.

Only his fears and doubts held him back.

The pictures in the album were his past, treasured memories. The future was all the blank pages, still to be filled however he chose to do it.

He could give up and end his story now. He could crawl back into his shell, hide out on his planet of pain.

But he wouldn't hurt David that way. His son expected more, and David's return had given him something to live for.

Julie and Kate had given him something to live for, too, if he chose to embrace all they offered.

He could hide away here safely the way he had these past two years, in fear of love and loss. Or he could reach out and reconnect to real life. A full life. He had that chance, that opportunity, though he knew the window would not be open forever.

Jack thought back to the night Julie had appeared at his door. He had just about reached rock bottom, and she walked in and hauled him up by his collar. He didn't expect that kind of miracle to happen twice in a lifetime. If he wanted her, he had to make some effort, to reach for what he wanted without fear of the consequences or the obstacles blocking his way.

She had called only once in the past week, to say she arrived safely in New York. He hadn't spoken to her since, distracted with David's visit and also unsure of what he should say to her.

The ball was in his court. She might refuse him, after all, and crush his heart. Or he might end up disappointing her and Kate in the long run, unable to give them both what they needed.

Jack picked up his dish and put it in the sink. Then went into his bedroom and got into bed, feeling bone weary. He couldn't have been more tired if he had been working outdoors in the cold all day.

He didn't typically pray, but in the darkened room, lying in bed, he closed his eyes and said a short prayer, asking God to please protect his son and keep him safe from harm wherever he traveled.

Then he silently added, *Please give me strength and show me the right thing to do about Julie.*

When he woke up, early morning sunlight slipped under the window shades. His sleep had been long and deep. He sat up, feeling refreshed, his head cleared of the cobwebs.

He took a quick shower and shaved, then dressed in khaki pants and the new shirt and sweater Julie had given him.

He faced himself in the mirror for one more appraising look. *You're a very handsome man, Jack,* he heard Julie say.

He smiled to himself. This might work out. It might work out after all.

He took her brother's address and typed it into the MapQuest site on the Internet, then printed out the directions. He was getting an early start. It would take about four or five hours to reach Long Island. He would make it there by noon, he thought. He didn't want to call; he wanted to surprise her. She should be around the house on New Year's Day, he thought.

Jack drove steadily down the New England Thruway. The traffic was light, and he was careful not to get too eager and exceed the speed limit. But even though he got hungry halfway through the ride, he didn't want to waste time and stop for lunch.

When he arrived at the condo development where Julie was staying, he had to laugh at himself as he drove around the suburban maze, trying to find the correct unit. Julie was right; they did all look the same. Finally, he found the house number and saw her beat-up little hatchback parked nearby.

He strode up to the front door and felt his heart begin to hammer. He rang the bell and waited for someone to answer, feeling suddenly as if he couldn't even breathe.

A man came to the door. He looked a lot like Julie. Jack knew it had to be her brother. "Peter Newton?" Jack asked.

The man nodded but didn't open the storm door, looking at him suspiciously. "Who are you?"

"Jack Sawyer, a friend of Julie's. From Massachusetts."

"Oh . . . right. Come on in." Peter opened the door and stepped aside.

The condo had three floors and plenty of rooms, but it was built on a small scale, Jack thought, looking around. The rooms were narrow and tight; all the furniture seemed close together. It was the complete opposite of his big, rambling house.

"Julie's downstairs, I'll let her know you're here. Is she expecting you?" Peter asked curiously.

"Uh, no. It's sort of a surprise," Jack admitted.

Peter gave him a skeptical glance then walked off. "Julie?" Jack heard him call. "Someone is here to see you."

Jack waited, his mouth going dry.

Finally he heard her coming down the short hallway. He turned and offered a smile, a pretty weak one at first. Then he met her eyes and knew he had done the right thing.

"Jack? What are you doing here?" She wore jeans and a simple brown sweater that brought out the rich color of her hair. Jack thought she had never looked more beautiful. And she was staring up at him as if he were a vision.

"I . . . I wanted to see you," he admitted. "I forgot to tell you something." He lowered his voice, then glanced at Julie's brother, who suddenly took the hint and left them alone.

Julie looked puzzled. "Why didn't you just call?"

Jack licked his lips. He swallowed hard. "I have to say this face-to-face. It's hard," he began. He cleared his throat again. "You see . . . the thing is, I had some time to think and I have to tell you something important. I know I said all that stuff about not wanting to disappoint you and that you needed some other type of guy. . . . But I don't want you to be with some other guy. I want you to be with me. I love you, Julie," he said finally. "With all my heart." He didn't dare glance at her as he spoke, afraid to see her reaction. He was on a roll now and just wanted to get it all out. The words he had carefully rehearsed for five hours on the ride down were getting all jumbled in his head. "I don't want to live without you. I can't. I wouldn't really be alive. . . ."

Finally, he looked at her. She leaned back, as if she had been hit with a gale-force wind. Her skin was white as paper. He thought she might faint. He reached for her shoulders and she pressed her hands to his chest.

Her words came out in a rush. "Jack, I was afraid, too. My first marriage was such a disaster, I was scared I might make another mistake. I kept telling myself what I feel for you couldn't be true. But ever since I left I've felt so empty without you. . . . I know it's true now. I know I love you." She put her arms around him and hugged him close. "I love you so much. . . ."

He cupped her face in his hand and kissed her. He felt like the luckiest, happiest man in the world. All his fears for the future vanished, and his heart filled with pure love and joy.

When he finally looked down at her, she was crying—tears of happiness. "I'm sorry, Julie. I was a total jerk to let you go. But you said that sometimes there are second chances. Thank God, I got one this time."

"I would have come up and knocked on your door again," she told him. "I wasn't going to let you go that easily."

He felt a thrill, knowing she really loved him. It seemed a miracle to him.

"Will you come back with me?" he asked quietly. "I know I told you I wasn't sure I could do it, but if you give me a chance . . . if you'll marry me . . . I'll do my best to make you happy every day. You and Katie," he added.

Julie stared at him in amazement again. She had not expected his proposal and before she could answer, they both heard Kate shouting at the top of the stairway.

"Jack! Jack! You're here! I told Mommy you would come."

He looked up to see Kate running down the stairs. She stopped a few steps from the bottom and flung herself into his open arms, without a shadow of doubt that he would catch her.

"Hey, Katie girl. Here I am." Jack hugged her to him.

"We missed you, Jack."

"I missed you, too," he confessed. "I missed you so much."

Katie pressed her head to Jack's shoulder and sighed happily. Jack glanced at Julie over Katie's head.

"You never answered my question. Need to think about it?"

Julie shook her head. Her eyes were bright, full of love. She put her arm around his shoulder and kissed his cheek. "No, I don't need to think about it. I want to go back with you, Jack. I want to take care of you and make you happy forever."

Holding Kate with one arm, he pulled Julie close with the other. He was so happy, he could have started singing. But he restrained himself. He would save that for later, to entertain Katie on the ride home. "It's settled then," he said quietly, hugging both Kate and Julie close. "Everything is just . . . perfect."

A SHORT TIME LATER, JULIE'S BELONGINGS WERE PACKED IN JACK'S truck. They decided to leave Julie's old car. It was barely running, and Jack wanted to buy her something new and reliable.

She said good-bye to her brother and his family. They seemed happy for her, Jack thought, as well as somewhat relieved to see her go.

Kate had been up very late the night before, waiting to bang pots and pans with her cousins at midnight. She fell asleep as they crossed the Whitestone Bridge and started on the turnpike back to New England.

Jack and Julie talked for hours, revealing their feelings and secret fears. Laughing about how silly they had sometimes both been. Jack talked about plans for the nursery, trips they could take together. The future had rarely looked better, and it was the best New Year's Day he could ever remember.

As he steered the truck up the long drive to the tree farm, he turned to Julie and she quietly smiled back at him. It seemed right to have Julie and Kate back at the house again. He carried their belongings inside, feeling a deep sense of peace and completion at their return.

When Katie's bedtime came, she was eager to hear a story. Jack sat on her bed with a book, Julie at his side. But before he read, he had something important to tell Kate.

"You know, Kate, I've always known that you're a very special girl. But now I know you have some real magic inside."

Kate looked puzzled. "What do you mean, Jack? Why am I magic?"

"Well . . . remember that time you pretended to be a Christmas elf and you gave me a wish?" He paused, watching her face. "I can tell you now. I wished for you and your mom to stay with me forever. And it really came true."

Kate's eyes were as wide as saucers. "Really?"

He nodded solemnly.

"Wow," she said. "Awesome."

"Yes. It is really awesome," Jack agreed.

Julie rested her hand on his shoulder. She leaned over and kissed his cheek. "So are you, Jack Sawyer. So are you."

EPILOGUE

S AM WALKED DOWN THE GRASSY HILL. HE HEARD DARRELL
and Tyler shouting and Sunny's loud barks before he could
see anyone. The marsh grass around the pond was very tall at this
time of year, deep in the middle of the summer. He hadn't had
much time lately to do any work down here, but maybe soon he
would at least trim some of the brush.

The boys didn't seem to mind. They liked the pond looking
wild. It made it feel like more of an adventure to swim here. Darrell was swimming on his back, a lazy backstroke. He saw Sam and
waved. Tyler was on the wooden float, preparing to dive in.

"Hey, Dad! Watch me. Look at this—cannonball!" he shouted.
His little body leaped off the float and he hugged his knees in the
air, creating a gigantic splash.

"Tyler, please! You're splashing me." Jessica jumped up from her
lawn chair. Sam hadn't even seen her sitting there.

He hadn't noticed Sunny either, who now jumped up and galloped toward him, her coat soaking wet, her big paws coated with mud. When she jumped up on Sam to lick his face, her paws practically rested on Sam's shoulders.

"Whoa, Sunny. Get down, girl," Sam said, laughing.

Jessica ran over and kissed his cheek. She wore one of his castoff shirts over her bathing suit. It hid her small round tummy. She was barely three months pregnant now, but she was still very self-conscious.

"Hi, honey. I was hoping you would quit work early today. It's so hot."

"Sure is. Even Madeleine Norris had to take pity on us," Sam said with a grin. He was almost done rebuilding the porch on Mrs. Norris's Victorian. A well-paying job, to be sure, though Mrs. Norris's nit-picking made him wish he had charged double.

Jessica took her seat again. "Are you going to jump in for a swim?"

Sam shook his head. "I don't think so. I just want a shower."

"I'll go up to the house with you. It's time the boys came out anyway. I bought some stuff for a barbecue. It seemed a good night to grill."

"Sounds good to me." Sam folded up Jessica's chair then carried it under one arm. He waved to the boys. "Come on in now. We're going up."

Tyler balked but Darrell came right away, yanking his little brother out of the water. Sunny helped, too, Sam noticed.

Sam took Jessica's hand as they walked up the hill. She suddenly stopped so he did, too.

"Feeling tired?" he asked

She shook her head. "I feel fine. I just wanted to stop a moment and look at our house."

They had come to the top of the hill and their new house was in full view. Sam gazed at it, too. It really was a good house. A gracious, elegant-looking house without being too formal or trying too hard to be a factory reproduction of a real Victorian. They had purposely chosen a design that was unlike their last house. They wanted something new. Something different.

There were large, long windows, a long front porch, and a back porch, too. A wide roof line and a turret. Sam had done much of the work himself, but the generous gift from Lillian had made it all possible.

It had plenty of bathrooms and bedrooms upstairs, and in some ways was much more convenient than their old house with all its charming quirks.

Most of all, they were happy here. Their life was back on track, and now they were looking forward to a baby.

"So, you still like the new house?" he teased her.

"You know I love it." She slipped her arm around his waist and squeezed him. "It's beautiful. Even my mother approves," she added, reminding him of Lillian's recent visit.

Sam leaned his head back and laughed. "So she does. I'm surprised Sara didn't put it on the front page of the *Messenger*. It's got to be a first in this town."

"Sam?" Jessica was fighting a smile, but also reminding him of his promise. He'd been pretty good these past few months, not criticizing Lillian . . . though it was often tempting.

But she had been generous and he would always be grateful.

They continued on their way toward the house, laughing together. Sunny barked and ran ahead, and Tyler gave chase.

Sam hoped they would spend many happy years in this house. And then, many more. The fire had taught him one thing: It was easy to take the blessings in his life for granted. He hoped this house would keep him mindful every day to cherish all he held dear.